THE WHITE CAMEL OF FEZ

A Captivating Adventure in Ancient Morocco

K. L. Vivian

DEDICATION

To Teresa and Jason

and

To my mother,
who helped with many hurdles
in this book and in life

.

ACKNOWLEDGMENTS

Thank you to all these people who helped me with this book. You all made more contributions than you know, and I appreciate your willingness to share your time, knowledge and support.

Gavin Hambly, Abraham Grossman, Loraine Bearden,
Peggy Browne, Tina Laningham, Jason Vivian,
Josephine Norton, Jackie Birkby, Michael Muchow,
Carol Janak, Todd Schomer, Sandi Simon,
E. Ann McDougall, Pir Vilayat Inayat Khan,
Henry Louis Gates, Jr.

11TH CENTURY MOROCCO

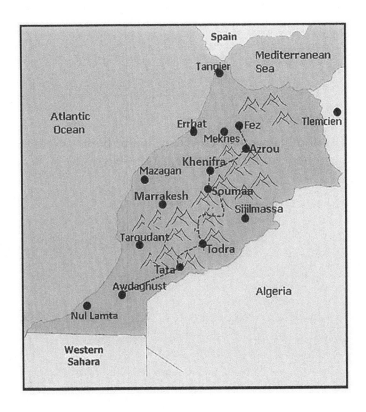

The ruins of Awdaghust were discovered in the 20th century in modern day Mauritania, further south than this map shows.

A list of names and terms used in this book (and their pronunciations) is provided at the end of the book.

Disclaimer

This book is a work of fiction. While there is an attempt to merge the story with historical locations, people and times, it is still a work of fiction. Any resemblance to anyone living is purely coincidence.

CHAPTER 1

The glaring sun scalded the great sand dunes stretching in every direction. Along the ridge lines, crystalline sand sparkled and danced in a light wind, adding a shimmer to the golden scene. The sand lifted and showered down like tossed sugar on the soldiers grouped in silent waiting.

Powerful armies on camels and horseback were in a civil war here, struggling to dominate the landscape and the rich trade routes. The waiting men were Almoravids, who raged on horseback from their base in Marrakesh across northwest Africa, conquering all the major cities on the western Sahara. They dominated the north-south gold and salt trade routes. Their enemies were the Almohads, mountain Berbers who were surging in the north and south.

"Ride, ride, you groveling infidels!" Emir Abdallah Ibn Yasin shouted toward a small caravan of donkeys in the distance.

He raised his sword, then kicked and whipped his black stallion to top speed across the sand, and shook his shining silver scimitar over his head in a fierce display of rage. The black veil wrapped tightly over his lower face matched his thick turban and stallion. The hundred or so mounted soldiers behind him sprang into action, raising their swords high and uttering fierce, shrill war cries as they thundered across the face of the dune.

"God is merciful, you cannot escape us!" Ibn Yasin shouted at the caravan. He was the leader of the Almoravids, and he intended to collect a tax from every Almohad caravan coming out of Fez.

The caravan had spotted them, and was running hard to get to safety, fearing slaughter and pillage from the imposing army closing behind. The riders' robes flapped in the wind as they kicked their animals, and the unhappy donkeys brayed in disgust at being rushed. Their steps threw up a large cloud of dust and confusion that could be seen for miles.

"Look at them run! Legs and arms flying everywhere!" Ibn Yasin shouted through the grit in his teeth. He was grinning a big smile behind his mask as he glanced over at his long-time friend General Malik..

"They are running like frightened sheep!" Malik shouted back. The general rode hard at Ibn Yasin's side, pace for pace, kicking his horse again and again with his heels. His bronze spiked turban was wrapped over his lower face in Almoravid style to keep out the dust. The burnished brass plates on his armor flashed brilliant signals in the sun.

Suddenly, Ibn Yasin threw his arm up to signal Malik, and sat back in his saddle. He pulled hard on the reins, forcing his powerful horse to a stop, and sheathed his blade.

"We have scared them, my friend, and they will think twice before watering freely at our wells again. Let these rabble go. I am in need of rest, and spilling blood doesn't interest me today. So few donkeys can't carry much of value anyway. We aren't losing much revenue," Ibn Yasin said, as he pulled his veil down to reveal shining, white teeth.

"That was a comical sight, yes? I think some of them will need clean pants." He wiped the dust from his face, and spat twice to get the sand out of his mouth. Ibn Yasin loved a chase.

General Malik signaled to the soldiers to divide up and make camp. It was a highly disciplined force. By the time the huge dust cloud from their riding had settled, the army was resting in low, makeshift tents made from their robes supported by riding whips. The camels and horses were hobbled around their front legs so they wouldn't run off, and most of them had already dropped their heads to rest. The sun was getting low and cast long shadows.

Ibn Yasin signaled for the soldiers to spread out their prayer rugs, and knelt facing East for evening prayers. He was their spiritual leader as well as head of government, and he made sure his army always followed the rituals of shari'a law without fail..

Afterwards, Malik made a small windbreak by spreading a riding blanket across two dry bushes, and built a small fire. The two leaders sat cross-legged on a rug, sharing dates and thick, black coffee. The darkness fell quickly, and so did the temperature. They pulled on woolen burnooses against the chill, and put the hoods up over their turbans.

Malik rubbed his hands together over the small flames to warm them.

Emir Ibn Yasin's Almoravids spent long days out in the desert, protecting what was theirs and raiding what was not. Despite his scholarly nature and the burden of administrative rule, Ibn Yasin enjoyed riding in the dunes with the soldiers most of all, plundering the infidels who refused to convert to Islam.

His biggest challenge, though, was not the infidels. It was the Berber confederation of Almohads from the mountain valleys. Most of them were Muslims, too, so they were considered brothers in the faith. But they openly challenged his religious authority and the rule of the Almoravid dynasty. Their interpretation of the *Holy Q'uran* differed from his. It was his duty to bring them to true understanding.

Since the Almohads had first appeared, Ibn Yasin had spent much of his time fighting them in the desert between his southern home in Awdaghust and Fez in the north. Fez was the greatest city in North Africa in the 11th century, and a sore spot for him, because the Almohads had stolen it. Fez was a jewel at the intersection of fifteen vast trans-Saharan trade routes, and a necessary stop for all merchants. He had lost a fortune in trade revenues when he lost the city.

More importantly for Ibn Yasin the scholar, Fez was the greatest center of learning in the world. It was home to the oldest university in existence and the magnificent Kairowiyyan Library, which rivaled the ancient Alexandrian Library in Egypt. The complex was already over two hundred years old. As a young man, Ibn Yasin had studied there. He was a revered theologian and scholar himself now, yet the Almohads denied him this one thing that mattered to him—access to the greatest library and university in the world. His own university. In his own territory. This irritated him like a blister that wouldn't heal..

Ibn Yasin's army patrolled the routes from the gates of Fez to the great southern cities of Marrakesh, Sijilmassa and Awdaghust, trying to squeeze the pockets of the Almohad interlopers enough to make them yield and return to the mountains. It was a contest Ibn Yasin and his generals would lose. Every dynasty has its day, and not a moment more. The Almoravids were strong today, but they were reaching the end of their power.

As the army bedded down for the night, the walls and buildings of the city of Fez were visible to the north along the horizon. The city was built on low hills and dipped into a valley divided by a river. The great mosque's landmark minaret, a square, stepped tower with a small dome, was over one hundred feet high, and featured ornate brick work and crenellations. It was visible from where they camped. The tower was plastered and whitewashed with a lustrous finish so its white brilliance could be seen for thirty miles in every direction under the bright sun.

Ibn Yasin sat with his back toward the city. It was a stubborn act of defiance. He didn't like to be reminded of all he was being denied.

Fez was the place most of the great thinkers and teachers from throughout the Islamic world came to teach and debate. All works of the greatest Muslim teachers, scientists and philosophers throughout time were available in the Kairowiyyan Library. Yet Ibn Yasin was now excluded from discussions with the other great scholars of his day. Losing access to the library and its myriad resources was bitter.

Visitors to the city loved to revel in the many treasures available in its tangle of twisting, narrow alleys. Even in the dusk, from a distance, the city glittered in the last rays of sun like a jewel with brilliant tile work and colorful mosaics everywhere. Walls, courtyards, alcoves and columns were adorned with intricate diamond, star and spiral shaped patterns in vivid, jewel-like colors.

The great main gate was covered in the deep blue, glazed tiles for which Fez was famous. The roofs of the mosque and university were a brilliant green. Lively markets flourished in every city square. The city was a beacon to travelers, traders and colorful characters as well as the learned, and its unique labyrinthine streets earned Fez the nickname, "the maze city."

And in the midst of the maze city lived Samir, young son of a salt miner.

CHAPTER 2

"Samir, come on! We will be locked in!" Saadi fidgeted on the red patterned rug in the great library, his eyes darting anxious looks toward the heavy carved exit doors. Long shadows lay across the floor. A hand bell jingled again.

Samir sighed, laid a marker on his place, and covered the scroll with a red and gold cloth to signal it was in use. "I'm coming, Saadi. I don't want to stop reading! The Angel of Reckoning is just about to swoop down and wipe out the city! Oh well." He stood up reluctantly from the low cedar table, stretching.

The reading room smelled of ancient parchment and tallow lamps. Two older students were moving through the reading room, extinguishing the pendant ceiling lamps and brass wall sconces for the night. Samir picked up his few belongings, and the boys scuttled through the large main doors just as the Lock Keepers arrived.

"Salaam aleikhum," the boys mumbled respectfully toward the four dignified men, and then turned and raced toward Samir's house, a few alleys away.

The thousands of rare scrolls and manuscripts in the library were greatly prized. To protect them, the great iron double doors at the entrance had four immense iron locks that were closed at dusk. Four iron bars slid across the doors into brackets, and a tail on each bar folded down into a large padlock. Each lock had its own giant iron key, and each unique key was in the keeping of one person from each of the four most powerful families of Fez.

Being a Lock Keeper was a great and solemn honor. The men came from their palaces every morning to unlock the giant locks and slide back the bars, and returned every evening to relock them. The ritual was known to scholars worldwide, as well as the citizens of Fez. Students who didn't get out before the doors closed were punished, and quickly learned to watch the hour.

Samir lived alone with his father Jamal, a poor man whose house was a meager two-room, mud brick hut in the shadow of the great library wall. On this side of town, the city had a peculiar smell—a mix of animal droppings, trapped heat, bread baking, mint tea and the pungent ammonia smell from the tannery. They lived near the tannery district, so the putrid smell of curing hides was always in the air. The narrow and twisting mud brick streets were barely wide enough for two pedestrians or one donkey to pass through.

Jamal wanted to increase his fortunes, so he maintained a few camels in a rented stable nearby. He hoped eventually to breed good racers. So far he had managed to breed only a few ordinary pack animals, but he did have one mare Alama who was small, but had the right body shape for a racer. He put his hopes in her, and had used his meager savings to pay a stud fee with a rather average racing male that belonged to another breeder across town.

"Insh'allah, God willing, you will deliver a champion tonight or tomorrow," he mumbled to Alama as he made sure there was plenty of straw in her pen for the night. She licked gently at the salt dust that covered his clothes. He patted the animal's neck and stroked her cheek with soft noises, wishing her well, and turned toward home.

Jamal almost bumped into Saadi and Samir at the front door. The boys whispered a few hurried words, then Saadi turned and sped home, his leather sandals slapping on the bricks as he ran. Samir slipped off his shoes, ducked inside and helped his father prepare their evening meal. It was almost dark, but the coals from the small cooking fire helped to light the room.

"What news do you have today, father?" Samir asked.

"I believe we will have a new calf by morning, son. Alama is showing signs. I would like you to sleep in her stall tonight, and let me know if there is any trouble."

Samir nodded. He had done this duty before. It was always interesting to see what would emerge from the mother. He hoped his father would get a good racer this time. That would help to make their life better.

Dinner was always the same—a kind of porridge of

wheat and barley flavored with a small portion of camel or goat meat. Sometimes there were a few root vegetables in it or some olives. There were also fresh flat breads to scoop up the stew. Samir loved the smell of the fresh bread, and put one to his nose with a deep breath. Jamal poured cardamom flavored coffee from a small copper pot placed near the fire. Father and son sat on the floor together and dipped bread into the stew.

"We have to pay the school fees again soon, father. It is almost the end of the month. The imam said we must pay by the fourth day."

Jamal sighed, and stopped eating for a moment. Even though the fees were low, it was hard for him to pay. "Samir, we may not have money for your school next month. I am sorry, but I spent our savings on the stud fee for Alama. If she produces a good racing animal, then we will have money again soon, and you can return to school. I wish it were not so, but you will have to give up your studies for a while."

"Oh no, father! No! The imam says I am doing very well. I am the second best boy in my class. We are about to start reading astronomy. I have been waiting for that. I need to be in school!"

"I am sorry, son. You are almost a man now, and I need you to help me build a future for our family. We will try to find money for your schooling again in a few months, but for now I don't see any way to do it." Father's voice had finality in it, and Samir knew not to question more.

Samir stood up abruptly. He wanted to get out of the house and be alone with his sorrow.

"I will go now to be with Alama, father, before it is too dark. I will get you if anything happens."

Jamal nodded and sipped his coffee. He was yawning, and Samir knew that once he was gone his father would be sound asleep.

CHAPTER 3

Samir grabbed his bedroll and a bowl of butter, and headed out to the camel pen. It was a short walk to the stable, and the stars were already out in the dark sky. He could see them between the buildings. Here and there around corners he could make out a few constellations he had already learned.

Samir had always loved looking at the stars, imagining stories of how they interacted with each other when humans were not watching. To him, they were characters in a great celestial battle between the sun and the moon or good and evil.

Alama was pacing in circles in her stall. He stopped to pat her neck and stroke her back. Her belly was very round and hard. She didn't want to kneel down to sleep as she usually did. She just paced. Samir stroked her nose and cheeks. She nuzzled his hand.

She was small for a racing camel, but her hump was still almost as high as Samir's hand could reach. Normally her belly was sleek, and her hump was fairly small. Now she looked inflated, and she was in obvious discomfort. The baby would appear soon, for sure.

Samir opened his bedroll in an alcove just outside of her walking track, and put the butter aside. "Now I wait," he said to himself.

He lay down on his rug and stared up at the dry reeds on the roof. A soft, warm breeze squeezed between the boards of his alcove. He was upset about having to give up his school, and started to think about ways he could make money himself to pay the tuition. Every thought failed, and finally he dozed off.

Samir awakened suddenly, wide awake, as if someone had called his name. Alama had knelt down on her forelegs and spread her back legs wide. Her breathing was labored. The baby was on the way. Her belly started contracting. First the front toes and spindly legs poked out and then the baby's nose. Quickly he lit a torch. The head came all the way out, and he could see the long split lip and tiny ears. It looked very pale.

Once the head was out, the rest followed quickly. The baby hit the ground with a jolt that helped it to start breathing. Some mothers turn and begin to lick and nuzzle their calf, but others do not. Alama did not. She sniffed the baby once and walked away from it. Samir grabbed his pocket knife, and cut the umbilical cord before it could injure the calf..

"Marhaba, little baby. Welcome to the world." He used straw to wipe the baby clean, and called to Alama.

"Come back now, little mother. Here is your baby. Come back now. Feed this little girl," he coaxed.

Alama stood her ground and refused to get closer. Samir could see that the calf was completely white, a rare white camel. Even her toes and nose were white. He didn't know if this was a sign of good luck or bad luck, but he now had a job ahead to make sure the baby and mother bonded. Otherwise, the baby could die.

"Look, little mother, she is white like the moon. You can see her in the dark. Come here now. Lick your baby. Come on, come." He walked over and tugged on her harness. Alama stayed where she was.

Camels are intelligent animals, but in some things they were ignorant. What to do with a new calf was not instinctive for camels the way it was for cows or horses. It was useful for a handler to be there and assist. Camel babies must be coaxed to nurse or they can die. Alama wasn't going to help.

The baby was lying on the straw. It rested with its tiny legs folded under its body. Samir pushed and nudged it to indicate that it should try to stand. It weighed almost as much as he did, and it wasn't ready. He went to the alcove and brought the bowl of butter.

"Here you go, baby. Little camel made of moon light. Have some nice butter to eat." He dipped his finger in the bowl and coated it with the soft butter. He then forced his finger into the baby's mouth so it would start to suck the butter off. The mother's teats are long to fit a baby's long jaw, so a finger is a perfect learning tool. Samir dipped his hand in the butter, and coaxed the baby to suck it clean many times.

"There you are. Now you've got it. Let's see if you can drink from your mother now." Samir nudged her to stand on her shaky legs, and guided her over to Alama, to introduce her to Alama's teats.

But Alama had a different idea. She wanted nothing to do with her calf. Each time Samir brought the baby near, the mother turned her body away. It was as if she didn't recognize her own baby. Perhaps she was confused because it was so white. She refused every aspect of it, and wouldn't let the baby near her milk. This was going to be a problem.

Samir ran home quickly and woke his father.

"Father! Wake up. We have a new calf, and she is all white! Alama is refusing her."

Jamal rubbed his eyes and stretched. He took a jug of milk from their stores, and they hurried together to the stable. For the next several hours, father and son tried to coax Alama to accept her calf, but she steadfastly refused, kicking it away whenever it came close. The baby needed food, and looked weak.

"Samir, we must raise this baby by hand. We can't afford to lose her. She will bring good money. Too bad she is a female. She will never have the big stride of a male racer. But her proportions look good. Maybe she will breed champions, God willing. What shall we call her?"

"Amuna!" Samir didn't miss a beat. It was obvious her whiteness came from the moonlight, so she should be named for the moon.

"We will have to feed Amuna every few hours for the next three months, and we will have to take milk from Alama for her, too. I need you to be responsible for this." Samir nodded. Jamal smiled to himself. Maybe this would help to make up for his schooling.

Samir sat with the baby's head in his lap, stroking her velvety nose and the soft curls on her head. Every now and then the camel made a soft, contented sound. It was clear that the camel and her boy had already bonded. From that moment on, the white camel was never far from Samir's side.

CHAPTER 4

For over a year Samir spent every hour he was not studying at the stable. The imam had allowed him to finish out the school year without paying, but now he was a full time stable boy.

Amuna ran to greet him each day as if he had been gone for years. She was getting tall and clumsy. Her nuzzle of affection nearly knocked him down, so he would grab around her neck and lift his feet and swing for a moment to greet her. He always brought her some sort of a treat...a date, a dried fig, a handful of wheat hidden in his pouch. She nudged him again and again until he laughed and produced the treat for her.

Although she was still very young, Samir had decided to start her training. Camels need to follow basic orders, like sit and kneel and up and stop. She was bright, and seemed eager to learn new things. He had no other responsibilities, so even though she was just over a year old, he had already taught her the basics.

"'Muna! Kneel" They did this many times each day. Samir pointed to the ground, and the white camel calf stood a moment longer before kneeling down in the sand with a disinterested look and a snort. She considered herself human, but she had managed to acquire the normal, grumpy vocals of a camel.

"Up, 'Muna! Stand up! Good girl. Now, down! Kneel!" The teenage camel was all unruly legs and long, sturdy neck, and threw out a long, hoarse gurgling bray at Samir. She was tired of this up and down game, and wanted to go walk. Her favorite thing was to run. She knelt as ordered once more and then shook her head strongly, rattling her harness. Samir understood.

"Okay, I know. You want to stretch those long legs out. Let's go for a run then, little girl," he said.

Amuna would not be an adult for nearly two more years, but she had most of her adult size. From the ground to the top of her hump was almost seven feet. Her legs were long, and she had the sleek belly line and big lungs of a racer, just as father had hoped. He tightened a hand strap around her middle as she kneeled, then threw a blanket over her back behind her hump, and leaned against it.

"Okay, girl, up, UP!" Amuna knew they were going to run now, and she responded with a happy toss of her head. Samir didn't weigh much. He perched over her back legs and swung his heels into her belly just in front of each leg. He sat up over her hips, and she swished her tail from side to side with excitement. The brushy end slapped him hard on the left, the right, the left. He rubbed his stinging legs.

Samir guided her slowly down a back ally, then turned right and then left through an opening in the city wall. He could feel Amuna's energy rising as her steps quickened. Before them lay a barren expanse of sand and rocky hills that ran all the way to the distant mountains. Amuna didn't need instructions. She leaped forward and began to pace and then to run. Samir's only job was to hold on.

The four footed rolling trot she used in town quickly broke into a full on gallop. Back feet hit the ground together like a spring and pushed her body forward through the air. All her weight landed on one stiff front leg and then the other, as the back legs shot forward to hit the ground and push off again.

A running camel is an amazing sight, and Samir enjoyed seeing the surprised faces that looked up as they flew by. Amuna might not be the size of the big male racers, but she ran like an arrow with her neck stretched out straight in front of her. Samir had to hang on to his hand strap with full concentration. He wasn't sure she would stop if he fell off.

Camels are not long distance runners. They can pace with their side to side gait all day without tiring, but their bodies are not made for flat out running. After a few kilometers, Amuna slowed down and Samir turned her head back toward town. She was gasping for breath, the air whistling in and out of her nostrils. White lather coated her lips. He knew he would have to groom her tonight before dinner.

As they walked back, he began to think about her speed. She seemed fast to him. He wondered if she was fast enough to enter a race. She would be old enough soon. He would have to talk to father about it. He put his head down on Amuna's hump rocking side to side, closed his eyes, and let the camel find her own way home.

CHAPTER 5

A few months later, Jamal came home from working in the mines with two flat packages. As usual, he was covered in salt dust, and his camels came to lick him clean. They needed the salt. He was carrying two small slabs of salt wrapped in cloth under his arms, and rested them against the stable wall.

"Salaam, father! Where did you get all that salt?" Samir's eyes were big. Father was a laborer who mined salt. It was rare if he was allowed to bring any home. These slabs were worth a fortune in gold.

Jamal smiled a tired smile. "I arranged to work extra hours if I could keep a one-tenth portion for myself. This week I shaped it into slabs, and here we are. We need the money, so I will let you take Amuna to Awdaghust tomorrow with your Uncle Moosa. He is taking six camels, and will keep you safe on the road, insh'allah. Amuna can carry these small slabs with no trouble, and Uncle Moosa will inquire about her value among merchants in Awdaghust. She is almost weaned, and it is time to think of our future."

"What? No, father! You don't mean to sell Amuna! She is a good racer, you will see. I have been teaching her. You have to let her race! You can't sell her. She is our best camel." His eyes pleaded.

"Samir, working in the mines is not easy for me anymore, and we have to do what we have to do to survive." Father walked away toward home, leaving the salt slabs leaning against the wall, and leaving Samir to suffer his heartbreak alone.

That night dinner was silent, and after they ate, Samir went back to the stable to sleep with Amuna. He was devastated, and could think of nothing but how he had fed the young camel every day with his hands, and how playful she could be. Surely Allah wouldn't tear her away. Samir knelt to do his nighttime prayers in the stable when he heard the adnaan, and he tried hard to get the words perfect, so Allah would smile on him with favor.

The next morning Jamal came to the stable to lash the slabs onto Amuna's back. He put a blanket on her back and fastened a small wooden pack frame over her hump, then tied a slab on each side for balance. The slabs were worth their weight in gold in Awdaghust where they had no salt mines, and he hoped to get a good return after the caravan leader was paid his portion. He added a large water skin on each side, then he padded the frame with straw and wool so it wouldn't chafe. He had left room for Samir to sit over her back legs.

Amuna didn't like this new game. She could smell the salt through its cloth wrapper, and kept trying to reach her head around and take a lick. Jamal was stern with her, and yanked her head away from the merchandise.

"Samir, you must train her not to do that. If she carries cargo, she must not turn and bite or lick, otherwise she will have to wear a muzzle strap to hold her head forward. She will not like that at all."

Samir was sulking. He was excited to go on caravan with his uncle, but not under the circumstances. His life looked very grim. First he had had to give up his school, and now the one thing he loved more than anything else, Amuna. It wasn't fair, and he wasn't going to smile about it. Maybe her color would be unlucky to the merchants, he thought with hope, and no one would want to offer a price. Even if they did, before he let his uncle sell her, he would steal her himself and run away. No one would be able to catch them!

"Come on, son. It's time to meet your uncle. I made you packets of dried meat, cheese, figs and dates, and filled two large skins with water," he said. "There is a bag of grain for Amuna. She is well fed, and one bag should be enough to last the journey. You will buy another for the return trip. The caravan leader will provide hay for the animals."

He continued, "The trip will take over six weeks each way, and there are only six stops for water. Be sure to fill your bags full whenever you can. It is important. You never know what can go wrong in the desert. Make sure you keep Amuna watered well. Do you have your knife? Stay close to your uncle, and follow his direction."

Samir nodded at the long list of instructions. He tucked his bedroll and prayer rug under the strap over one of the salt slabs.

"Father," he pleaded one last time, "I don't want to sell Amuna. Please don't sell her."

His father put his hand on Samir's shoulder and said, "We are only asking the prices. Moosa will bring her back once we know her value. Now go with the blessing of Allah, my son. Here are three silver shekels to tuck into your belt for an emergency."

Samir took them with surprise. Father had never given him money of his own. Just then Uncle Moosa in a long striped shirt walked up to them with his arms outstretched and a wide grin on his face. He was a plump man with an expansive personality.

In a jolly, booming voice he asked, "Are we ready to go? Let's move then." He rubbed his hands together with glee and clapped.

"Greetings uncle," Samir said with a small bow.

Moosa ruffled his hair, and grinned over his head to Jamal. "I was about your age when I made my first caravan, youngling. You will learn a lot and see many interesting things. You won't miss your school at all. Let's go have some fun! See you in a few months, brother."

CHAPTER 6

Uncle Moosa turned back toward the caravan, leading Amuna to her place behind his front two camels. Most of the camels had rings through their noses, and a rope went from each nose ring to the tail of the animal in front of them.

A few like Amuna had no ring, and were tied by their harness. All the camels Samir could see were shades of brown and gold and very plump. They had been well fed in preparation for the arduous journey. Amuna, with her slim white body and long legs, was hard to miss. She was the only white spot in a line of animals that stretched as far as Samir could see in either direction.

There must be thousands, he thought with amazement. Armored Almohad soldiers hired by the caravan leader rode up and down the line on their horses, ordering everyone to get into place.

Samir turned with a forced smile for his father, and gave him a quick hug. He still felt anxious. He would try to do as his father asked, but he would also utter earnest prayers five times each day that Amuna was the ugliest camel in Awdaghust.

The caravan was slow to get underway. The first animals moved out long before the last ones took their first step. The rhythmic swaying of the endless line of camels had a mesmerizing effect. They rocked side to side like ships broadside to the waves. The pace was slow, but relentless. They left camp each day long before the sun was up, and rested in the heat of the day. Riders dozed on rugs in the small shade their camels cast. Some stretched their cloaks out from the camel saddle and created little tents to rest in.

Amuna had settled into the routine well so far. This was more walking than she had ever done, so she was glad of the rest breaks, too. It was building her stamina and toughening her body. Samir fastened his cloak on top of her pack, and lay under it with his head on her neck when they rested. The thick fur on the back of her neck crest was curly, but in the crook near her body where he rested, it was smooth and soft.

The caravan was guarded by several dozen mounted Almohad soldiers who rode up and down the line. They would be paid well for this journey, and seemed conscientious. Samir struck up a conversation with a stocky young soldier called Ali from the Harghi tribe south of Marrakesh. He was a muscular young man a few years older than Samir, with dark skin, broad shoulders and a heavy black moustache like most of the southern Berbers.

Ali was interested in Amuna. She was the first white camel he had ever seen. Samir told him a little about her, and explained she was a racer, not a pack animal.

"Do you know there is to be a race day in Awdaghust after we arrive?" Ali seemed pleased to be able to pass along information that was new to Samir. "Sayyid Walid, that merchant over there with the camels in red blankets," he gestured, "he is planning to wager on the races, and bring back some racing camels if he does well, he says. You should talk to him."

Samir got all the details Ali knew about the race, and decided he would find a way to go to watch. He wasn't sure whether he would talk to the merchant or not. He had an uneasy feeling about discussing Amuna with a stranger. Especially one interested in camel racing and buying camels. He had never seen a real camel race, though, and thought he should take advantage of any knowledge he could get. Maybe he could talk to some riders and groomers in Awdaghust, and get information that would help his father understand what a great camel Amuna was.

One evening he decided to mention the races to his uncle. "Amo, I hear that there will be a race day in Awdaghust after we arrive. Do you know anything about it?" He sat cross-legged near his uncle's small fire, chewing on dried figs. The night was still, and the stars were starting to blink into view.

"Hmm. No, but I am not surprised," Moosa replied. "Soon it will be the *mawlid*, the celebration of the birth of the Prophet Mohammed, peace be upon him. That would be a likely time for a festival and a race day. Especially if a caravan as large as this one arrives in town and money is loose. Why do you ask, nephew?"

Moosa sipped thick, black coffee from a small cup.

"I would like to see some camel races. It would help father if I were able to watch other racing camels run, and see how their riders coax them to win."

"Hahaha!" Moosa laughed a big belly laugh and slapped his knee. "Coax! That is far from the right word. You will see how they beat them and kick them so that the animals can scarcely breathe. And the ones that end up at the end of the pack will end up as someone's stew and sandals within the week. Better you should think about how to get the most money you can from those salt slabs. That will help your father the most!"

Samir's eyes became very big. This was not at all what he had imagined. He imagined all handlers were kind like him, and all racing camels were pets like Amuna. It sounded like a terrible business, and suddenly he found himself wanting to return home with Amuna and continue life as before. But there was no way to do that now. He hid his misery and prayed even harder each day that Amuna would be considered ugly and unlucky, so he could bring her back home.

CHAPTER 7

As days passed, Samir noticed his uncle often sat in conversation with Sayyid Walid, the merchant interested in racing. Sometimes they wiled away the rest time playing backgammon or alemungala. Sometimes they just shared a small pot of boiled coffee or tea. Sometimes he could overhear a few words, and it sounded as if they were bartering. Once he saw them facing Amuna and talking, but when they saw him looking, Uncle Moosa just waved and turned away.

Every week or so the supply camels would drop bales of hay for the merchants to take to their animals. Then they would pour barrels of water into a trough for the camels, and place out barrels for the humans to refill their water bags. Merchants hurried to refill their small water bags and bring their camels to drink at the trough. Camels could go two weeks without water if they had to, but it was better to let them drink more often. When they refilled, they could each drink up to thirty gallons at a time, but on the road they were usually limited to about half that. Samir made sure that Amuna and Uncle Moosa's camels stayed well-watered.

Each rest stop, camel after camel knelt down on their elbows and knees with groans, growls and snorts. They were noisy animals. They had thick callous pads to protect them from resting on the hot sand, but Amuna was still young, and her pads were still forming. She often remained standing during the heat of the day to protect her belly from the burning sand. Sometimes Samir spread his own rug under her so she could lie down. She complained when they walked on rocky ground, because she didn't yet have the thick cushioning on her feet that the older camels had. It was not an easy trip for a young camel.

Even at rest, the camels were not still. They ruminated like cattle, chewing their cud with an odd, jerking side-to-side jaw movement. Like cattle, they had more than one stomach, and they could eat pretty much anything, even thorny brush that other animals avoided.

Sometimes two camels would disagree over something and would spit the vile contents of their stomachs at each other. Amuna was not suffering from lack of food, and though she was freshly weaned, she chewed her cud when she rested like the other camels did. Fortunately, she had not yet learned to spit.

Samir had never felt so dusty. His brown hands were so dry they had become almost white. His elbows and knees were constantly tender, as if they had been scraped bare by sandpaper. Each day he would squint into the distance and hope for the first hint of palm trees. It had been almost a week, and they were due to arrive at the first oasis Azrou any day now.

The steady left-right-left sway of the camels walking, and the bright sun beating down, had a hypnotic effect. When trees finally did appear on the horizon, he thought it was a mirage. He was too worn out to get excited about what he might see there. Right now, all Samir could think about was walking straight into a welcoming pool with all his clothes on and sitting in the water for the rest of the day.

Azrou was built at the base of ancient cliffs in the rocky hills. Instead of palm trees, there were tall cedar trees in the surrounding countryside. The cedars could be seen from thirty kilometers away as a low, dark smear across the sand in the distance where the rocky ground turned up toward the cliff and the mountains beyond. Remarkably there were monkeys in the trees! Samir spotted a family swinging through the branches, and ran to ask Uncle Moosa about them.

"Yes," he said, "these monkeys were here when this area was still alive and green. The advancing desert cut them off from their families in the south, but they continue to thrive here." Experienced caravaners learned that when they were in Azrou, they should never leave anything lying loose or unattended. The monkeys were bold, and would slip in and steal things, especially in the night.

The shimmering haze on the horizon soon solidified into shady groves and the buildings of Azrou village. As excitement began to travel down the caravan from the leaders, everyone's pace picked up a little, and the handlers had to rein in the camels to keep things orderly. The animals smelled water, and were eager to get to it. Camels never forget a place where they have found water, and most of these camels had been to Azrou before. Even Amuna started to dance a little in her walk, as if she wanted to trot, but it was too hot to make the effort.

Attacks in an oasis violate the rules of the desert, so everyone uncomfortably put aside their weapons for the duration of their visit when they entered. Almoravid guards eyed the Almohad caravan suspiciously, but allowed them to pass. The permanent residents got their primary income from the fees paid by caravans for using their water, but the residents also grew ample dates, pomegranates and vegetables from small family patches, and sold any excess to the travelers.

The oasis village occupied the western side of the large palm-fringed pool, and extended up the side of a low hill toward the ruins, where it received some shade in the afternoon. Fortified mud brick buildings were divided by a complicated braid of irrigation channels. A small enclave of artisan craftsman provided rudimentary tools and repairs.

The eastern side of the pool was empty except for groves of date palms fading away into cedars. This is where the caravans pulled up to water their animals and fill their water barrels. A few small muddy creeks marked by reed beds ran off from the pool in several directions.

Caravans normally rested in an oasis for two or three days. On the third day, the caravan leader rode through the area telling everyone to load up. They would head out before sunrise. Ali told him Khenifra, the next oasis, was a long eight days away. He fell asleep marking the days off in his mind. This would be his routine for the rest of the journey.

Two days later, Samir was surprised by a change in the landscape. Misshapen pillars of red sandstone began to appear in all directions, like lost legions of giant soldiers frozen in place. The wind had eroded them over centuries, and they were every imaginable size and shape. Samir entertained himself with imagined stories of an ancient war on this plain where the armies were unexpectedly turned to stone. Perhaps they were demons who had been frozen by Allah. Perhaps these were the evil forces who fought with the army of stars at night.

A week later, the sea of sand soon gave way to a flat valley with patches of green that led to an ancient Roman ruin. Khenifra emerged like a vision out of the sand. This oasis was an early Almoravid military encampment built in the ruins with a wadi running through it. The Romans had dammed the water centuries before, and created a huge pool on the edge of which the village had grown up. An octagonal minaret of rough stone rose high above the small oasis mosque, and did double duty as a lookout tower. It could be seen from several kilometers out.

The walled sanctuary of Khenifra was known for its olives, milk and colorful hand woven rugs. It had been the wintering headquarters for Berber tribes until Ibn Yasin conquered the great trade routes. Now the turbans and veils of the Almoravids were everywhere, and there was only grudging peace. The caravan's routine in each oasis was the same. The animals were fed and watered thoroughly, the humans bathed in the river or the hammam, and some limited trading was done. Remarkably, they were all uneventful stops.

When a big caravan like this one came through, the oasis guards moved among the animals to keep an orderly flow around the water. They were especially necessary in this Almoravid oasis when a caravan was guarded by Almohad. Tensions between the two factions were always high. Heat and travel fatigue made it worse. Even Samir was aware that his friend Ali and many of the older merchants were tense.

After a few hours, though, the soothing shade from the many date palms and the cool green of the valley brought calm and good spirits to the weary travelers. Off to one side, some local boys were jumping into a covered water cistern and laughing.

After watering Amuna and helping Uncle Moosa to settle his camels, Samir wandered over to join them. Soon, he was wet and clean and felt renewed. It was good to splash in water and talk freely among boys his own age. When the muezzin sang the adaan from the minaret, Samir bowed down gratefully to pray with everyone in the oasis.

Two days later, the camel leader rode through to tell them to load up. Samir took Amuna for a last long drink at the pool. He fed her two dates and hobbled her for the night. He was happy for a few more hours of resting in the cool grass before facing the relentless heat of the desert again.

A brief four-day journey took them to the tiny village of Soumaa. It was only a quick stop to refill water containers, not a real oasis. There was a single well with a hand operated pump, and a small pool they had to refill manually for the animals to drink from. It was important to water the animals well for the next leg of the journey, and it took two full days to water all their animals. The next oasis was over a week away, through the Atlas mountains, at Todra.

As they moved east toward the mountains, they crossed a section of deep sand dunes. The road was less packed or noticeable here, so the caravan strung out across the ridges of the dunes like fringe on a blanket. It took less effort to walk the tops than to go up and down all the slopes. It was a striking picture to see the very long line of camels and men stretched out as far as the eye could see across the ragged tops of the dunes.

Dust floated constantly in the air. Precocious winds blew it from one side to another so it waved like an erratic, wispy veil. The wind often crossed the crest of big dunes with a strong whoosh and blew sparkling particles ten feet out that then showered down with a sssssss sound on the travelers like crystalline rain.

Samir loved to stare into the distance and watch the glinting sun sparkle on the sand, and then see the sand swirl suddenly up into dust devils that danced and twirled across the flats like sinuous dancers.

Amuna's nostrils were often closed against the dust, and her eyelashes were coated with it. Even her white fur was a dirty beige color. Samir was coated with dust, too. Everyone was.

Uncle Moosa looked fatigued. He walked beside his camels most of the time, and his trudging steps scuffed up the dust as he walked. He was often drenched with sweat, so he had to drink a lot.

Samir was less affected by the heat, but he made sure to offer his uncle water when they walked together. He had seen men pass out from heat exhaustion before, and knew it was dangerous. He didn't want anything to happen to his uncle. Moosa's only comment on the long, hot stretches was, "The desert will test the limits of a man." Some were tested worse than others.

The caravan leader knew the best route through the mountains, and managed to keep the caravan at lower levels on flat areas that lay between sharply rising slopes on both sides. They made good time, but it was still a very long trek to the far side. At least the morning and afternoon shade cast by the mountains helped them to keep moving during the heat of the day and sped up the journey.

On the eighth day, the caravan rounded a sharp bend. The camels were starting to be thirsty, and in the distance they could see the walled forts of Todra nestled at the base of the mountains with an endless flat plain spreading out before it to the Sahara. The pace of the caravan picked up noticeably with their destination in sight.

Todra was a point where Morocco connected to so-called black Africa, and the dark skinned races were dominant. It was a gateway city, and would have been a major trading center like Awdaghust if it were not so remote from the other centers of civilization.

Todra consisted of four walled fortresses with small villages lying in between. The fortresses were made from stacked rocks and had small windows. Each fortress had a broad, three-level square tower with caps at the top corners. Todra had been founded centuries before to grow date palms, and the palms were evident everywhere, along with grape vines and fig trees.

As the caravan pulled into the oasis, the variety of people and cultures found in a gateway city was obvious. The dark skinned people were probably the original and most ancient citizens, and the lighter or "clear skin" Berbers were probably the second group of residents. The Berbers had imposed their culture and language on the existing population.

Interestingly for Samir, the third group present were Jews who had come to Morocco a thousand years before. Even though they adopted the Berber language, the Jews retained their monotheistic religion and traditions.

Samir knew that they were called 'people of the Book', and treated with respect, but he had not seen Jews before. When the Muslims came to southern Morocco a century earlier, Islam replaced the animistic Berber worship in the area, but Arab culture did not penetrate far beneath the surface in this region. Traditional Berber and Jewish laws continued to be applied with only some influences of shari'a law.

Todra was a true melting pot and very prosperous. Its main wealth came from silver mining. There were mines in the nearby mountains, and the residents got good prices for it from caravans heading north. Cities like Fez that used both silver and gold currency were hungry for silver. So were the rich families who bought silver ornaments and jewelry.

Most of the local residents were miners, laborers, tanners and leather curriers. Samir enjoyed going from village to village during their three day stay and seeing all the strange and unique goods for sale. Even in Fez he had not seen some of the unusual art and weaving done by the residents. Or some of the animals in cages. He liked to spend time watching them. On the third day, they loaded up the caravan again, and prepared for the five day trek to Tata, the final oasis before Awdaghust.

CHAPTER 8

Tata was the oasis Samir enjoyed the most. The caravan moved southwest along the mountains from Todra, and on the fifth day detoured sharply from the main track to the east. Within half a day they were in a canyon hidden in the side of a free standing mountain.

The narrow defile they entered suddenly widened out into a large, grassy space around a huge lake that was fed from three mountain streams. Tata was an old Berber stronghold, and was controlled by the Almohads.

About thirty small villages were built against the rocky walls of the steep canyon surrounding the lake, and tall cedars and date palms created cooling shade in the heat of the day. Most of the houses were built from pink clay, and had large green gardens and animal pens containing sheep and goats. Lemons, oranges, and almonds grew among the palm groves. There were even fish in the lake.

Almohad guards could be spotted in the surrounding areas of the village. Tata was a wealthy oasis, not only for its natural beauty and lush vegetation, but also because of its slave market. Tata was the largest slave market in southern Morocco, and twice a year the oasis was filled with representatives for nobility all over the country—especially from Awdaghust and Marrakesh—vying to purchase more slaves. Everyone who traveled along the caravan routes made a point to stop over in Tata. Ali also seemed to enjoy Tata, and spent a lot of time talking with the Almohad soldiers there. He liked hearing their stories and rumors of battles.

Unlike most of the other oases on the route, Tata was a mixture of Muslims and pagan Berbers who lived together in relative toleration. This meant that all travelers felt welcome there, and less restricted than in the Almoravid oases.

In these more southern oases, only about half of the residents responded to the calls to prayer. When Almoravid caravans or army units visited, there was greater tension, since the Almoravids were orthodox Muslims and didn't tolerate heathen infidels well. But normal oasis rules and peaceful interactions usually prevailed. Samir had begun to realize that even feuding forces actually did respect the sanctuary of oasis.

When they loaded up to leave Tata, Samir began to get excited. The next stop would be Awdaghust. But he was also anxious. For weeks now he had been able to relax and enjoy the novelty of the journey, but in a week more they would be at their destination, and he didn't know what to expect there for Amuna. The only bright spot was anticipation of the race day and what he would learn.

Ali rode beside him as they left the canyon. "How did you enjoy Tata, little brother?" Ali asked.

"This has been a very interesting journey over all, Ali, but I liked Tata the best," Samir replied.

"Well, get ready for a few hard days ahead. The last leg of this journey is not the longest, but it is the worst. Your camel will need her water, and so will you. Everyone will be hot and tired, and tempers will flare. You might want to be especially kind to your uncle," Ali smiled. "And to me!" He smiled again, saluted and rode away.

Everyone on the caravan was getting restless now. They were anxious to get to their destination. The animals were more bad tempered, and camels regularly snapped and snarled and spat at each other. Ali was right. Everyone was irritable, and seemed to want to hurry, but the caravan leader kept them at a steady, even pace.

On the second day on the route, the sandy ground became rocky, with many large rocks the size of water barrels. Off in the distance Samir could spot a few red clay two-story houses.

Samir usually walked beside Amuna on difficult ground. He was guiding her through the open spaces between the rocks when he saw a strange mark on one of them. He walked over to look and thought it looked like a bird's head. He looked a little closer and discovered that many of the rocks in this area had markings on them. He tied Amuna to a nearby camel, and took one of the smaller stones to Uncle Moosa.

"Yes," Moosa said, "these are petroglyphs of the ancient people who lived in this area from the time of the first men. They carved these symbols into the rocks. When we were boys, your father and I used to run through these rock fields and see how many different types of animals and figures we could find."

Samir busied himself for the next two days doing exactly the same thing. He found birds, many images of antelopes, spiders, snakes, scorpions and carved on one rock a rhinoceros with two horns. There were also random symbols he didn't understand, but he thought one might be the moon and others stars.

By the time the landscape returned to sand, they were over halfway to Awdaghust. There was nothing on the horizon in any direction as far as he could see, and the sun beat down on them like through a glass lens. They crossed a gravel pan that amplified the heat even more. The heat rose from the rocky road like an oven. Once again they returned to traveling by night and resting in the heat of the day as best they could. They were all feeling depleted from the long, difficult trek.

CHAPTER 9

Two days later, over six weeks into the journey, the sun rose revealing the outline of a city wall and several large towers to the south near a large mountain. Finally they were approaching Awdaghust. They had made good time.

Ali rode over close to Samir and pointed. "There you are, my young friend. We have made it to safety. Perhaps I will see you again on the return journey."

Samir was full of questions. "Ali, is it true that fountains shoot water into the air in Awdaghust? I heard that they have peacocks as big as goats there! Do you know where they keep the racing camels? Will I be able to get close to them?"

"Slow down, my friend!" Ali smiled. "Yes, there are such fountains and peacocks. About the camels I don't know, but I'm sure there will be many there, since they will have a race day. No doubt you will be able to examine them. All will be known to you very soon. We should arrive there by midday tomorrow."

Ali's small turban was wrapped loosely around his head and neck in the Almohad style, and a tail hung down in the back to protect his neck from the sun. He pulled the tail around and wiped his dusty face with it. He was looking forward to bathing in the hammams.

"I can't wait to see this city!" Samir exclaimed. "I wonder if it is like Fez? Are the streets of sand or stone? What kind of wonderful foods are there to eat? Is it a safe place? Do they really use coins of gold?"

"Insh'allah, all will be known in due course," Ali said with a smile. "Emir Ibn Yasin himself lives here. He rules Awdaghust, and doesn't like the Almohad. We must observe the shari'a laws strictly. Mind your behavior— Awdaghust is a very conservative religious city, even though the entertainments and gold keep everything lively. Keep your hands clean. Take care of your camel, and tie your belongings well. Salaam." Ali bowed slightly with a touch to his forehead and rode away.

Uncle Moosa walked up beside him and said, "There we are at last! Awdaghust. Now we will have some fun! The trading is the best part of all this hard journey. And I will be thankful to sleep in a soft bed for a few nights. My old bones tire of these long, hot treks in the sun. I want you to stay near me while we barter. You may learn a thing or two, youngling."

"I will, Amo. How long will we stay here? When will we go home?"

"You are ready to go home already when we are just arriving? Such a boy!" Moosa laughed. "That reminds me of a Mullah Baba story." As long as he could remember, Samir remembered Uncle Moosa telling him Mullah Baba stories. He had one for every situation, even if it was impossible to find the sense in it!

"Mullah Baba's friend asked him, 'Mullah, which is wiser, camel or man?' Mullah answered him, 'Camel.' 'Why?' his friend asked. 'Because a camel carries loads, but does not ask for more, whereas man, even if he is overwhelmed by responsibility, often chooses to add more.'"

Samir smiled as if he had not heard the story before. "I guess that is true, and I feel the burden of my responsibility. So when do you think we will go home?"

"We will probably be here a week. You were right. There is to be a race day in four days. We will probably leave three or four days after that. I will pay for us to enter the race grounds so you can look around the track. Our friend Walid will be looking for some camels to buy, so I will accompany him and see what the dealers offer. But be careful," he said and turned to grip both of Samir's shoulders, "Even though they can lose their right hands, there are many pickpockets in this city. Keep your belongings out of sight and tightly tied."

Awdaghust was also an oasis city, but a rich one, built upon sand, and almost barren of vegetation. Its wealth of water was in a large, clear underground aquifer and numerous artesian wells located throughout the city. Cucumbers, wheat and millet grew in abundance, but the only crops that grew without hand watering were date palms and henna trees. The citizens appeared to be even wealthier than those in Fez.

Awdaghust was a great crossroads trading city. All the major trade routes from a dozen directions flowed into Awdaghust. Tens of thousands of people lived there, and a large percentage of them were slaves working for rich masters. Slaves far outnumbered the owners.

Salt came from the Muslim countries north and east. All the countries to the south came to Awdaghust to purchase salt, because they had no salt mines of their own. Gold mines lay in the south, however, and everyone desired gold, so Awdaghust was a thriving north-south trade center. Commerce was conducted in gold dinars, and everyone took a percentage from every trade. There were many rich people. Most of the wealthiest lived in great palaces in the lush center of town, with lavish gardens and fountains, supported by thousands of slaves.

Ali was right. They arrived when the sun was high the next day. The city had several caravanserais around its walls—large, walled shelters with an open thatch roof where caravans could unload and house their camels for their stay. Samir's caravan was so large it had to be split into two groups.

Sayyid Walid went to the other caravanserai, and Samir discovered that he was relieved. He was still bothered by the things Uncle Moosa had said, and seeing how Walid looked at Amuna didn't make him feel better. He felt uneasy. He intended to stay with her as much as possible, but this night Uncle Moosa had invited him to stay in an inn and sleep on a real bed. It was a temptation he could not resist. He had never slept on a soft bed.

The caravanserai was two levels. The lower level was a large open room with a reed and palm roof. The roof was for protection from the sun, so it was possible to see the sky in places. Air could flow freely and the thatch blanketed the interior in dark shade with small patches of sunlight coming through.

In the back by the wall was a long, deep watering trough for the animals. About thirty at a time could drink. The trough was kept full by a channel that ran from one of the underground springs. Long stone benches ran along each of the side walls. The wide entrance was the only way into the caravanserai, and one or two soldiers were stationed at the entrance day and night.

Outside there was a stairway up to a second floor area that contained small, rustic sleeping rooms with string cots. Merchants were assigned a sleeping room by the caravan leader and were charged a small fee by the city for the luxury of privacy. Valuable items could be kept in the sleeping rooms and guarded.

Many merchants opted to save the cost, and slept with their animals in the lower area like they did on the road. Others decided to hire guards to protect their valuables, and went into town to sleep more comfortably at one of the many inns. Young men like Samir usually bedded down with the animals.

Samir helped Uncle Moosa unload and tend to his camels, and secure his trade goods. Almohad guards were posted at the one entrance to the caravanserai, and as darkness fell, most of the traders and camel handlers poured into the town with excitement. There would be good food and baths, bubble pipes to smoke, and old acquaintances to meet that night.

The ultra-conservative Almoravids didn't allow wine or music, but visitors were welcome and found plenty of other activities to lighten their purses. There were food carts and restaurants, gambling, entertainments, brothels, jugglers, magicians, tumblers and fortune tellers vying to separate a traveler from his gold. Rickety merchant stalls made from spindly poles and reed or palm leaf awnings were set up selling food and drinks throughout the town. Tea sellers strolled through the streets with large, hot vats strapped on their backs, selling tea by the cup.

Piles of dates and fragrant spices could be found on nearly every corner, along with coffee and mint tea. The aromas of cinnamon, garlic, cardamom, peppers and fresh mint swirled through the air near the markets in waves. There were strange items like dried camel heads, monkey paws, ostrich eggs, hand painted pottery, strings of strangely shaped beads, brightly colored leather slippers, and kilim bags woven in exotic patterns.

In the squares, acrobats tumbled and animal traders from the south presented exotic, colorful birds and animals in cages. There were baskets of all sizes and shapes piled high everywhere. Samir didn't even know what most of them could be used for.

A much loved feature of every desert town had been introduced by the Romans—the large public bath houses or hammams. The men from the caravans poured into the baths, where they steamed and scraped and scrubbed themselves clean before going for dinner. Moosa went to the hammam immediately, then off to dinner with some acquaintances.

Samir was left on his own. He wandered the streets for a while, taking in all the sights and smells. He found it was easier to get around in this symmetrical city than Fez. Fez had been designed deliberately as a maze of twisting alleys centuries before to confuse marauders and prevent them from pouring rapidly into the town to overwhelm it. Awdaghust had wide paved streets in large, concentric circles.

Everything cost money, but Samir held on to his. The browsing and people-watching were free. In addition to his caravan, two other large caravans had arrived from the south. They had all decided to stay over the week because of the Prophet's birthday holiday.

There were Moors from Spain and black Africans from Ethiopia and Ghana, elaborately tattooed Yoruba artisans from Ile-Ife, nomadic blue men from the south who herded camels, and men of all colors and shapes wearing every imaginable type of dress. Merchants came up to him and waved sheer cotton and wool shirts and pants at him. Many were in vibrant colors. They were disappointed when he said no, and kept walking.

Samir wandered around the streets with wide eyes and amazement for several hours. Even in Fez he had never seen so much diversity.

Throughout the city, the Almoravid soldiers in their fat, spiked turbans and fitted face veils were constantly visible. The *Qur'an* says, "Turbans are the crowns of Muslims, turbans are the dignity of believers," but it was against the law for anyone but an Almoravid to wear this distinctive dress. They were a notable presence since Awdaghust was a major Almoravid city.

The Almohad soldiers who rode with Samir's caravan were forced to remain outside the city wall. The Almoravids let them move freely only within their own barracks, except to enter the mosque to pray at appointed hours. Even hated enemies were allowed to pray.

CHAPTER 10

Awdaghust had many thousands of inhabitants, laid out in roughly rings of prominence. The outer wall of the city was near the sandstone escarpment of the single mountain nearby. Soldiers' barracks and the caravanserais were just outside the wall.

The outermost ring of roads was for the artisans, merchants and shopkeepers. The innermost rings were for the aspiring and the wealthy. The houses and citizens became grander the closer Samir walked to the center of town.

Each residence was surrounded by high walls protecting its grand inner courtyards from prying eyes. The doors into the high walls around courtyards and homes were arched, and often painted or tiled in bright colors. Many doorways were framed in glazed tiles or ornate bronze work. The grandest homes had elaborate wrought iron gates surrounded by colorful enameled tile patterns and ornate pendant lanterns hanging from elaborately carved brackets. Samir drank in all the variety and detail.

He passed dozens of wells and fountains, and even though it had been dark for several hours, he could still hear loud haggling underway in the many market squares. There were smaller mosques and craftsmen's shops of all kinds, with signs indicating where to get a saddle or iron tools or armor and weapons or pottery. Knives and swords and hilts on display everywhere were inlaid with precious agate, amazonite and garnets.

Samir took his time looking at all the wares. In one shop he discovered special saddles and blankets for horse and camel racing, as well as padded straps in bright colors to protect the animals' faces and necks from rough handling.

He asked the saddle shop owner where the races would be. "Over in the track by the west gate. Day after tomorrow," the man said.

He took Samir by the sleeve and pulled him aside, saying in a low voice, "Are you planning to wager? My brother has a real beauty in the second race. The camel's name is Jabbar al-Takruri…'Strong man from Takrur'. He would be a good bet. A sure winner."

The man winked and poked Samir in the shoulder, then turned away. Samir took note of the information, and planned to tell Uncle Moosa later. The shop owner would probably get a percentage of any bets on that camel.

It was late when he got to the inn where Uncle Moosa had rented a room. The night prayers had finished well before. The inn was called The Peacock's Nest, and had turquoise tiles set around the dark blue, arched wooden door. Big, ornate copper lanterns were mounted on the wall on either side of the doorway, making it hard for anyone to slip in or out of the inn unnoticed.

He entered and asked the innkeeper for his uncle's room. The winding stairway was steep. He knocked on the door. When he entered, Moosa was in a big bed with carved wooden columns on each corner. A sheer curtain surrounded it, and fluttered like butterfly wings in the soft breeze from the window.

"Oh, Amo! What a bed!" Samir exclaimed. He approached it with his eyes wide, and touched the sheer fabrics on the bedding and curtains with respect. "It is for an Emir!"

Moosa laughed and said, "Then this night I am an Emir! Bring me pomegranates and a dancing girl!"

Samir laughed.

"There is a bath behind that screen, Samir. Make use of it. You look part camel yourself right now, and smell like one. You will sleep on that small bed under the window."

By the time Samir had bathed in the cool water and soaked his skin for a while, Moosa was fast asleep and snoring. Samir poked his uncle so he would turn over, and then got into his own bed.

As he expected, it was like a dream. He was floating on soft clouds, and being blown about by the warm desert wind. He was asleep in minutes, and the next thing he knew, the sun was beating down on his face through the carved wooden window screen.

Moosa was already gone. Samir had missed the morning prayers, and breakfast, so he decided to run out to check on Amuna and his salt slabs. With a little effort, he found the caravanserai. His friend Ali was currently standing guard.

"Salaam aleikhum, little brother," Ali said. "You are late today. And you apparently found the hammam." He laughed.

"Aleikhum salaam, brother," said Samir. "Yes, at last I am clean again. What a city! I have seen so many things. I slept on the softest bed of pillows you can imagine this night. I never knew it was possible to sleep in such a way. The rich must sleep like this every night. No wonder they look so happy!"

Ali nodded and smiled at the boy's enthusiasm. "I remember when I first slept on a real bed. You will never forget it. Are you here to check on your camel? She has been looking for you."

Samir nodded, and ran inside. Amuna stood out immediately. In the dimly lit shelter, she was a pale spot standing alone. She snorted when she saw him, and tried to come forward, but she was hobbled. She stopped and gurgled loudly at him. He came up and hung from her neck, then stroked her nose and cheeks. He could see the double row of long eyelashes protecting her big brown eyes. She stared intently at him as if trying to tell him something.

"Amuna, Amuna. Little moon. You are upset with me for being gone, aren't you? I wish you could have seen me. I was lying like a prince on the softest pillows. But now you are hungry, aren't you? Oh…what? Ouch!" She nipped his arm with her big teeth. "What was that for? Ahhh…you want your treat, eh? Did you think I would forget you?"

He reached into his pouch and pulled out three fresh dates he had found on the streets as he walked along. The trees were fruiting in the parks, and he had managed to collect them before the birds and rats did.

He fed them to her one by one. It seemed to cheer her up. She was well rested now, and wanted to go for a run. She nudged Samir several times. After pushing her away several times, he decided it would be okay to take her out, so he removed the hobbles, had her kneel, and he climbed up on her back. She started walking toward the door before he even had a chance to settle himself.

Ali waved as they went through the door. Samir barely had time to lift his hand back. Amuna took off into an immediate trot, then broke into a full gallop.

She had not been able to run much for weeks, and it was exhilarating. Amuna thundered across the desert at a breakneck speed that literally took Samir's breath away. Sand and rocks were flung out in a torrent behind them in every direction. Amuna had transformed in that moment from a bored-looking teenaged camel to a strong, fiery racing beast.

For a split second, Samir caught the mischievous look in her brown eyes, and knew that any attempt on his part to stop her would be futile. He wrapped his legs tightly around her soft underbelly, grabbed a wad of thick fur in each hand, and held on for dear life.

This was as close to flying as he had ever been in his dreams. At that very moment, nothing else in the world mattered more to him than the thundering sounds of his camel racing like a champion through that stretch of deserted sands in the wilderness and the feel of the wind on his face. He closed his eyes and let the speed wash over him.

Amuna finally slowed down foaming, snorting and breathless. Her whole body quivered as she danced sideways through the sand hills, shaking her head and blowing air loudly out of her nostrils. Samir patted her furry back and smiled. He had been right about this magnificent animal. They would have many exciting races ahead of them. She was amazing.

It had felt good to stretch out her legs, but Samir didn't want to go too far from the city walls, so he turned her back toward town. No telling who or what was out here in this unknown place.

He was right to worry. Behind a dune, a small band of Almoravid soldiers were watching him with interest. One was Ibn Yasin himself.

CHAPTER 11

Mansur ibn Abdallah was the oldest son of Emir ibn Yasin, the ruler of the Almoravids. Even as a young boy, Mansur had preferred the quiet pursuits of reading, writing and imagination to the rough and tumble ones of his younger brothers. He had his father's temperament. Most people believed that he would follow in his father's footsteps and become a religious scholar or jurist.

Ibn Yasin favored Mansur, and spent many hours with the boy, discussing religion, politics and the governance of people. Although the Almoravid emirate was not hereditary, most people assumed that if Ibn Yasin lived long enough for his son to acquire his full education, Mansur would rise to replace him. He showed great promise. Ifs are always big unknowns in a world in flux, but Ibn Yasin invested what time he had to guide his son as wisely as he could.

Like his father, Mansur was completely comfortable being in libraries, studies and quiet places to read and reflect. Unlike his son, Ibn Yasin had a warrior streak in him that left him craving to join his armies in the field. Often he did.

By the time Mansur was a teenager, Ibn Yasin had started demanding that the boy join him on his forays into the desert. He insisted that Mansur needed to know how to ride and to understand how his armies lived, plus how nature, human and otherwise, affects campaigns and discipline. He also wanted Mansur to enjoy the company of older men, so he could start to assess for himself the qualities of leaders and the values that those around him should have.

The private family residence in Awdaghust was in the center of town, on a large estate fed by one of the natural springs. The great stone residence was built around a large, central courtyard ornamented with flowering vines, clusters of tall trees and three large pools. An army of gardeners watered and trimmed everything meticulously. Lavender wisteria and crimson bougainvillea draped over the walls. Roses and jasmine bloomed profusely, and scented the entire courtyard at night. Most official visits and parties occurred in this courtyard.

The family's private apartments surrounded a variety of smaller, more intimate courtyards with private gardens featuring elaborate fountains, pergolas and reflection pools. The rooms became heated during the day with the sun beating relentlessly on the stones, so all the rooms were deep and had large openings facing the courtyard. Inner doors in the back of each room connected one room to the next and were kept open. Any slight breezes could flow through unimpeded and cool them all down. Privacy was maintained by placing screens with silk panels or woven tapestries at strategic spots.

Mansur's room was on the second floor, which gave him a sight line out toward the mountain. He liked to sit on his balcony and look through the elaborately carved balustrades to watch a family of peacocks that lived in the courtyard below. Sometimes he would throw grain down to feed them, or he would mimic their piercing call. They created brilliant displays of turquoise and blue against the green grass and trees.

There were large, elaborately carved cedar doors on either side of his room that stood open against the inner walls. They were never closed in this safe place. The doors were draped with sheer blue silk cloth that hung on either side and could be pulled across the opening if the occupant desired privacy. Mansur rarely noticed whether they were open or closed. He was happy as long as he had a low reading table in a brightly lit area, a cushion or two to lean on, and a sheaf of scrolls to read.

On the day of his recent foray into the desert, he had been sleeping in his room with a cool breeze blowing. It was still dark when his father came into his room.

"Mansur, wake up," Ibn Yasin said loudly, "we are going to the desert. Dress quickly. There is little time."

With that, he was gone. Mansur had no choice. He dragged himself out of his warm bed and scratched his scalp, shaking his head and blinking his eyes to rouse himself. He ran his fingers through his long brown hair to smooth it, then tied a leather strap around it to hold it out of his face. He used the chamber pot and was pulling on the first tunic that came to hand when a slave slipped quietly into the room and lit the wall sconces. Strange shadows from the candles danced on the half-lit walls.

The slave handed him a fresh burnoose with a slight bow. It would be too hot for it later, but while the cool was still in the air, he would need it. He grabbed his turban from the chest where he had left it the night before, and slipped sandals on his bare feet as he left the room. He headed down to the kitchen.

This morning he was hungry, and he would have to eat fast. Father was probably already pacing at the door ready to go. With luck, they could get to the city wall before the muezzin sang the adnaan. They would have to stop to pray.

Mansur had no idea where they were going, but then he rarely did on these unexpected excursions. Usually they were just an excuse to get his father out of the house and onto a horse.

Mansur grabbed a loaf of flat bread from a platter, and sliced off a thick piece of cheese to go with it. Even the servants were slow this morning. Usually they had something ready for him as he went out the door.

Ibn Yasin strode into the room, saying, "Let's ride!" Mansur threw his turban on his head crookedly, stuffed his food into his sash, and was right behind him out the door.

"Salaam aleikhum," Malik said with a brief salute to Ibn Yasin. He was standing outside the door and holding the reins to their three horses. Malik was Ibn Yasin's right hand and commander of the militia.

"Aleikhum salaam, Malik. Shall we give the horses a stretch? We haven't been on a hard ride in two weeks," Ibn Yasin replied.

"Maybe we can find some fun out there today. I heard there might be a small caravan leaving for Meknes," Malik replied. "I have a company of light cavalry at the ready, in case you are eager for a skirmish."

Malik smiled at Ibn Yasin. They were old friends, and Malik knew that, despite his scholarly responsibilities, the Emir was always up for a skirmish.

Ibn Yasin turned to look at his son. "Let's go and show Mansur some action. Soon he will be in university and will forget all his riding skills," Ibn Yasin said. "I think a company might be too many men, though. Dismiss half and let's ride light."

Malik nodded, and with a slight bow, mounted smoothly and turned his horse out of the rounded gate to address the men beyond. Mansur enjoyed being out with the men. His brothers were too young yet, and it was time that he could have alone with his father—something he didn't get much of.

"Father, why do you pursue the caravans? They bring goods and gold to our city."

"Yes, they do bring goods and gold, but they also carry gold away," his father replied. "If they are enemy merchants or infidels, their gold should stay here, where it will do the most good. We just help them to make that decision before they head back home. We don't take it all. Just a 'departure' tax," he smiled.

"The main thing is we don't want them using our water without paying. They very often try to do it stealthily, so we remind them that we must be paid our due. People often need to fear the consequences so they will do the right thing. Let's mount."

As if choreographed, they each put their left foot into the stirrup and swung their right legs across their saddles. In that moment, it became obvious that Mansur was the young version of his father. He had already attained his father's height and mannerisms, and sat in the saddle with the same straight posture.

Father and son rode through the arched gate, and Malik came toward them. "We are ready, Emir. These men will accompany us." He waved toward a contingent of twenty mounted warriors.

Ibn Yasin saluted formally to the men. He pulled his veil up over his nose and mouth, and all the men followed suit. Then he pressed his heels into the sides of his horse and took off at a gallop. He wanted to be outside the city walls before the call to prayer, as Mansur knew, and the sun was just about to break the horizon.

Malik's information proved true. About two hours later, they spotted a small donkey caravan heading north toward the Todra oasis. It had only a few guards whose affiliation was uncertain. Probably mercenaries.

Ibn Yasin gestured to go after the caravan. The men drew their scimitars and with a great shout, they ran full speed toward the donkeys. Ibn Yasin was in the lead. They were spotted almost immediately, and the caravan took off running down the great trade route. It was flat here and hard packed. Easy riding for the horsemen, who gained quickly on the caravan.

Malik and a few men rode to the head of the train, and forced it to stop. The other men subdued the few guards with practiced efficiency. Ibn Yasin rode to the fore.

Malik said, "Esteemed brothers, you appear to have forgotten to pay the departure tax for your animals when you left Awdaghust. Where are you headed?"

The caravan leader knew it was a shakedown, and replied with resignation, "Meknes."

Malik replied, "Ah, the queen of oasis cities. Well, I see that you have about thirty donkeys. Fully loaded, so your trading was successful, yes? Your departure tax is 150 gold dinars."

The caravan leader stared angrily at Malik for a moment, then over at Ibn Yasin and Mansur. He started to protest, and gripped his saddle horn so tightly his knuckles turned white. He clenched his teeth, and then gave a small, sharp nod. He reached into a purse in his belt and counted out the coins.

"Do you rob all caravans that leave your city like this?" he asked as he handed over the gold.

Malik replied, "Only those of infidels. If you were Muslim, you would be on your way now with your gold intact. Salaam." He bowed and backed his horse away from the caravan leader, and made a gesture of waving him on.

The donkeys were reluctant at first to get moving again in the heat and brayed loudly, but they eventually began to walk. Malik rode over to Ibn Yasin and handed him the gold. He pulled down his veil and wiped his dusty face with the tail of his turban.

"A profitable morning," Ibn Yasin said as he tucked the money into his belt. "Are your men up for some competition, Malik?"

"They always are, sir," Malik replied. "What do you have in mind?"

For the next few hours, Ibn Yasin devised a variety of races and exercises designed to show the men's strength and stamina. He enjoyed watching the determination on their faces, and he knew that giving them a chance to perform before their Emir was reward enough. Soon they were all sweating as the sun moved overhead.

"Let us find a place to rest and pray," Ibn Yasin said to Malik. "The sun is approaching midday. Find us some shade."

The soldiers rode east a few miles across the tops of the dunes, and spotted some scrub trees ahead. They went down the slope to the small shady grove to rest and drink. The horses were glad of the shade, and the men were glad to stretch their legs. The walls and minarets of the city were just visible above the long, barren expanse of sand to the south.

Ibn Yasin, Mansur and Malik had not yet dismounted when Mansur turned to face south abruptly and cocked his head as if listening. Immediately the men fell silent. Malik nodded and scurried forward up a small dune, gesturing for the others to mount and follow quietly.

In the distance, he saw a single camel. A camel as white as snow was running straight toward them. As they watched in amazement, it slowed and turned back toward town. Ibn Yasin nodded, and the horsemen charged the camel, waving their scimitars.

CHAPTER 12

Samir steered Amuna back toward Awdaghust, and as Amuna's run slowed to a walk, Ibn Yasin and his men ran up from behind him on their horses. They rode in a circle around him, and fired questions at him all at once, like drum roll. Their veils hid their mouths, and their armor flashed like fiery jewels in the sun, making them very intimidating. Samir was terrified, and tried to answer. Meanwhile, Ibn Yasin rode around and around Amuna, studying her lines and manner.

He raised his hand for silence. "Boy, is this your camel?" he asked.

"Yes, mawlawi," he said with deference and lowered his head. "I have raised her from birth."

Ibn Yasin gestured and a boy on a sand colored horse came forward. He was wearing a smaller version of the Almoravid turban and veil. He was obviously the son of the leader.

"What do you think, Mansur," Ibn Yasin asked. "These Almohads and their camels. Maybe we should think about expanding our herd. We do not have a white camel.

Camel troops are quite effective in battle." The boy nodded.
He watched Samir with curiosity.

"I will buy her," Ibn Yasin announced, turning back to
Samir. "Twenty-eight gold dinars. She is a good animal."

That was an astonishing amount of money, and Samir
was suddenly very afraid. "Sir, I cannot sell her. She is the
best camel of my father's lot. We are poor people, and she
will mother our future stock. I don't think she is powerful
or large enough for someone of your stature. Perhaps you
could find a better one in the market."

Ibn Yasin smiled behind his veil, but stood up in his
saddle. "Do you know who I am?" he thundered.

Samir shook his head, "No, mawla, I only arrived last
night. I have met no one like you before."

"That is true, and you are unlikely to." Ibn Yasin sat
down in his saddle again. "I am Abdallah Ibn Yasin, the
leader of all the Almoravids, and the lawful ruler of Fez,
Awdaghust, Sijilmassa and Marrakesh. I do not shop in
markets," he said with growl. "People bring me gifts of
their best stores so I will keep the peace and protect the
trade routes. Perhaps you would like to give me this camel
in exchange for your life, and save me the trouble of going
to a market?"

Samir's eyes got very big. He nearly slid off Amuna in
fear. This was not going well at all. Amuna whipped her
head around quickly and nipped his leg. He had to do
whatever he could to keep her safe.

"Mawlawi," he said using the most formal title of respect and dropping his eyes, "this camel is very young and unskilled. She is my only friend and my responsibility. I cannot go home to my father without her. I ask you please to let us go. We will leave in a few days, and I will speak only kind words of you to all I see."

Ibn Yasin's men were having trouble to keep from laughing out loud. They could see the boy was about to wet himself with fear. Even young Mansur had an amused look.

Ibn Yasin threw the men a look that said, *Control yourselves*, and turned to address Samir. "Boy, what is your name?"

"Samir ibn Jamal, mawla, I am from Fez," Samir answered.

"I will let you go on one condition, Samir ibn Jamal. You will bring me the first calf of this white camel. I like horses. I don't raise camels, but I think she will produce good stock. Bring me her first calf when it is weaned, and settle our debt. If I do not see you in due course with a fine camel, I will come to Fez myself to claim this one."

Ibn Yasin pulled his scimitar from its sheath. Samir could see it was encrusted with jewels that flashed in the light of the sun.

"Mawlawi, I will breed her with the best camel in Fez, and I will bring you her calf as you ask. Thank you for sparing me. I will not forget." Samir bowed respectfully.

Samir and Mansur locked eyes again for a moment, then Ibn Yasin and his men began to gallop again in a wide circle around Samir, waving their weapons in the air and shouting a shrill war cry.

Ibn Yasin charged at him one last time, pointed at his chest with his scimitar, and called, "Remember!" Then he and his men took off riding to the north at top speed.

Samir slumped down on Amuna's hump in relief. "Oh Amuna, I was so afraid! Now what have I done?" he said. "Father will be so angry that I have given away one of his camels! I cannot say anything to Uncle Moosa about this meeting. He will be furious! We should never have come out here."

He turned Amuna back toward town and let her run again until she tired. Her lips and cheeks were covered in white lather from the run.

Samir watered Amuna in the caravanserai and groomed her, then replaced her hobbles, promising her he would return that night.

The muezzin sounded the call for evening prayers, so he went outside to pray under the open sky. He knelt facing east, and gave thanks for his narrow escape, praying that no one else would take serious notice of Amuna again.

CHAPTER 13

Uncle Moosa woke Samir the next morning with a kick that made Amuna bray.

"Wake up, nephew! We have an appointment with Walid to visit camel markets today. It is the Prophet's birthday, peace be upon him, and no sales can be made, but all the sellers will be out showing their animals and taking wagers for the races tomorrow. Even those blue camel nomads from the south have come. Bring your camel. We will see what they say she is worth."

Samir's heart sank. This was the day he had feared. And now he really had to make sure nothing happened to Amuna. He owed Ibn Yasin a calf, and he didn't think the man would forget! He put on Amuna's harness, unfastened her hobbles and led her out of the shelter. Today he wished she weren't so white! She had no blankets on, and her color was startling in the bright sun.

As they walked through town to the market, many people stopped to stare at her and mutter. Walid approached from the crowd and greeted Moosa and Samir cheerfully.

"Salaam, my friends!" he said, and they all smiled and nodded to each other. Samir was wishing the earth would open up and swallow him and Amuna.

"Let's go in and see what's for sale," Walid said, "and we will see what the buyers have to say about this snowflake of a camel."

The biggest camel markets in southern Morocco were held in the village of Nul Lamta every Saturday at daybreak. The town was home of the Amazigh, the indigenous people of the south, and the site of an important annual camel-trading fair. Nomadic herding of camels is commonplace throughout the region south and west of Awdaghust. As luck would have it, a large caravan of camels had arrived just yesterday from Nul Lamta.

Accompanying them were Tuaregs, or "blue men of the desert". They got their name from the clothes they wore. The blue color was pounded into the cloth instead of boiled to save water, so the cloth rubbed its excess pigment onto the owner's skin. The garments the blue men wore were tinted with indigo, a very scarce and expensive plant dye, and the men's skin became blue from constant contact with the pigment. Dark blue hues on a man's skin were considered an indication of great wealth.

Samir had to work hard not to stare at the blue men, especially when they inspected Amuna. Many of them did. They were fierce looking men with very dark skin made even darker from the indigo dye. Their hands were dark blue up to the elbows, and they rubbed the blue on their faces as well. They were a mixed race that traveled freely throughout Morocco and the Sahara, and despite their dark skin, many of them had blue or grey eyes.

Samir knew he shouldn't think such thoughts, but he wondered if their private parts were blue, too. He didn't think he would like to be blue like that. He surreptitiously checked Amuna's fur where they touched her to see if the blue rubbed off onto her. It didn't.

The marketplace was teeming with activity. For hours buyers went up and down the rows, lifting camel's feet to inspect them, opening their mouths to check their teeth, feeling down their legs and backs for any signs of malformity or old injuries. Many of the camels were bad tempered, and snorted and growled. Some even nipped at their handlers and prospective buyers repeatedly, or spit violently. Really mean ones wore leather muzzles. Samir hoped seeing these bad mannered animals would not give Amuna ideas.

Although she didn't like it, Amuna allowed strangers to put their hands on her and open her mouth. Several of the merchants commented that her lines were good and her legs were strong, but they thought the white color represented a weakness that would show up later in her calves. Samir started to squirm as the buyers got personal about Amuna. He didn't want anyone to be interested in buying her or breeding her. He would run away before letting anyone buy her.

One merchant chattered about the coming races, and Samir heard him mention a good camel named Jabbar in the second race. He took a double take to see if it was the shopkeeper who mentioned the same camel. It wasn't. Perhaps Uncle Moosa could make money if he bet on Jabbar. He had to try to remember to mention it to him later.

Two of the merchants thought Amuna might be able to race in smaller, local races, but didn't hold out much hope that she could ever be a champion. She was much smaller than the best male racers, so they would outpace her. This discouraged Samir. It was the answer to his prayers to Allah, but secretly he had wanted to learn that Amuna was the most beautiful and desirable racing camel ever.

Despite Amuna's flaws, the two merchants expressed willingness to overlook them and buy her after the *mawlid*, making Samir look at Moosa with wild eyes. The prices offered were good, more than 30 gold dinars, but Samir absolutely did not want to discuss selling her. Period. Moosa sensed his discomfort, and eventually led the boy and camel out of the market.

"At least we know our answers now, boy, eh? Your father has the start of his racing herd." He ruffled Samir's hair and though it was a sign of affection, today it annoyed Samir.

They bid goodbye to Sayyid Walid. He and Moosa had a few private words, and the boy and his uncle returned to the caravanserai. Tomorrow would be a busy trade day, so he hobbled Amuna and helped his uncle to organize his trade goods.

All Samir had to sell were the two salt slabs, and they could easily be tied onto Amuna's back to take to the market tomorrow. And then it would be time to go to the races! Samir could hardly contain his excitement.

Moosa headed back into town for dinner and another night sleeping at the inn. Samir stayed behind. He thought maybe he would have an early night so he could be up early and ready for the next day.

Night came quickly for boy and camel. They were tired. He unrolled his bedroll. A boy Samir had not seen came over to stare at Amuna. After a few questions, he invited Samir to go into town to check out the location of the racetrack for the next day. Samir eagerly accepted. He was tired of adult conversations, and his fatigue miraculously disappeared.

He patted Amuna, who was already kneeling, rubbed her tiny ears, and the boys left. There was a new guard at the door, and he nodded at them as they passed. No one paid much attention to a couple of young boys coming and going. They easily found the track, and after a few hours went their separate ways to bed down for the night. Samir made his way through the sleeping camels and piles of trade goods in the caravanserai to the spot where he had left Amuna.

She was gone!

CHAPTER 14

Samir stopped in his tracks and stared anxiously around in all directions, thinking perhaps her hobbles had loosened and she had wandered. She was nowhere to be seen. He panicked. Perhaps she had just wandered out and decided to run.

He asked the guard if he had seen the white camel, and the man said, "No, but I just came on duty half an hour ago, and no one has gone in or come out." Samir ran to a camel handler sleeping nearby and woke him.

"Brother, did you see anyone come in here and take away my white camel?" The man shook his head, and said, "I saw and heard nothing." He didn't want to talk, and turned away to resume his sleep.

Samir didn't know where to go next. Uncle Moosa was still sleeping at the inn, but Samir knew he would be cross to be awakened. Instead, he ran out the door and far into the desert, calling, "Amuna! Muna come back now. Come! Amuna!"

He waited and listened. The half-moon was up and he looked in all directions as far as he could see. There was no familiar camel shape anywhere. His heart pounding in his throat, Samir trudged back to the caravanserai. Perhaps the guard who was there before had seen something. He asked the new guard if he could identify the last guard so he could go and find him. No luck. The new guard only passed the other guard in the dark with a salute as the shift changed. He said he didn't know the man, but he had likely gone back to the Almohad barracks. Samir headed that direction.

It is intimidating to walk into a soldier's barracks when you don't even have a beard yet. The barracks was a large, squared off area full of tents and gear. Samir was conscious that it was late, and he was very out of place. He walked smack into the guard seated near the entrance.

"Oh, excuse me! I didn't see you there. Salaam aleikhum, brother. Do you know which man was guarding caravanserai six tonight? His duty ended a few hours ago," Samir said.

The man sat down again on his box and continued carving on a stick with his knife. He paused to stare at Samir for a moment, and then resumed carving, saying only, "Nope."

Samir tried again. "Is there someone here who keeps a list of the soldiers on duty? Perhaps you could check the list, or I could talk to him." The man remained silent, as if Samir had vanished.

"Brother, I am sorry to disturb your excellent whittling, but an emergency has occurred, and I need to find the guard." Samir tried to hold his ground and stared at the soldier's face. The guard shrugged. "Come back in the morning," he said and turned away.

At this moment Ali came around the corner of one of the tents. He walked over and greeted Samir. "Salaam, rider of the moon. What brings you to our barracks at this time of night?" Samir beckoned urgently to him to follow, and went a few yards away so the other soldier couldn't hear.

"Ali, greetings and gratitude. I...," Samir's voice broke, "my camel was stolen while I was in the city tonight. I was with her all day in the market, and bedded her down. Now she is gone. I want to find the guard who was there while I was in town tonight, and ask if he saw anyone take her out. Can you help me?"

Ali tugged on his moustache a moment, and said, "Tonight was my duty night, but I was told that someone had volunteered to take my shift, so I went to bed early. I didn't see the man who volunteered, and no one mentioned a name. Wait here. I will go and see if I can find an answer." Samir felt relief to be in the presence of a familiar face, and sat down on a nearby barrel to wait.

A short time later, Ali emerged.

"My friend," he said, "there is a mystery here. No one in the company seems to know who took my shift tonight. Everyone is accounted for." Samir's eyes widened in disbelief.

"If your camel is gone and not strayed, then she has likely been stolen," Ali said. "She is an unusual animal, and no doubt caught the eye of many strangers this day when you were out. Did anyone offer to buy her, or spend an unusual amount of time touching her and studying her features?"

Samir told him of the last two merchants who had offered thirty gold dinars for her. He also mentioned Sayyid Walid, who often looked at Amuna as if he would like to have her himself.

"Thirty gold dinars is a good price, but if that was their first offer, I suspect your camel would sell for double that to the right buyer. She has a racer's body, and should breed good stock with unusual markings. Let's see if we can find anyone who saw anything unusual tonight. I will go with you to the caravanserai," Ali said. Samir nodded, and jumped up to lead the way.

They walked around in the caravanserai for more than an hour, waking camel handlers and body guards to see if anyone had noticed Amuna leaving. Finally, there was a small breakthrough.

One of the handlers who slept near the entrance had awakened briefly when he felt movement close by. He had nearly been stepped on by a camel, and it turned out to be the white camel he knew from the caravan. He had not seen the man leading her clearly, because he was wearing a burnoose and had the hood up. He had noticed his feet, however, since his head was near the ground, and saw that one dark strap on his right sandal had pulled loose from the sole.

Samir thanked the man, bowed, and walked outside with Ali.

"Well, we have a few clues now," Ali said. "We know she was taken, and we know the man didn't want to be seen, and that he has a broken sandal strap. That isn't a lot, but maybe we can find another clue in the market. They have to keep her somewhere, and she is quite visible, even at night. I think we should stroll the market you visited today, and look in the camel stalls as we go. Maybe we will get lucky. Here, drink some water," Ali said. He smiled at Samir and offered him a water bag. Samir discovered he was very thirsty, and nearly drained it dry.

Ali had grown fond of Samir and his wide-eyed enthusiasm for life. It reminded him of his two younger brothers at home in the mountains south of Marrakesh. He wanted to help Samir find his beloved camel.

As Ali and Samir cautiously approached each camel stable around the market, they looked for a camel sheltered from sight, or fully covered in blankets. The walk around the empty market produced no Amuna. They also checked sandals resting outside the doors. No luck.

Ali had another idea. "Perhaps it is one of the rich merchants in the center of town who has her. They have private barns and stables. If a thief brought such a prize to the right buyer, his price would be paid, no questions asked. This town is dripping in gold. Let's go visit some palaces and see what we can find. Perhaps my uniform will work in our favor, unless we run into a gang of Almoravids. They will know I am supposed to be outside the walls, and might get pushy, but perhaps the common people will be kind and assist us."

By then it was midnight, and most of the shops and inns were closing or dark. They kept to the shadows, and moved into the lush inner circle of town unmolested.

"Shh!" Samir stopped suddenly and tugged on Ali's arm. They froze. For several minutes they stood completely still, breathing silently.

Finally, Samir said, "I thought I heard Amuna bray. I know her voice. Perhaps she senses me nearby. Or maybe she is just calling for me. I only heard it once. I think it was that way." Samir pointed down a dark paved road that curved off to the left.

The road was wide, and there were leafy gardens here and there along the way between the massive walled compounds. The heavy sweet scent of night blooming jasmine and honeysuckle filled the air. It felt cooler in this part of town. Here and there they could hear the soft sound of running water.

Well-kept corrals and barns appeared on both sides of the road between palatial compounds, and the two slipped quietly from one to the next, trying not to attract attention. All of the stables and barns had open windows or low doors to let the breezes through to cool the animals. They moved smoothly without disturbing even the peacocks roosting in the eaves or trees. Mostly the stables were filled with horses and a few goats.

They came upon one large stable that was different from the others. It was very long, and held many more animal stalls. It was whitewashed and could easily be seen in the soft light of the moon. They weren't sure if they could enter and move through without disturbing the animals and alerting the guards.

"What do you think, Ali? I want to look inside," Samir whispered softly. "I feel like she could be here."

"It's a promising spot. That looks like a room of some kind at the far end, but we will have to be cautious. Guards could be inside. Move smoothly so we do not startle any of the animals," Ali said. "We will go in together, but if anything happens, I will come out and try to distract anyone who comes to check. You must hide inside until it is clear. When you can, make a run for the caravanserai. I will meet you there as soon as I can."

Samir nodded. They crept up to the stable door. It was pitch black outside, but someone had left a small lamp burning at each end of the building. Perhaps that would be enough light to help them avoid stepping on any cats or rats inside. They entered, then stopped to listen. All they could hear was the occasional stamping of hoof or shifting of straw. They hoped there were no handlers bedded down with the animals. Samir led the way. If he were spotted first, he would be less likely to cause alarm.

The corridor was long, with thirty stalls on each side. The floor was covered in deep straw and it smelled like a stable. Mostly there were horses in each stall, but occasionally one was empty, and sometimes a goat or a cat slept near a horse. As he approached the end of the corridor, he could see that the room at the end was closed. There was no visible lock on the door, but there was a wooden latch that only a human would be able to open.

Samir pointed to the latch, and Ali shrugged. This was the most dangerous moment. If they opened the door and Amuna was there, a handler in the room with her would be aroused. If Amuna was not there, a guard might be inside sleeping. The unknown was what Amuna might do if Samir entered the room, with or without a guard being there. If she made a noisy greeting, it would alert the nearby guards or create noisy responses from the horses outside. Samir didn't know how to silence Amuna except to greet her and stroke her nose.

Opening the door was a big risk.

CHAPTER 15

Ali signaled that he was going back near the entrance, and would try to distract any guards so that Samir could escape with Amuna if she were in the room. Samir waited for him to get down to the other end, and then put his hand on the latch, closed his eyes for a brief prayer, and then quietly twisted the latch and slid it open. He paused a moment to listen, held his breath, then opened the door very slowly. The hairs on his arms rose.

The room was darker than the corridor where he stood, and it took a moment for his eyes to adjust. But there was no denying what he saw inside--a large white shape. He let out his breath and quickly glanced around for a human, but saw no one. Amuna smelled him and started to get to her feet to greet him. He patted her and said, "Down, Muna. Kneel." She resumed her kneeling position.

He went around and petted her neck and stroked her soft nose. She still had her rope harness on. "I am so happy to find you! We must be quiet, and we must leave this place now, before they see us."

Samir moved behind her and leaned into her hump, saying softly, "Up Muna." She raised her back end, and then lifted the front and turned her head around to gently nip his leg. He positioned his heels in the soft belly inside her back legs. "Let's go, girl. Walk softly and don't scare the horses." He pulled the door closed behind them to delay a guard, if any should come.

They reached the far door without making a disturbance. Since camels have soft feet, Amuna made barely a sound as she walked through. Suddenly, he heard Ali's voice.

"Greetings, friend, I took a wrong turn in the dark and somehow ended up in this place. I don't know how to get back to my barracks. I'm glad you were sleeping in that hut," Ali said.

Another voice mumbled something Samir couldn't hear, and then Ali said, "Thank you, brother. Would you be good enough to lead me back to the road? I'm not sure I can find it on my own in this darkness. My commander will be furious if I am not on duty when the sun rises." Ali had given Samir the clues he needed to escape.

The men set off straight for the road, so Samir guided Amuna to the right and tried to stay behind trees or buildings as they moved further down and closer to the main gate. As soon as he could get onto the road safely, Samir kicked Amuna and said, "Run, Muna. Run." She had never run in town or at night, but she picked up her pace to a trot.

There was just enough moonlight for Samir to see the road. They made it to the center of town without seeing anyone. Samir slowed Amuna to a walk and took some deep breaths. His heart was pounding.

A few more turns and they were back at the caravanserai. He waited inside in silence for a few minutes to see if he had been followed, but everything remained quiet. He jumped off and led Amuna to her place.

Samir knew what he had to do. He had Amuna kneel, and quickly placed a blanket and the pack frame on her back. He grabbed a water bag and some food. He threw his bedroll up on her back, and borrowed one of his uncle's large burnooses from a nearby chest. Then he dragged his two salt slabs over and leaned them on his uncle's trade goods. His uncle would understand, and sell the slabs in the market later that day. Samir was ready. He led Amuna out of the caravanserai just as Ali walked around the corner.

"That was exciting," Ali said, full of enthusiasm. "It looks like you heard me and were able to go the other way. Well done, little brother. We are unscathed, and now we are both thieves!" Samir nodded, rubbing his right hand anxiously. A thief who is caught would lose his right hand to the sword.

"Where are you going?" Ali asked.

Samir said, "I will go north into the desert for the night. No one will find us there, Insh'allah, and I will decide what to do after that to keep Amuna safe. I want to see the races tomorrow. It will help my father. Maybe I can find a place to hide her so I can come into town. What about you? What will you do?"

Ali answered, "I will do what I always do. I will take my work shift now, and perhaps I will go into town to the races for a while tomorrow. If you bring Amuna back to the caravanserai, I will stay with her and guard her myself."

"Shukran, Ali, thank you. I am in your debt. I will not forget. I will see you in a few hours in the caravanserai."

Samir kicked Amuna to let her know she should go. He turned to wave at Ali, and then grabbed his safety strap. Amuna didn't need an invitation to run. Run, she did, until finally she tired and was ready to walk. By then, only the night sky and brilliant stars were visible in all directions. The walls of Awdaghust were out of sight. There was not even a glow in the sky. Samir noticed a few scrub trees and some grasses behind a dune. They would rest there.

He dismounted and pulled out a date treat for Amuna and stroked her neck. She kneeled down to rest, and he covered her back with his uncle's ample cloak. It was brown, and would keep Amuna from shining quite so brightly. He unrolled his rug and put his head on her neck for a pillow. Yes, this would do just fine. He studied the stars until his eyes closed, and together, they slept.

CHAPTER 16

Samir woke to the blistering heat of the sun on his face through a break in the tree branches above. He was annoyed that he had overslept, and hoped he had not missed the races. Uncle Moosa would be worried by now. He was probably already in the market selling his goods. Or maybe he had already finished, and was looking for him.

Samir quickly loaded up Amuna and rode south toward town. They entered the caravanserai before noon, and found Ali was already asleep in Amuna's place. Uncle Moosa's trade goods were gone, including the salt slabs, and Samir guiltily hoped that his uncle had made good profits this day. Samir hobbled Amuna, settled her for a rest, and thanked Ali for his offer to guard her.

"You had better be here when I come back," he said affectionately to Amuna, and pulled gently on her tiny ear.

He was in luck. This race day was not like normal race days. Usually, the races alternated between horses and camels. The organizers had decided to run all the horse races first in the morning. He had not missed any of the camel races at all. The first one was about to start. Since his uncle was not around to pay his entry, he waited until the guards were busy with other patrons, and he slipped in unnoticed. He worked his way down to the track area, and scanned the audience for his uncle.

Finally, he spotted him. Uncle Moosa was seated on the far side, about half way up, next to Sayyid Walid. Down to their left was the box where the wealthy sat near the finish line. Large banners of colorful silk were spread overhead to keep the sun at bay for the nobility. Samir could see the large poles on either side of the track where the starting and finish line banner was strung across.

On all sides, handlers and jockeys walked and groomed camels dressed in dazzling colors. Many of the camels wore tall, padded saddles with high fronts and backs over their humps. This was a traditional style, where the rider would hook his right leg around the front saddle post and then lock it in place with his left leg over the ankle. It left both arms free to manage the reins and the riding prod or whip.

Others wore sleek, contoured saddles behind their humps. Those jockeys sat low and hooked their heels into the belly of their camels, like Samir had been doing instinctively.

Camels were moving about everywhere, and many of them complained loudly, despite their colorful muzzles. With all the bellows and snorts and grumbles, it was a noisy and chaotic scene. Samir loved it.

Suddenly a horn blew, and about twenty-five camels filed out onto the track to stand under the starting banner.

Samir's heart leaped. The first race was about to begin. The camels were pressed tightly side to side and most of them struggled with being in a pack like sardines. They bumped and jostled, snorting and growling, and swung their heads as if to bite. Miraculously, they all ended up behind the line for one moment.

Someone in the private box struck a gong to signal the start, and the camels bolted off the line, their jockeys whipping and goading them to make a fast start.

The power of the running pack of animals was staggering. The ground vibrated beneath Samir's feet like heavy thunder as they passed. The onlookers cheered wildly as the camels galloped by. Some led with their left legs and some with their right, but they all had the long three-point gallop of a racer. The extended necks bobbed up and down as they ran, creating visual confusion. It was impossible to tell one camel's parts from another, except for the blur of the blue numbers painted on their necks.

He tried to analyze their gaits to see if the best ones did anything different from the others. It was hard to tell. The two back legs landed together and gave a forward springing action. As the animals flew through the air, one front leg extended vertically to the ground and absorbed all the landing force and shock of the momentum. The other leg carried through and became the platform from which the next push of the back legs would propel the animal forward. Their long curved necks extended forward until they became almost straight.

It was an odd and awkward looking gait, and yet these

camels could run as fast as the best horses, especially on packed sand like this track. Their two-toed feet spread wider than a big man's outstretched fingers as they hit the ground, and helped to hold the camels steady. It was an amazing thing to watch. Samir understood why so many people were fascinated with camel races.

Behind Samir a man cried, "Last call for bets. When they round the end, betting is closed."

An elderly man rushed up and pushed some gold at the bookie, "Here! Put three gold dinars on number seven."

The bookie took the bet and gave the man a receipt. "Good luck. Number seven is favored."

Samir quickly figured out that the bookie said that about whatever number the fools bet on. Praising the choice of the wager seemed to be good for his business.

In this race it was obvious who the winner would be. Camel number five had led from the start and couldn't be caught by the others. Samir watched his rider carefully, to see how he guided his animal through the turns, in the pack and when he was out front alone. He observed how the rider had a fluid movement of hands and hips. He would pull the camel slightly back and then shoot him forward like an arrow to pass, all the while speaking to the camel with his heels in its belly.

Samir wanted to go over to Uncle Moosa after the race was over, but the infield was mobbed with winners and well-wishers, grooms and handlers. Samir had forgotten to tell him to bet on Jabbar in the second race. But more than that, Samir was really anxious to enter Amuna in the race now, and wanted his uncle's support.

Although she is young and inexperienced, he thought, *I will not have this chance again soon. I don't think she will win, but I want to know what she can do.*

He turned toward the park entrance and found the place where contestants register to race. Samir told the man in the booth that he wanted to enter his camel in the third race.

The man looked at him for a moment and said, "The third race is full, but we have a spot in the fourth. That will be the last open race before the Champions Final race for all the winners."

Samir didn't hesitate. He said, "I wish to enter my camel in the fourth race."

The man said, "That will be five gold dinars."

Samir gulped. He had only the three silver shekels in his belt. He held out the shekels and said, "Will you accept this?"

The man shook his head. "You won't be racing this day unless you have the proper fee. If you can get the money, get here fast, before the last position is sold." He turned back to his paperwork.

Samir's heart sank.

CHAPTER 17

Samir was deeply disappointed. More than anything, he wanted to race. If Amuna finished well in a big race like this, his father could get better prices on her calves.

He returned to his spot by the track. He knew he wouldn't have another chance like this to race. *Five gold dinars is as much money as father makes in six months*, he thought. The taste of defeat was bitter in his mouth. He heard the bookie behind him again, and walked over.

"Salaam, Sayyid. Can you tell me how much I would need to bet on the next race?"

"Salaam, young brother. You can bet any amount, large or small. It's up to you. What you get back is up to the odds on the winning camel. But of course, you have to choose a winning camel, or you will lose all your money. Don't bet if you are afraid to lose your money," the man said kindly. "I will not be afraid to keep it, if you do."

Samir reached into his pouch and hesitated a moment. He thought of what his father would say if he found out that the first money he had ever given Samir had been spent on a wager. He knew no other way to get the entry fee, though. He pulled out his three silver shekels and said, "I want to bet."

The man was amused, but took the small amount of money, and said, "Who is your favorite camel in the race?"

Samir paused, a little panicked by the question. He hadn't thought to pick a camel as he walked around the track. The only camel he knew in race number two was the one the shopkeeper had mentioned, Jabbar "the strong."

"I will choose Jabbar," he said. Now it was in God's hands.

The man held his face in check. He didn't want to take the money. Jabbar was the worst camel running in race two. The boy would lose everything. But this was his business, so he said, "Okay, three silver shekels on Jabbar," and handed him a receipt.

"How much will I get back if he wins?" Samir asked.

"About five gold dinars," he said. "Good luck! Jabbar is the favorite."

The race was not scheduled to start right away, so Samir decided to seek out Jabbar in the preparation area. He wanted to whisper good wishes to him and tell him to win. He noticed an opening where some camels in colorful livery were starting to walk out.

Perhaps the camels for the second race are in there, he thought, and slipped in when the guard wasn't looking. He walked around studying all the sleek, well-fed animals and he admired their condition. Their saddles and harnesses were brightly colored and elaborately decorated. Even their clumps of left over winter coat had been trimmed neatly.

He wound his way through the pack and came to a scruffy looking animal in plain brown leathers in the back, kneeling and waiting for his saddle to be tightened. Of course, it was Jabbar.

Samir was aghast. He would have laughed out loud if he hadn't been so shocked. Jabbar was a caricature! He had a scrawny looking body and big, clumsy feet. He had probably spent his life hauling water to the vegetable fields. He looked like he had not had a good meal in years, and his face had no sparkle of life in it. His teeth were especially bad.

He even looks too old to be running, he thought. Betrayal is a bitter pill. The shopkeeper had misled him, and the merchant in the market was wrong. Amuna could beat this old camel without even hitting her full stride.

Nevertheless, this was his choice, and now all Samir's hopes were riding on his bony back.

Samir gulped and addressed the jockey. "How is he feeling today?"

The jockey answered, "He is feeling strong today, God is great, and I think he will be able to finish the race."

Samir nodded with his face blank, trying to mask his despair.

He approached Jabbar and patted his neck kindly. He whispered to the old camel in a soft voice, "Jabbar, beloved of Allah, pour out your heart this day and win. We must win, you and I. I will give you my beautiful camel to be your mate if you win. You are sure to win, God willing. Go out and run like the wind!" He silently begged him again to try hard, and left sadly to find Uncle Moosa.

Moosa was relieved to see his nephew appear. "Where were you all night and all day? I have been worried sick," he said. His eyes looked like storm clouds. "And how did you get into the track without money? I think we have some serious talking to do."

Samir apologized to his uncle. "I'm sorry you were worried, Amo. Someone stole Amuna last night, and I hunted for her all night. I didn't want to wake you when I discovered she was gone." Samir watched Walid out of the corner of his eye to see if he would react. He didn't.

"Did you find her?" Uncle Moosa looked surprised and distressed. "Who would do such a thing? Where is she now?"

Samir said, "Yes, I found her. I have left her with one of our guards. I will tell you the story later. Amo, I want to race her this afternoon, but I have no money for the entry fee," he blurted out. "Could you loan five gold to me from my father's salt profits?"

Moosa paused and pulled on his beard. He appeared to think hard about it. "Samir, I cannot do this. Your father would not spend five gold just to learn that his camel is not a good racer. She is too young to succeed, and she might get injured. That is a lot of money to him. I think it is better to go home with his profits and his camel intact. I'm sorry to disappoint you, but you will have to talk with your father about this and race her another time, if he is willing."

Anger stirred inside Samir. But he dropped his eyes, bowed with respect and walked away. He would find a way to enter the race, and show his uncle just how wrong he was. *Now I really need Jabbar to win,* he thought.

The horn blew again, and the second race was about to start. Samir watched the lining up with great attention, since he hoped to be lining up himself in the fourth race. It looked like the bigger camels tried to fight for inside places on the line near the wooden rail. They shoved and slung their heads to hit their neighbors.

The smaller and weaker animals were pushed to the outside. Samir would try to get Amuna on the inside, though he wasn't sure how she would react to being crammed into such tight quarters with so many other camels.

Well, I'll deal with that when the time comes, he thought.

Bong! The starting gong was struck, and the camels bolted off the line. The riders whipped and kicked their animals with violent jerks and wildly flailing arms. Their yelling could be heard above the roar of the crowd as they thundered by. Jabbar had a pretty good start. He was in the middle of the pack, and not yet being jostled too much by the bigger males on the inner track.

Samir shouted to him, "Go! Move up now. Don't fall so far back. You can do it! Show them what your name means. Go! Go! You are doing well, Jabbar. You can do it!"

Jabbar began to gain ground inch by inch. When he rounded the last curve, he was in fourth place. Two big males were in front of him, and a smaller one was on his right, hemming him in on the rail. Their long, long legs flew out in front of them, and their necks stretched forward past their feet. It was impossible at that speed to see which legs belonged to which camel. They were moving too fast.

As they entered the home stretch, the unthinkable happened. The two camels in front of Jabbar tangled their front feet in mid-stride, and went down. Jabbar managed to clear them only because he had just pushed off on his stride and was already in the air. One of them fell into the other camel beside Jabbar, knocking him out of his place in the pack, too.

Samir's eyes got very round and his mouth opened in astonishment as Jabbar crossed the finish line—in first place!

CHAPTER 18

Samir went wild! He was screaming and jumping with delight and thanking God for this gift. He ran as fast as he could down the track to where his bookie was. When he handed the man his ticket, the bookie gave him a little smile with the five gold dinars, and wished him well. Samir ran immediately to the registration booth. He put his five gold on the table and said, "I want to register my camel in the fourth race."

The man behind the table looked up at him. It was a different man. He checked the list and said, "Yes, there is an opening, but since two races have passed, and this is the last opening, the entry fee is ten gold dinars."

"No! That is impossible! The other man told me five, and I went to get it. I can only pay five. Please!" The man shook his head, and said only "Ten gold dinars."

Samir turned to walk away. He had no other options. The man said one more thing to his back. "Perhaps you can find a sponsor." His uncle had already told him no. He refused to ask Sayyid Walid. He would probably want Amuna herself for loaning him the fee. He knew only one other person.

He ran back across the track, and this time he approached the box of the nobility. Guards held him back. He kept repeating, "I want to see Emir Ibn Yasin. Please. Let me see Ibn Yasin. It's about his camel. I must see him."

Eventually, the scuffling caught the attention of Mansur, Ibn Yasin's son, who pointed Samir out to his father. Ibn Yasin sent a slave down to see what was going on. When the slave returned, Ibn Yasin scrutinized the boy below, and asked the slave his business.

"It appears the boy is seeking a sponsor for his camel in the final race. The fee taker raised the entry fee to ten gold, and he doesn't have enough," the slave said with a bow.

Samir was still arguing earnestly with the guard.

Ibn Yasin was amused by the boy's brashness. He turned to Mansur and said, "What do you think? Should we waste ten gold on that camel from the desert?"

Mansur responded immediately, "Yes, father! She was very fast, and if she makes a good name here, they will get better males, and you will have a better calf. And he seemed an honest boy."

Ibn Yasin smiled at his son's logic, and nodded. "Go down and guarantee the fee then. Let's see what this white camel can do." Mansur and the slave went down to Samir.

Samir recognized Mansur even though he was wearing the Almoravid head garb and mask. "As-salaam aleikhum, Sayyid," he said with a slight bow.

Mansur's eyes twinkled at being called sayyid, and he returned the formal greeting, "Wa-aleikhum salaam. My father has agreed to sponsor your camel. We think she looks very fast. I will go with you to the registration table to guarantee the fee."

They went to the booth, and the slave handled the transaction. He received the participation papers, and handed them to Samir with Amuna's number. Samir was overjoyed! He struggled to hold back his urge to jump with glee.

"Thank you, thank you!!" Samir exclaimed to both the slave and Mansur, waving the papers excitedly. "Please wait here. I must go get my camel." He stuffed the papers into his belt. "Please! I will return very soon. Thank his eminence greatly for me. He will see his investment was a good one. Please wait! I will be back very soon!"

He took off running as fast as he could through the racetrack crowds, dodging people, dogs, goats and children in the streets as he hurried to the caravanserai. He burst into the shelter, and ran to Ali, who was still guarding Amuna.

"Ali, I am going to race in the fourth race! Come to watch. I don't know how we will do, but perhaps you can make some money if you bet. I have to go. Now!"

"What?" Ali asked with surprise. "How did you get the registration fee?"

"I'll tell you everything later. I don't have time now. I have to go to the ready area right away." Samir's fingers fumbled with Amuna's hobbles.

Amuna was agitated by Samir's excitement, and reached around to nip his leg with her big teeth. He brushed her away, and said, "Not now, Muna! We are going to run!"

She snorted and made a loud gurgling noise in the back of her throat.

Samir threw his blanket on her back and fastened the safety strap around her middle. He leaned onto her back and said "Up, Muna, UP!"

Amuna lumbered to her feet and bumped Ali with her nose, as if to say thank you, and they walked out into the sun. Samir was unaware that he had been followed from the track by two burly men.

He got Amuna safely through the entrance gate by showing his race papers, and was directed to the waiting area for the fourth race. He saw the general's slave waiting, but Mansur had returned to the stands. Samir signaled for the slave to follow.

The other jockeys and handlers all turned to look as they entered the pen. They didn't know this white camel or her rider, but they did recognize the markings of Ibn Yasin on the slave's armband. It created a buzz of conversation.

Samir found an empty spot, and guided Amuna to kneel down. The slave came over and produced a paint pot. With a brush, Samir drew a big twenty-four on both sides of Amuna's neck. The blue paint stood out in sharp contrast against her white fur.

The slave bowed and wished Samir success, then left to return to his place. Just then a big roar went up from the crowd as the third race ended. Samir knelt down by Amuna's neck and stroked her cheeks and nose. Her tiny ears twitched.

"This will be new to you, girl. Don't be afraid," he mumbled in a comforting voice. "Those big camels will push you and try to hold you in, but you can run as fast as they can. Don't pay attention. Run away from them. Just run, like you run in the desert. Do your best. I will be with you, and we will show them how good you are." He was reassuring himself more than her.

He suddenly realized as he looked around that he was a boy among experienced men with much bigger camels. They were adult, professional racers. Who was he to ride against them? He knew nothing. He could feel his palms start to sweat. Whatever had he been thinking to enter this race? His heart was sinking fast.

The rider next to him leaned over and said, "Hey, are you okay? You with the white camel. You look like you are going to puke."

"I think I am," Samir replied. He felt a lump rising in his throat, and said a quick prayer, *Oh God, please, please don't let me throw up here!"*

The wave of uncertainty was about to swamp him, but then an organizer appeared in the doorway and shouted, "All camels for race number four to the starting line!" He didn't have any more time to waste on doubt.

Grunting, snorting, growling and bellowing, the camels lumbered awkwardly to standing positions. Their riders shifted and adjusted their straps a final time, pushed into a line, and in their swaying stride, filed out toward the starting point. There was very little conversation. It was time for business. Even the camels seemed more alert and tense. It would be a few minutes more before the animals from the previous race cleared the track, and the bookies paid off their bets.

Samir's thoughts were spinning. He felt like he was going to faint, so gave an extra tug on the strap. *"What was I thinking? I can't protect Amuna from all these rough animals. I'm so scared! What if I fall off? What if Amuna is knocked down and breaks her leg? What if I break my leg? What if someone hits me in the eye and puts my eye out!"* His heart was pounding in his chest faster than Amuna could run. It was too late to back out now.

Samir sat on Amuna's back feeling more and more tense. Each second that passed was an eternity. Sweat was pouring down his forehead. Several times he reached down to dry his wet palms on his pants legs. Amuna sensed something was wrong, because she turned her head backwards and nibbled on his knee with affection. He reached down to stroke her nose, and smiled. Whatever is happening, she seemed to say, we are in this together. He relaxed a little.

Samir looked toward the stands. A banner of vivid blue silk cloth hid Ibn Yasin and Mansur from view. He did see uncle Moosa, however. He was waving both arms frantically to attract Samir's attention. His face showed disbelief mixed with rage and amazement. There was no way for him to have missed that white camel in the field for the next race. Samir was racing against his uncle's wishes. He raised his hand in a hesitant wave to acknowledge his uncle, and then pumped his fist in the air enthusiastically to show that he was feeling strong.

There wasn't anything to do now but wait. By the grace of God and Ibn Yasin, he was about to race. Amuna would have a chance to show her talent.

Minutes later, a horn blew and the organizer waved the camels through the gate onto the track. They filed up to the starting line. Samir did not look into the stands again. He had to pay attention to everything around Amuna.

Many of the big camels didn't like being lined up shoulder to shoulder with other males, and they struggled and bellowed, stomping their feet and shaking their heads, disturbing the entire line. A few tried to bite the others with their long teeth, but most were wearing muzzles.

Samir found himself pushed farther and farther from the rail in the center. He wondered how the riders would get their camels behind the line and ready, so the starting gong could be struck. It seemed impossible. He could see that all the riders were struggling to control their animals.

Amuna didn't like being compressed in the line either, and began dancing in place. Her ears went flat back, and she was showing her teeth. She was pinned between two big males, and their sides scraped against Samir's bare legs. Her fleshy tail twitched from side to side violently, smacking Samir like a whip on his thighs.

He talked to her to calm her, and her tiny ears swung back to listen. He knew she would be okay if she could hear his voice, so he kept talking. She rattled her harness a few times, but seemed to calm down. The animals magically fell into line for one moment, and a sudden gong strike rang out. The camels bolted off the line. There was no more time to think. This was the critical moment.

Some of the riders had difficulty breaking their camels free from the others in the line for a second, but Amuna didn't wear a special saddle or gear, and her smaller size left her free to slide forward and get out of the start with the leaders. Samir leaned forward on her hump and held on to his strap tightly. He kicked her hard in the belly and she jumped forward. They were finally racing!

CHAPTER 19

"Go Amuna, go girl! Run your heart out. Get in front of these other camels. Go, go!"

Samir was kicking her hard and fast with his heels in her belly, and she knew what that meant. She stretched out her neck straight in front of her and ran. They went around the first curve and she swung a little wide.

Samir guided her back in to the left, and her nose was on the back of the second place camel. The three were a length ahead of the pack behind them, but some looked ready to make a move on the leaders.

Both leaders were experienced, and knew how to handle a newcomer. They ran tightly together, holding Amuna in check. She couldn't squeeze in, and couldn't get around without going very wide and losing ground. They would save their fight with each other for the final stretch. Right now they cooperated to keep Amuna back.

Samir could feel that Amuna was not tiring yet as they rounded the track for the first time. He decided to take a chance and run her around the outside. He felt like he had already proved what he came to prove. She was as good as the best big racers, and father could sell her calves for big money. Now he just wanted to see what she could really do.

Two camels from the pack started to move up on Amuna from behind, and pin her in. Samir veered her to the right, outside the four big animals, and gave her her head. "Okay, girl, this is your chance. Give it all you have! You can get around these big boys. They will tire soon. Go!" He kicked her again and again.

Amuna began to gain on the leaders, and as they rounded the last curve, she was in line with them. The two leaders were tiring and had only expected to be racing each other at the end. This unexpected white camel was still there, and created a little confusion for them.

Amuna began to pull ahead, and the camel next to her veered sharply over to bump her off stride. Samir shouted at the jockey, who ignored him. He bumped her again. Samir shouted to Amuna to run harder.

She managed to pull up just a bit more, and the next bump by her opponent missed. He jerked his camel back toward the inner rail and flailed his arms in the air to make his camel regain his spot. All the riders where whipping and kicking and shouting at their animals as hard as they could now. Huge, long legs flew everywhere. Great long necks stretched forward, bobbing up and down, and all the camels gave their last push down the stretch.

Samir knew Amuna was running as hard as she could, so he put his head down on her hump and just hung on. There was nothing else he could do to get speed from her.

It was in God's hands. He closed his eyes and prayed for her just to finish the race in good health. His heart was thundering in his ears louder than the sound of the camels' feet hitting the ground.

A sudden roar from the crowd made him sit up, and he discovered that Amuna had won! Not by much, it seemed, but she had won.

Next time, he thought, *I will not close my eyes at the end!*

The crowd was shouting and jumping, waving scarves and hands in the air. Some people were angry, many were elated. He tried to find uncle Moosa, but he went by the spot too fast. He pulled Amuna back gently, and let her trot for a distance before slowing her to a walk. She was still breathing hard, and white lather ringed her lips. As they rounded the track to the finish again, an organizer came out to take her reins and walked her over to the spectators' box.

Mansur came down to join the race director, who walked over and handed Samir a prize purse with Ibn Yasin's seal on it. He congratulated Samir on the win, but Samir didn't hear anything he said. He looked up into the stands behind the director and saw Ibn Yasin grinning.

Samir bowed to him and touched his heart, then smiled and nodded to Mansur, and turned to go back to find Uncle Moosa. He wanted to savor this moment of victory, but was afraid to face the wrath of his uncle.

Moosa was nowhere to be seen. Well-wishers and the curious mobbed Amuna at once. They all wanted to touch the white camel. There was no way that he would ever be able to sneak around town unrecognized with her again.

He thanked the people and smiled as he urged Amuna toward the gate. He tried to be gracious, but he wanted to get out of there as fast as possible. He felt exhausted. He could barely hold on. Finally, they exited the park, and he was able to trot her back to the caravanserai. A few stragglers followed, but the guards kept them out. He didn't notice that the two burly men were still following him.

Samir led Amuna to the water trough in the back of the caravanserai, and, for a few minutes, he had a breather while she drank. He stroked her neck and with a wet cloth scrubbed to remove the numbers from each side. It was water based dye, and came off easily with a little rubbing.

He took her back to her place and wiped her down with fresh straw, then sat down and leaned against her back.

"You did well, my little Amuna! Now father will be able to get a good price for your babies. After I tell him about Jabbar and Ibn Yasin, he may not be so happy, though! If we can mate you with Jabbar and then give that calf to Ibn Yasin, we will be done with this city for once and for all, if God is merciful. I want to go home."

CHAPTER 20

Samir closed his eyes a moment, and then remembered the purse he had won. In the confusion, he had not had time to check it. He slipped it from his belt, and saw the crest of Ibn Yasin stamped into the leather. It felt heavy and warm in his hand. He opened it.

His eyes widened in disbelief. He was looking at fifty gold dinars! And if he added the five he had won from his bet, he had fifty-five gold dinars! That was more gold than he had ever seen, and his stomach wrenched in fear. He didn't know how to hide so much money, and he needed Uncle Moosa here to advise him. Right now he wished he could close his eyes and ride on a magic carpet back to Fez. He wanted to be home in his own stable, and back to his simple routine. He wanted to give this money to father, so he could leave the salt mines and have a better life. He could imagine the joy and disbelief on his father's face when he handed him the purse.

The excitement finally caught up with him. He felt the burn of tears in his eyes. He was overcome with emotion.

Quickly, he stuffed the gold back into the purse. No! That leather purse would be too obvious. He pulled out two dinars to put in his belt. Then he tore off a piece of dirty cotton used to wipe down Uncle Moosa's trade goods, and wrapped the purse in that. He buried the small bundle under the straw where he slept, and put his rug over it. Maybe it would be safe there until they left town.

Just then, Ali came running in to find him and congratulated him with a big grin and slap on the back. "She is fast, little brother, just as you said. Did you see the faces of the people? They were stunned. The whole city is on its ear talking about the white camel that appeared from nowhere and suddenly vanished. She is already a legend! Now you are expected to run in the final race of the champions. There will be a big purse, offered by Ibn Yasin himself."

"No, Ali. We will not run again. I proved she is fast, and that is all I wanted. Now I just want to go home," Samir said.

Ali looked closely at the boy and realized he was near tears. "Sit down, little brother. Let's make a plan."

Samir nodded with gratitude, and they sat near Amuna. She was already dozing, with her double row of long eyelashes lying on her cheeks. There was a knot in his stomach, and he felt swamped with emotion. It was a relief to be told what to do.

Just then, Ali heard people talking at the door. He said, "Stay here and stay out of sight. I will go see what's happening. Sounds like the guard might need help."

Ali emerged into the sunlight to find the guard arguing with two burly men. He stepped over, and asked, "Can I help you, brother? Is there a problem with these men?" The other guard appeared grateful for the unexpected support.

The men turned to Ali and said, "We are here to take back our camel that was stolen."

He felt a chill, and said, "Describe this camel, and why you think it is here."

"She is a white female. Our master bought her yesterday, and she was stolen from our stable last night. We are here to claim her and take her back...with force if it will be necessary." Ali's eyes dropped, and he noticed the man had a broken strap on his sandal. "We followed a boy leading her yesterday, and saw him ride her back here a few minutes ago. She is in this caravanserai."

"Friends, you are mistaken. There must be another white camel in Awdaghust. The one inside came with me from Fez by caravan. Her owner did not sell her, and he told me he plans to return to Fez with her. I suggest that you look in other quarters." He stepped forward to imply that the conversation was over and they should depart.

"Almohad, we are not through with this camel, and we will have her back. You will not stop us." The man stepped forward and rested his hand aggressively on his sword. Ali held his ground and put his hand on his hilt, as did the other guard. They faced each other eye to eye for a long time. Finally, the burly men backed down.

"We will be back to claim her. She is not to leave this caravanserai. Our master will not be ignored."

"Who is your master?" Ali asked.

"Emir Abdallah Ibn Yasin."

Ali swallowed, and then said, "We will be glad to speak with his representative or the man himself, if he wishes to come here and discuss the matter." Inside, Ali was churning. This was a bad situation. He did not want to face the violent ruler of the Almoravids! It would not end well for him.

The men turned away, glancing over their shoulders with annoyance and said, "We will return." Ali went inside to join Samir.

"Brother, where is your uncle?" Ali questioned.

"I don't know. I saw him in the stands before my race, but he was gone when I went back to find him after," Samir replied.

"You are in danger. You need to get out of town fast, with Amuna. The men at the door have been following you since yesterday. One has a broken sandal. They are trying to recover the white camel that was stolen from them last night, and they have found her here. I will not be able to help with this problem. They are Almoravids. Even worse, they work for the man who bought the camel, Emir Ibn Yasin himself." Ali studied Samir's face as various shades of surprise washed over it. It was clear the boy knew nothing of this.

"Ali, I met Ibn Yasin in the desert three days ago. He and his men rode up on me when I was running Amuna. We made a deal. He would let me go, and I would present her first calf to him. We agreed. And today, when the organizers raised the price for me to race, he sponsored me and paid the fee." Samir paused to let his words sink in.

"Ibn Yasin watched Amuna run. He did not steal her. He seems to be an honorable man. He offered to buy her from me in the desert," Samir said. "Perhaps these two men are thieves, and they hid Amuna and planned to sell her to him themselves, and they have lost their prize."

Ali shook his head in disbelief and smiled a big grin. "You have a magic shield around you, brother," he said.

"Whatever the truth of the story," Ali replied in a serious voice, "Amuna cannot hide. She is too visible. You must run away with her after dark. I will stay here with you until then. If your uncle comes back by nightfall, he can help you. If not, then I will remain here to explain what happened. You need to expect the worst and plan for it," Ali said.

"Most likely," he continued, "since the races are over, the caravan will restock tomorrow and depart the day after. Take enough water to last you a week, plus food for you and feed for Amuna. Tata, the first oasis on the trade route, is only four days ride for a single camel."

Samir nodded and said, "Yes, when I was in the desert the other night I was thinking about how to find the oasis. I believe I can use the stars to find it. If I must hide in the desert for a few days, I can do it. I will try to rejoin the caravan when it passes. But if not, I will wait at Tata for Allah to guide me. When you are in Fez, go to meet my father Jamal. We live in the shadow of the eastern wall of the great library, near the tannery." Ali nodded. He put his hand on Samir's shoulder and squeezed.

"God is merciful, you will not need to go to the oasis alone, brother. Tonight ride northeast until you reach a safe distance. Cover Amuna so she will blend in better. Stay there tomorrow or continue further northeast until you see the mountain. Late on the third day, you should see the rocky fields with the petroglyphs. Look for the canyon entrance in the west side of the mountain. You should spot the trade route that cuts over. But be careful. Cross the dunes with caution. Travel at night. The desert is full of bandits and Almoravid armies when the caravans are leaving Awdaghust. They are rich targets for robbing, and there will be robbers about."

Ali continued, "I will be with the caravan, and I will try to place pieces of cloth along our route to help guide you to where we are."

Ali walked to the entrance again to talk to the guard on duty. Samir began to put together his provisions for the journey. He stood Amuna up and walked her to the water trough again. "Drink, 'Muna, drink a lot. You need to be full tonight." Amuna drank, and when she had finished, Samir took her back and bedded her down.

He sat down on his rug and thought through everything he might need. He took another of uncle

Moosa's large cloaks from the chest, just in case, and tucked it into a saddlebag. Then he topped off his two large water bags and filled a saddlebag with dried meat and fruits. There was an open feed bag against the wall, and he decided to take it for Amuna as well. Most camels can go two weeks without food, but Amuna was still growing and her hump was small. He wanted to be sure she could eat.

Without the two salt slabs to worry about, Samir knew he could balance the load over her front legs so he could ride on her back if he needed to. He didn't weigh that much, and the load was not heavy. They should be okay.

Now they just had to wait for dark. He lay down on his rug and closed his eyes. He tried to relax by taking slow, deep breaths. The straw beneath him molded to his body, and his muscles began to unwind. It had been a very long day and it wasn't over yet. He prayed for Uncle Moosa to show up soon. He began to doze.

CHAPTER 21

It was not yet dark when Uncle Moosa returned. Samir heard him coming in the entrance speaking in a loud voice, and sat up quickly. He wasn't sure what Uncle Moosa's greeting would be, and felt apprehensive.

Moosa strode over to him with big steps and outstretched arms to greet him like a prodigal son. He said in a booming voice, "Nephew! Allahu akbar! God is great, you are safe. You have had a big adventure. Let's go where we can talk. I want to know what happened, and how you got into that race."

Samir could feel tension under his uncle's words, and he wasn't sure what was causing it. He followed him to a bench by the wall. When they sat down, Moosa grabbed him by the arm, and pinned it to the wall firmly.

In a low, rough voice, he said, "You are an ungrateful boy! You left with no word, you return and help yourself to my belongings, and you don't even ask permission to run your camel in a dangerous race. I am responsible for you, and you have worried me sick!"

Samir wasn't sure that was exactly true, but he hung his head in penance, and started to tell his uncle about his adventures. He left out the part about meeting Ibn Yasin in the desert and his promise to deliver a calf. He also left out the parts about stealing Amuna back and hiding in the desert. Something didn't feel right about sharing that with his uncle. He still wasn't sure if Moosa had a hidden agenda. with his friend Walid.

He apologized for missing the market, and not being able to sell his father's salt slabs or help his uncle.

Moosa replied, "The market was good. I didn't miss your help. Everything sold right away, and we got good prices. Your father's salt was worth fifty gold dinars. I will keep twenty per cent to contribute to the price for the caravan leader, plus one gold for me for my effort, and give him thirty-nine gold. It should make him very happy. I bought more goods to take home to Fez. It was a good day."

Samir said, "Amo, I want to leave Awdaghust. I am worried about Amuna. People followed me here. When will the caravan leave?"

"Not for two or three days yet," his uncle replied. "And why would you want to leave so soon? You are a hero in this town. People want to see you, and many people are interested in buying your camel. If you sell her now, you could make enough money so your father would not have to work again, and you could return to school."

"I don't want to sell Amuna," he said in a forceful voice. "I will return her to father, and let him decide how to use her the best." His uncle shrugged.

"It's your loss," Moosa said, "but you are a good boy for taking care of your father's interests. Now tell me about the race. How did you get the money to enter? How did you know what to do? How did you manage to win?"

Samir told him the story, but left out the part about promising the camel Jabbar a chance to mate with Amuna if he won, and the part about betting with the bookie. He didn't think Uncle Moosa would approve of that.

Moosa was very interested to learn about Ibn Yasin's sponsorship. "What?! How did you dare to go to ask him after I told you no? And why would he sponsor a poor boy he doesn't know?"

"I passed him in town the other day when I had Amuna," Samir lied. "He was with his son, and he stopped me and asked about the white camel. I told him my father will breed her to have racing camels. He said he is a horseman himself, and let me go on my way. Maybe he recognized my face today. Or maybe he just wanted to see a white camel run. He sent a slave to talk to me and to pay the fee. Perhaps he wagered on her. I don't know."

Moosa smiled showing all his teeth, and said, "I wagered on her! I figured if Allah is crazy enough to let you enter the race, he has plans for Amuna, so I bet just before the start. Not a lot, but the odds were long, and I won a lot of money." He smiled with satisfaction. "A lot." He nodded and patted his money belt and its secrets. "Maybe we should go into the racing business with her."

Samir didn't like the direction the conversation was

going, so he said, "She is father's camel. Let's see what he says when we are home." Moosa nodded.

For the next two hours, Samir helped Uncle Moosa to gather up and organize his belongings. He filled heavy water bags at the trough, and led each of Moosa's camels over to drink. It took a long time, about twenty minutes for each camel to drink its fill, but drinking was necessary so they would have reserves stored when they started back on the journey home.

The sun was setting when Uncle Moosa said he was going into town for dinner, and would be back later. Ali was no longer on guard at the entrance. Samir decided to remain in the caravanserai and rest until everyone settled for the night. The day had been very tiring.

Uncle Moosa left in good spirits. Samir heard the muezzin singing the call to prayer, so he took his rug out of the caravanserai and knelt for evening prayers. He would need Allah's blessing for the rest of this journey, and he wanted to give thanks for his success and apologize for lying to his uncle.

Dark settles in quickly in the desert, and with only a half moon rising, even with the starlight it is not easy to find one's way. Two torches were lit inside the caravanserai to prevent people from tripping over animals or goods on the ground, but the effect was dim and a little spooky. Everything moving cast big shadows on the walls.

Samir quietly started loading Amuna for their escape. He put a blanket over her hump, and strapped down the wooden frame over it. He hung woven saddlebags of food on one side of the frame, and put Amuna's feed bag on the far side. He loaded one water bag on each side for balance, and strapped it all down snugly. He tucked his bedroll across Amuna's shoulders in front of the frame, along with the cloak he had used to cover her the previous night. He needed to be able to pull it out fast to hide her if they saw anything in the desert. It was not a heavy load, and there was still room for him over her back legs. He was satisfied. Now he just had to wait for Ali.

He didn't have to wait long. Ali appeared in a clean uniform, and came to sit with him. He smiled with approval at the preparations, and asked, "Are you ready, my friend? What has happened since I left?"

Samir told him about his uncle and their conversation. "Uncle says the caravan will leave in two or three days. I will try to stay hidden in the desert that long, and meet you on the road, or if not, Insh'allah, at the oasis."

Ali gripped Samir's shoulder again, and said, "Go with God, little brother. If He wills, we will meet each other again on the road. Stay low and be safe."

Samir nodded and took a deep breath. As Ali walked away, he remembered his winnings, and hurried to pull out the dirty cloth bundle. He stuffed it into a food saddlebag. That would have to do for now.

He leaned onto Amuna's loaded hump and said, "'Muna, UP." He would give Ali a minute to distract the guard, and then they would run northeast. One thing was sure. Amuna was getting her share of running this day.

CHAPTER 22

The desert had an eerie feel. It was harder to see this night than last, and after Amuna stopped running, she settled into a slow, easy trot. Eventually, she slowed to a walk, and Samir slid off her back to lighten her load. They walked for another hour or more. It was impossible to see more than a few yards in any direction, so he couldn't spot any scrub growth to rest in. He would have to choose the base of a big dune and try to shelter there. Perhaps they would avoid any notice.

He didn't know how far they had gone, only that they were still heading northeast. Yildun, the guiding star, was visible off to his left. It would set soon, so they needed to camp. They crested a large dune and descended a steep slope. He decided that would be a good place. He told Amuna to kneel, and removed the load and the pack frame. He gave her a light feed from his hands and took a big drink of water. Even at night the desert sapped away moisture, and it was important to drink a lot. Every small child who lived near the desert knew this.

Next he pulled the brown cloak from the pack and spread it over Amuna's back to blunt her whiteness. The night was chilly, so he took out the other cloak from his saddlebag and drew it across her neck with a stick to make a small shelter. He used her neck for a pillow, and soon they were both fast asleep.

This time he awoke before the heat rose. He placed the frame on Amuna's back and reloaded it. They were ready to go. He only had to consider how far they had come, and whether they should wander looking for better cover or whether they should just ride northeast another day. Now he was less concerned about being followed than about bumping into bad characters in the desert. Especially bad characters who rode horses and wore spiked turbans with wrapped veils.

They started up the side of the next dune and Samir decided to take a chance and walk along the crests for a while. It was easier, and even though they were visible, they would make more progress to the north. As the sun rose high overhead, Samir looked for a place to shelter and rest. He thought he saw some vegetation ahead, so he moved cautiously forward. If anyone else was in the area, they might also be looking to rest in a shady spot. He got up on Amuna's back so he would have a farther view, and so he could run away if there was trouble.

To his relief, there were no inhabitants except a sand snake and a few scorpions, which he quickly eliminated. They settled into the meager shade, and he covered Amuna's whiteness again with the brown cloak. He drank, and munched on some dried lamb and fruit. He gave Amuna two dates, to show he hadn't forgotten her. A few hours later as the sun was setting, they started off again. He was riding, and as soon as it was fully dark, they passed along the winding dune ridges for a time. They were very quiet. One camel without fancy harness makes almost no noise as it passes. All Samir could hear was the soft, sibilant shoosh, shoosh as the sand slid away down the slope with each rhythmic step.

That was how they almost ran into trouble. Just as they passed over a big sand slope, he froze and stopped Amuna. He thought he could hear low voices to the left. No voices could be good for him, so he turned her and moved down the long slope to the right. A few hundred meters later, they turned northeast again. He rode until they were well away from being discovered.

They nearly tripped over another small cluster of trees in the darkness, so Samir dismounted and bedded Amuna down. This time he didn't remove her pack. He fed her and had a bit of food and water himself, then he sat leaning against her warm body. The desert chill had set in.

It occurred to him that anyone who spotted them and captured them would go through his belongings. They wouldn't expect much. He was a poor boy, after all, even though he did have a good camel. They were likely to steal Amuna, and if they found the gold in his saddlebag, they would take that, too. Disguising Amuna was the only way he had to protect her. Now he needed a way to protect the money.

Samir had an idea. No one was likely to abandon him without water, even if they took the camel. He unwrapped the cloth and took out the gold purse. One by one he dropped the gold coins into his half empty water bag. No one would think to look there. He kept two gold dinars in the prize purse tucked into his belt for an emergency. He tied two more into a corner of his head wrapping. This was the best he would be able to do. Anyone who wanted his belongings would take them, and he would not be able to stop them.

Suddenly he felt overwhelmed. He was vulnerable and foolish. He should have waited to go with the caravan. At least Uncle Moosa and the army guards would be there to help him. With luck, tomorrow he would continue on his heading and find the trade route to the canyon. Today he had seen the peak of the mountain, but it was a long way ahead. He would find a place to hide near the trade route into the canyon until he saw the caravan pass in a day or two. Insh'allah.

Samir woke with the first light. He was cold and stiff. Amuna wanted to stand. He scanned the area, and it seemed clear. They would not stop to eat now. He had a hurried drink and placed the bag on her back. Again he decided to ride. The only way they could escape was if he were already mounted.

He continued north until the sun was overhead. This was the third day. The caravan should be on the road now. He felt optimistic that he would intersect them the next evening or the following morning.

Amuna was holding up well to the pace. Her stamina had improved greatly since they left Fez. Samir started to imagine seeing the city walls of home in the distance. He would be so happy to see father and give him the gold. He couldn't wait to tell Saadi of his adventures, and to return to school. If he had studied astronomy already, he would know more of the night sky. The stars were still a mystery. He drifted into a light sleep.

CHAPTER 23

Ali had not always wanted to be a soldier. He was born in the High Atlas mountains in southern Morocco, grandson of the al-Harghi Berber leader of the Masmuda tribal confederation. His grandfather ruled the entire valley region south of Marrakesh, and played an important role in bringing the rule of Islam to Northwest Africa.

Unfortunately, Ali's father Wujallid was the second son of his famous father Abdul Rahman, just as Ali was the second son of Wujallid. There was no benefit for them from his grandfather's station.

Life as the second son was not easy for Ali. Second sons had no rights or benefits of their family's station according to Berber tribal tradition. Since his father was the second son of Abdal Rahman, there was no dynastic role to play, and Ali's family received no preferential status.

Only the first son inherited lands, rights and titles from his father, and any other sons had to find their own ways in life. Wujallid had found his as a shepherd. Ali's older brother Mahmud would inherit their father's small land holdings and flocks, so Ali had to look elsewhere for his destiny.

Some second sons joined the clergy or became scholars, and many joined the army, hoping to make a name for themselves. Unlike his father and older brother, Ali had a hunger for knowledge, so he happily attended religious school at the local madrasa. From childhood he was well educated, and like all boys his age, he had memorized and could recite the *Holy Qur'an*.

When he got older, he studied at the madrasa in the great mosque in Marrakesh with his brothers and cousins. Spirited discussion and debate, principles and theology were their daily routine. They didn't know at the time, but he and his generation were defining the distinctive religious and political views that would be their legacy when they later became the Almohad ruling class.

Most of the well-to-do boys from his school eventually traveled north to Fez to study for a time in the renowned Kairowiyyan University. Ali showed promise as a scholar, so his father managed to save money for him to go with his friends. It was in Fez that Ali realized his true calling.

At the request of the imams, General Yusuf ibn Rahim came to Fez to be a guest lecturer at the university. General Yusuf was a tall and charismatic young man only twenty-five years old. He was of mixed Arab heritage, and had a youthful flamboyance radically different from the serious, thoughtful old scholars in the university. He had an innate understanding of human nature and military strategy. He lectured the students with the passion of his youth on the importance of bringing the order and law of Islam to the native people, by force if they resisted.

Yusuf also had a sense of humor. As he described his adventures and battles, his eyes sparkled and he captivated his audience with his anecdotes and his zeal. Being young himself, he still had optimism and enthusiasm for what he believed was Allah's work, and his ideas were contagious.

Something about his presence inspired the students, as much as it did his soldiers. General Yusuf would eventually expand his victories and the rule of Islam to include most of northern Africa and the southern half of Spain, but none of that mattered to Ali. He only knew the first time he heard him that he had found a hero. He decided to become a soldier. He was eighteen.

Ali was average size, but he made up for his ordinary stature with muscle. He sought out mock fights daily with the other enlistees, and could often be seen running up and down the nearby steep hills to strengthen his legs and heart, or perfecting his scimitar swings on practice dummies in the yard. He had a kind face, and had inherited his grandfather's dark Berber skin. His almost black, probing eyes seemed to scrutinize all details and see through lies. They could be soft and kind when he smiled, though, so he tried to keep smiling to a minimum and cultivated a serious, intimidating image.

Beards came early to the men in Ali's family, so by the time he was twenty, he had a thick black moustache worn down the sides of his mouth. It gave him a stern appearance, and that is what he wanted.

Like all the mountain tribesmen, Ali was an excellent horseman. The Berbers of the flat lands and deserts preferred camels for their stamina and ability to carry heavy loads, but the hill tribes preferred the speed and maneuverability of horses. Both animals were widely used by armies and traders. Ali progressed through his military training, and one day realized that he wanted to ride with the horsemen instead of fight with the infantry. But he had no horse.

A few weeks later, Ali received a summons from the city commander as he was working in the practice yard.

"Al-Harghi, Allah is generous and watches out for you," he said, and handed him the reins of a beautiful, dark brown gelding.

His father had sent him the gift from the stables of his grandfather. He must have known his son would need a horse. The three-year-old was called Gawa, meaning coffee—perfect for his color. Gawa had already been trained in warfare, and Ali threw himself vigorously into learning all the moves and techniques needed by cavalrymen. Gawa taught Ali many things he needed to know about being a horse soldier.

General Yusuf came often to Fez, and on one of his trips, Ali caught his eye. Ali was in the training yard as usual, attacking a practice dummy. The general watched him for a few minutes, then signaled to his followers to be silent. He drew his scimitar and came up behind Ali, raising the scimitar over his head as if to strike.

Ali turned quickly and blocked the blow. He was startled, but his instincts reacted to the threat. He fought vigorously to defend himself. When he became aware of the surrounding audience, and at last saw the face of his opponent, he lowered his sword and held it out to his side in the posture of surrender. Yusuf laughed and clapped Ali on the shoulder.

"Well done, soldier. I wish that all my troops were as prepared and as serious as you about their work. What is your name?" he asked.

Ali replied, "Ali ibn Wujallid al-Harghi, General."

"Al-Harghi? Masuda Confederation? Isn't that the tribe of Commander Abdal Rahman?"

"Yes, General. He is my grandfather," Ali replied.

Yusuf studied Ali's face for a moment, then said, "Your grandfather is a wise and capable leader. We are lucky to have you both in this army." His smile flickered briefly at Ali's stern manner and formality.

"Would you like to join me on our next campaign as a Lieutenant, Ali al-Harghi? I tire of having these old men fussing around me. It will be good to see a new young officer's face."

He turned to smile at his entourage. They knew the young general was always seeking young officers to befriend. It was one of his most effective traits, and won devotion from his men.

"We are pushing north to consolidate the Maghrib, and I need good men like you," Yusuf continued. "Good *young* men," he emphasized with a grin tossed to his second in command.

Ali maintained his stoic face and gave a crisp salute. "Yes, sir. I would be honored." His heart was pounding in his chest. This was his dream come true.

And that was how Ali started his rise in the Almohad Army.

CHAPTER 24

General Yusuf was delayed in his desire to move north by pressing needs and serious resistance on the western coast, so Ali remained in Fez with his unit for several months and waited for orders. Meanwhile, his commanding officer offered him a job to occupy his time.

"Lieutenant, the roads to the south are becoming more and more unsafe for caravans. Merchants are being harassed by the Almoravids and forced to pay exorbitant fees for traveling the great trade route. A very large caravan to Awdaghust is planned in a few days. They have requested a military escort. I would like you to take a company of men and go with them. It will be good long distance riding practice for all of you."

Ali saluted and replied, "Certainly, commander. Permission to speak." The officer nodded.

"I want to be available to join General Yusuf when he sends for me," Ali said. "This caravan will have me on the road for three months or more. A lot can happen in such a long time."

"Yes, I know your desire, Lieutenant, but if we can't

keep the trade routes open, the merchants will revolt and rejoin the Almoravids. That is what Ibn Yasin and his men want. We can't allow that. If General Yusuf sends for you, I will send a messenger at once. It looks like he will be busy on the coast for a long time, though. I believe you will return in plenty of time. Be ready to leave in two days," the commander said.

"Thank you, Sir. I will be ready." Ali saluted. He went to the barracks to gather his belongings and prepare Gawa for the long ride and the uncertain months ahead.

CHAPTER 25

Sometime around dawn, Samir woke up fully alert. He had dozed off on Amuna's back and she had continued to walk northeast. He didn't know how far they had come, but the mountain was closer.

Far on the hazy horizon, figures were moving. It looked like a large band of horsemen. There was no place for him to hide. He pulled Amuna down low, and threw the covering over her back. The horses were moving perpendicular to his path, so perhaps he and Amuna had not been spotted. He could only wait and watch. And pray. He bowed down and earnestly beseeched Allah to let him reach his caravan with Amuna in one piece.

Fate was on his side. The band passed, and after several hours, Samir decided it was safe to move toward the trade route again. It was now the heat of the day, and anyone roaming in the desert was likely to stop to rest. He would keep going.

The sun was cruel. The light dazzled his eyes. He drank and drank, and splashed a little precious water over his head and face. The loose ends of his head covering made a small breeze and evaporated the water, cooling his neck.

They were now crossing the rocky plain where he had seen the petroglyphs, and the footing became tricky and uneven. The rocks stretched as far as Samir could see in every direction, and were sharp under Amuna's feet. The rocks absorbed more heat than the sand, and reflected it back to the travelers. It was like being in an oven and baking on two sides at once.

Even Amuna started to sweat. It had to be extremely hot for a camel to sweat. The ever-present, wind-swept sand stuck to their damp bodies. It helped to dull her white color. At least Amuna had an inner eye membrane to protect her eyes, and she could close her nostrils.

Samir couldn't close his nostrils, so he tightened his head cloth around his face and pulled his turban lower on his forehead to help shelter his eyes from the unrelenting brilliance of the sun. After a few hours, the rocky fields gave way to the hard uneven ground of a gravel pan. It wasn't much better.

Amuna took small prancing steps through the rocky field and gurgled with discontent. The hot sand and rocks burned her feet since her foot pads had not yet grown to adult thickness.

"I know this is stressful, girl," Samir croaked, "but we have to keep moving." His mouth was dry like paper and his lips were cracked. He could barely speak, and there was no place here to rest.

They walked at a slow pace for hours. Soon the sun would set. He wondered how far they were from the trade route. The mountain was growing larger on their right. He hadn't thought about this part of the journey. There were no road signs in the Sahara. He wasn't sure how Ali would leave the markers for him. Tracks didn't last in sand. The Berbers and bedouins knew how to read the signs of sand, sun and well markers. Samir did not.

Another two hours passed with Amuna suffering through the gravel pan. Finally, it ended and the ground turned again to soft, loose sand just as the sun moved low. The mountain was still distant, and he hoped he would spot the trade route to the canyon entrance sometime in the morning. He began to look for a good resting place.

They would rest now and in a few hours, they would move northeast once more and hope to intersect the long caravan at rest on the road. Or at least find a safe spot near the canyon where they could hide and wait. The caravan would rest in the oasis for three days. That would give him time to catch up if they were ahead, or he would wait if they had not yet arrived. Right now, finding either the caravan or the entrance to the oasis would make him happy.

Samir spotted some brush, and they knelt down to rest. He covered Amuna, and gave her water from his full water bag. Camels could go weeks without water, but she was still young, and he didn't want her to suffer. She sucked it down like she had drunk her milk when she was a baby.

He put up his makeshift tent. Then they slept, his hand on the pouch in his belt and his head on the curve of

Amuna's neck. He had no idea what would happen next. Too many things could go wrong, and he was now responsible for not only himself, but for his camel and for his father's fate.

Samir became chilled as the temperature fell, so he stood with stiffened joints to look around. He put on a cloak and told Amuna to stand. He made sure the pack was secure, and then got on her back. Her hump provided a little warmth as he leaned against it. He pulled his burnoose tightly around him, and they started walking toward the dark mountain just visible against the night sky.

The sand was relatively level, and Samir realized he should probably eat something. He fished in his saddlebag and pulled out some dried fruit, a small lump of dried cheese, and goat meat. By the time he had finished them, they were crossing land that was very flat and felt packed. It ran due east.

He didn't know if this was the trade route, but he decided to make up some time since it went in the right direction. He told Amuna to run and pushed his heels into her belly. She started to trot and then to run. He knew she would slow when she tired, so he just hung on and let her go. The faster he got to the oasis the better, even though he would be vulnerable there alone.

After running for fifteen minutes, Amuna slowed to a walk, and he dropped off her back to walk beside her. It wasn't hard to travel this way, on an even surface in the cool of night. They continued walking for several hours.

As the sun began to lighten the sky, Samir became alert to their exposure on the flat plain. He decided to veer off and shelter for a few hours. They walked for a kilometer or so and came upon a low wash with a vertical face on the north side where they could sit and be out of sight of casual travelers. He covered Amuna, made his small tent, and dozed for a short time. Amuna shook her head vigorously and woke him. He heard the sound of voices and camels.

He raised his eyes above the ground cautiously and saw a caravan, but it was coming from the east. The wrong way. He knew there would be soldiers riding guard, so he dropped below ground level again, and hoped they would be looking in the far distances and not nearby.

A few came close, but he wasn't discovered. The caravan was about half the size of the one Samir had come on, so it passed by quickly.

"At least we found the trade route, Amuna. Now we just have to wait a while longer. If our caravan doesn't pass within the day, we will head east and take our chances with the oasis. You will be able to drink your fill, and we will have cool shade to rest in."

He patted her neck, and she threw her head back to nibble on his shoulder. He remembered he had not given her a treat since yesterday, so he rummaged in his food bags and pulled out two dried figs. She made happy noises, and he patted her neck. The sun was still beating down, so he crawled back under his tent and waited.

CHAPTER 26

Hours passed. Still no caravan. Samir had been thinking about the Tata oasis. He remembered it because it was the first one where he had seen a lot of Almohad soldiers. This area was dominated by them, and his Almohad guards had been eager to arrive there. The shopkeepers and merchants would sell to anyone, but they were distinctly more friendly to his caravan.

Now he wondered if he would be safe going in there alone. If he stayed outside the oasis, but got too close, the oasis guards would find him and take him in. If he rode in like a customer, no one would believe a young boy on a white camel just happened to show up from a casual ride in the desert. If any of them had been to the race in Awdaghust, they would recognize Amuna and perhaps try to steal her. No, it wasn't a good idea to wait in the oasis. And he would be exposed once he started into the canyon.

He remembered what Ali had said about placing cloth markers along the way. Samir wasn't sure how he would do it. Perhaps he would have made a small rock pyramid and anchored the cloth there. But he had not seen any cloth or any kind of marker on this road, so that probably meant the caravan had not yet arrived. Perhaps they got a later start than they planned. He just needed to wait. Sitting in this hole was as good a place as any, he decided. But Amuna was restless and needed to stretch. He left the pack in the hole, and decided to let her run.

"Come on, girl. You need to move. Let's go walk." He got on her back, and they took off east for a short distance and then circled back. They knelt down again, and waited. And waited. The sun passed from overhead to near the horizon.

It was dusk before he heard sounds from the road again. Amuna's ears twitched. Samir stayed low and they remained covered. This time the sounds were coming from the west. Samir was excited, but didn't want to show himself too soon. He would wait until he saw Ali or Uncle Moosa to be sure this was the right caravan.

He slipped his eyes just above the protective bank. The caravan was a long one, and stretched far into the distance. After a few days in the desert, though, all loaded camels and their handlers looked the same. They were covered in sand and wrapped in sand coated cloth. It was only possible to make out the richest merchants, because they used bright colors, and a little of the color showed through the sand. Sometimes they had special saddles like small houses with curtains that they rode in.

Samir couldn't tell if this was his caravan or not. Judging from their head coverings, the escort soldiers were Almohad, though, which was encouraging.

It was quite dark when the end of the caravan appeared. He had seen no sign of Uncle Moosa or Ali, but with all the dust and the low light, he might have missed them. He decided to wait until morning, and then ride boldly into the oasis, and join this caravan if it was going north.

"Any caravan going north to Fez will get me home," he mused. "And I have some gold to pay for my passage."

Samir settled down to sleep by Amuna after giving her a little feed and more water. He dozed off, secure in the knowledge that they would be safe again tomorrow.

He awoke to a sharp kick. Two Almoravid soldiers in spiked turbans stood over him, scimitars drawn.

"And what do we have here, I wonder," one of them said in a gruff voice. "It looks like the Emir's white camel and the thief who stole her."

CHAPTER 27

Emir Ibn Yasin was lounging in his private study, sprawled on a low couch with gold covered legs and crimson embroidered cushions. He wore a blue silk kaftan and his embroidered leather babouches lay on the floor near his feet. He was leaning against a fat tubular bolster covered in red pleats with big gold tassels.

The elaborately tiled walls of the room were covered by scroll racks, and the polished cedar floor was layered with fine woven rugs in simple geometric patterns. Like most of the Almoravids, Ibn Yasin was orthodox, and a strict follower of shari'a law. He preferred simple, solid colors with no life form designs at all. He favored geometric patterns with an occasional touch of Quranic calligraphy along a border.

The doors to his private garden were open. A slight breeze fluttered the long, gold silk curtains. Just outside the window was an ornate mesh screen of carved Spanish marble over which water flowed constantly. It cooled the air that passed through it, and provided a soothing background sound.

Tomorrow would be his judicial day, and Ibn Yasin flipped idly through the papers for the cases he would hear.

Mostly they were ordinary thefts or disputes between merchants over some sale or other. He knew how to dispose of those quickly.

A soft knock on his door caught his attention. "Come," he said aloud.

A guard opened the door to admit Mansur. "Salaam, father," he said. "May I disturb your studies?"

Ibn Yasin smiled, put aside his reading, and pointed to a plump cushioned stool nearby. "It will be a welcome change," he said. "Come sit. There is pomegranate juice here, and it still has snow from the mountains in it."

Mansur poured a small glass, then perched on the edge of the stool, as if he didn't intend to stay long. His brown hair was pulled back tightly from his face, but a few strands had managed to escape, and he nudged them behind his ear with his fingers. He bathed every day, yet he always managed to have dirt under his fingernails. He looked like he had run through the dunes to get there. His house slippers were even dusty.

Ibn Yasin took note of all the details of his son's appearance, but said nothing. Soon he would have to send Mansur to the university, and truthfully, he enjoyed having his impulsive and intelligent son around, as sloppy as he was. He chose not to spoil the visit with parental instructions.

"What can I do for you, my son?" Ibn Yasin asked.

"Father, I'd like to talk about my studies. My imam is a good teacher and an admirable man, but he doesn't have energy in what he teaches. He is old. Yes, yes," Mansur quickly interjected, "he is also wise and I have no right to judge him, but he has no enthusiasm for life! He is dry like dust, and I want to learn from someone who has inner fire! It is so boring to sit day after day and listen to the imam's soft, dry voice...all one tone, no excitement. Flat like the horizon."

Ibn Yasin stroked his beard in silence and watched his son's face.

"Last week we had a teacher from the Kairowiyyan University in Fez, and he was completely different. He showed us all kinds of puzzles with mathematics and explained how mathematics is behind the patterns of the stars." Mansur was unusually animated, gesturing broadly.

"He talked of planets and the arc of the sun, and how stars change position over time, and how great the distances are in space! And of comets! Did you know that they pass through our heavens and vanish, and yet it is possible to know when they will appear again? I want to know more about these things."

Mansur's hands swooped and arched as he mimicked the movement of the comets. He clearly loved what he had learned from the visiting teacher.

"It is Allah's will that you should come to me today and tell me these things, my son. I have just been thinking about your education," Ibn Yasin said. "When I was your age, my father, peace be upon him, sent me to Fez to study. The greatest teachers come there, and it is the best place to learn the new discoveries of science. I miss that I cannot enter Fez now and visit that great library again. The Almohads would turn me away at the gate, or worse! But you, on the other hand..." His voice trailed off into thought.

"Father, yes! Could I go to Fez and study? I will make you proud. They have so many more things I can learn there than we have here. They even have an observatory! I'm sure it would be possible to find a place to stay at the university. Surely they would not keep me away because you are my father. I am a good Muslim, and all Muslims should be welcomed to university, right? My imam would give me a letter of recommendation."

And so Mansur started on the path to the next phase of his life. His father knew someone who knew someone, and they agreed that Mansur could go to Fez and stay with a family of distant relatives for the next three years of his study.

Within a few weeks, Mansur would find himself on the road, heading north to the start of the work that would consume his life. But he didn't know that part yet.

CHAPTER 28

Samir stood up quickly and brushed sand off his clothes. He was frightened and tried to control his voice, saying simply, "There has been a mistake. This is my camel. I brought her from Fez and raced her in Awdaghust just three days ago. Some men stole her from me. I am waiting here to meet my caravan and return home."

The soldiers slid down the slope and sheathed their scimitars brusquely. They towered over Samir. One grabbed him by the arm and the other began tugging hard on Amuna's lead trying to force her to stand. She resisted, and put her head in the air and started to bray loudly.

Samir shouted, "Please, don't hurt her! We will go with you. Let me lead her. She will follow me."

Samir took the rope and said softly, "Up Muna." She lifted her back legs, then her front and stood quietly.

One soldier nodded, and said, "This way," and started to walk around the embankment and up the dune where they had left their horses. Samir followed, leading Amuna. The other soldier followed with his hand on his sword, as if expecting Samir to run at any minute.

They ascended the rise and Samir told Amuna to kneel. Amuna had no nose ring with which they could lead her, so the soldiers attached a rope to each side of her harness and tied the ends to their saddles. They mounted their horses.

Samir climbed on Amuna's back and told her to stand. She lumbered to her feet, and the soldier on her right gave a tug on the line, and said, "No funny business. You ride straight between us all the way, and we will have no trouble. You understand?"

Samir nodded.

They began to walk. Inside his brain was spinning. Was there anything he could do to escape? What would happen when he got to Awdaghust? Would Ibn Yasin claim Amuna as his and cut off his hand for stealing her? Would he pass his caravan on the trade route, and would Uncle Moosa or Ali see him and rescue him? Could he get free from these men and outrun them in the desert? Would they find the gold in his water bag? All he could do was put his head down on Amuna's hump and let his misery wash over him. There was a knot in his stomach. He was afraid.

The journey on horseback or camel is much faster than a caravan moves. Amuna kept up with the horses easily, and didn't get winded. From Tata to Awdaghust was six days by caravan, but just over three days traveling as fast as they were. The soldiers apparently watched for approaching caravans, because they left the trade route several times to cut through the desert.

Samir didn't know if his uncle was now at the oasis or still on the road. He began to realize just how alone he was. That was a kick in the backside that he needed. He started thinking about what he could do with his situation.

The trio camped out only two nights under the stars. The men offered to share their food, but Samir stuck to his own and his own water. They bedded down after eating.

The men tied Amuna to the leg of one of the soldiers, and threatened Samir not to run off in the night. They didn't really expect him to. He would get lost, they surmised, and they would find him in the morning. The men talked a while in low voices.

Samir made his usual tent by Amuna's neck and slept against her. He hoped this would not be the last time they would sleep like this.

It was still dark on the second night when the soldiers roused him. They wanted to get to town before the heat of the day. He drank some water, and fumbled in his saddlebag for some dates for Amuna. He gave them to her to let her know everything was okay, and then loaded her pack frame again. It only took a few minutes, and they set out immediately.

As the sun rose, he could see the familiar wall of Awdaghust ahead. Only one week before, he had been a hero and winner of a camel race. Today he was a prisoner, and Amuna might be taken from him forever. He couldn't bear that thought.

As they approached the city gate, Samir suddenly had an idea. He remembered the son of Ibn Yasin from the race. He had seemed friendly in a quiet sort of way. Perhaps he would be willing to help or to testify for him about Amuna being his camel. But, he thought, that means he would speak against the interests of his father. He doubted that would happen. He was back to square one.

The men rode through the broad streets of the town to a section Samir had not seen before. It was apparently the area where the Almoravid soldiers had their barracks. There were many buildings and large stables there, and one of the men gestured toward a stall. "Put the camel in there."

"Shall I leave her feed and pack frame here as well?" he asked. The man nodded.

"No one will bother your things," he said with a gruff voice. "Once the judgment is made, you may return here to claim what is yours, if you are innocent. We will see that the animal is fed and watered. She will remain in the stall until then."

Samir nodded, and removed the items from Amuna's back with care, then stood the wooden frame in a corner. He treated his water bag nonchalantly, but made sure the one with the gold was on the bottom, just in case. He untied the ropes from Amuna's harness and gave her a big hug and rubbed her nose. He wrappd his arm around her front leg and quickly gave her two more dates.

"I will be back as soon as I can, girl. Don't make trouble or worry. I will be back," Samir said. He tried not to let his tears show, and rubbed his face on her neck to wipe them. She bumped him with her nose as if to say, Get going. He smiled and pulled her ear, and turned to the soldiers outside the stall. "I am ready. Please be gentle with her. She responds to kindness."

The man took Samir's arm and said, "Now we will lock you up until the court is ready to hear your case." They led him to a mud brick cell behind the barracks. Two big uniformed men stood up as they came in.

"Salaam aleikhum. We have a new prisoner. A thief. Accused of stealing Ibn Yasin's white camel. We found him on the road to Tata. The camel is in a stall. They haven't made any trouble on the trip. He should probably be a good prisoner." He turned to stare at Samir. "Yes?" he asked.

"Yes," Samir replied. His voice shook a little.

The prison cell was small and poorly lit. He was in the tiny room alone. He had a bedroll and a chamber pot, and they brought him some porridge once a day, with a small bag of water. The mud bricks were cool in the shade, and kept him cool if he leaned against them. It was kind of like being at home, except he couldn't leave.

Day after day passed. There were only two tiny windows on opposite walls, but they were higher than he could reach, so he couldn't see out. He could only gauge the movement of the sun by the shadows on his floor, and see two small patches of the night sky. He hoped they would call him soon. This was all a mistake, and he desperately wanted it to end.

Twice he heard Amuna call for him. She didn't know where he was, and this was the longest he had ever been away from her. He hoped they were taking good care of her.

After two weeks, he overheard one of the soldiers say as he passed his cell, "The camel thief will go before the court tomorrow." That night when he prayed, he asked earnestly to face a judge who would see the truth of the story and set him free.

He pressed his forehead down on his rug, and prayed out loud. "Lord, I am afraid of having my right hand cut off! How will I get back home? And what will happen to Amuna? Where will she go? How will she understand if I can't go back to her?" This time he did cry. There was no one to see or hear, and it all came pouring out.

His sleep was uneasy that night. The guard came for him early, and said to wash and clean as best he could. They would go to the judge soon.

"May I please see my camel before I go?" he asked. The guard shook his head.

"No. She isn't your camel. If the court finds in your favor, she will be here when you come back." That was all he had to say.

Samir quickly prayed his morning prayers, and tried hard not to worry about the outcome of his trial. He was anxious, and kept fidgeting with his hands. He knew he was telling the truth, and if the judge was an honest man, he would see it, too. That's all he had to hold on to when the guard came for him and they set out for the court.

He wondered if he might see Mansur in the streets, and he watched all the faces intently as they walked, hoping to spot him. His only hope was if Mansur would speak for him. He had no other witnesses. Not a single one. He had never felt so miserable or so alone.

CHAPTER 29

Although Mansur had been raised under orthodox Islamic law, he enjoyed reading or reciting passages from the *Holy Qur'an* and thinking about them for himself. He had come to believe in the unity of all creation. It said in the *Qur'an* that Muslims were to befriend the other people of the book, meaning Muslims, Christians and Jews, and yet it seemed these religions were always warring with each other. He thought a lot about religion, his relationship to God, and the meaning of life.

Mansur's father, being the ruler and chief jurist of the region, held traditional, conservative religious views, and enforced them strictly. He had been known to whip Muslims who didn't say their prayers properly or omitted words. Piety and asceticism governed the Almoravids' actions, and kept them from erecting elaborate palaces and magnificent monuments. Their art and architecture were functional. They sought to be the ideal, conservative Islamic state.

It troubled Ibn Yasin that his son held a more mystical view than the strict shari'a law allowed, but young men have to resist a father's teaching in order to find their own way.

Ibn Yasin withheld his criticism and didn't seek to discourage his son, because he thought the boy might become hardened in his views if he did. So he waited for Mansur to mature in his beliefs, and meanwhile, he exposed him to all the things a leader should know. He hoped Mansur would pass through this rebellious phase quickly. Especially since he planned to send Mansur to study in Fez at the Kairowiyyan University and he would not be there to help guide his son.

From early childhood, Mansur had had a different view of the world. He saw beauty and order in all things. He felt himself to be only one of the myriad possibilities of creation. Life around him was a source of richness and joy. Ibn Yasin remembered one conversation they had had riding together in the desert when Mansur was only about ten years old.

"Father, why are men more special to Allah than all of the rest of creation," he had asked.

"The Prophet taught us that Allah made men in his own image. Therefore, we are closest to Him, and we rule over the rest of His creation as he instructed Adem," Ibn Yasin replied.

"But it says that all creation is one. If He created it all, why does He need our help to rule it? Why can't he do it Himself if it is all Himself? And we don't know how Allah looks, so how do we know man was made in His image? Wouldn't that mean that He would have a body like ours and talk like we do? We are not supposed to make images of Allah, yet if we imagine He is like us, then isn't that making an image of Him in our minds? And why would he choose men to rule over His creation? Why not birds, who can fly above it all? Why not snakes that are the most humble?"

Ibn Yasin answered according to the teachings of all the wise men who had studied the inspired words given by the Prophet, but he could tell that his son didn't fully accept his answers. Mansur continued to stand in his own ideas. From that moment, Ibn Yasin knew that his son would follow his path as a religious leader. Mansur's ideas needed some training, but he thought for himself, and sought his own explanations. Ibn Yasin's face remained impassive, but his secret heart was smiling with pride.

CHAPTER 30

Samir approached the palatial court building with dread. Outside the large carved doors to the courtroom, long benches ran along the walls. About a dozen prisoners and guards were seated, and his guard motioned to a place for him to sit. He went to check with the door keeper, and came back to say, "You will be the fourth case. Now we just wait."

Samir spotted the two burly men who had pursued him across the hall at the far end, and realized that they had made the claim against him. His only witnesses were all on the caravan to Fez. There was a knot in his stomach. He wanted to throw up.

The first three cases were decided quickly, and soon he was called. He entered the grand courtroom with all of his muscles rigid. He was intimidated by the high seat of the judge, and the stern faces of everyone in the room. When he finally turned to look up at the judge, he saw with mixed feelings of relief and anxiety that it was Ibn Yasin himself. He had not looked up since Samir entered the room, so Samir didn't know if he would recognize him or not. He hoped he would.

Off to his left, he noticed Mansur seated on one of the side benches! Periodically Ibn Yasin had him come and sit in the court to watch the people and proceedings. They would then discuss the cases and the decisions afterwards over dinner. It was part of Mansur's leadership training. Today was one of those days. Samir tried to catch his eye, but he, too, was absorbed in reading something.

The steward of the court stood and said in a loud voice, "Bismillah er-rahman, er-rahim. We begin in the name of Allah, the merciful and compassionate. The defendant Samir ibn Jamal of Fez is accused of camel theft by Vakil ibn Masud and Mohammed ibn Abdul of Awdaghust. The parties please stand."

He turned first to Samir, and said, "How do you plead?"

"I am innocent, your excellency. She is my camel and she was stolen from me…"

The steward interrupted, "Not now. You will have a chance to tell your story in a minute. Be seated." Samir and the two burly men sat in their respective areas and waited.

When Samir had started to speak, both Ibn Yasin and Mansur had looked up and squinted to see his face clearly. Mansur had a puzzled expression. They did recognize him. His heart pounded in his chest. Maybe he would be okay after all.

Ibn Yasin paused for a moment to review the documents in front of him, then turned to the accusers. "Please state your case," he said in a stern, formal voice.

"Your eminence, on the night of the mawlid of the Prophet, peace be upon him, we purchased a camel from a merchant from Fez. He said he was having trouble selling the camel because she was white, and many breeders and racers are superstitious about white camels. We thought we knew a buyer, so we offered him thirty gold dinars, and he agreed to the sale. We waited until after dark to make the transaction because of the holiday."

"The man told us where the camel was housed," he continued. "It was in caravanserai six, which was guarded by Almohad soldiers. As soon as we paid, we went to collect the camel. She was there, and we led her out to her new owner. Your excellency, the man who purchased the camel from us was your own stable master."

Ibn Yasin looked surprised, and asked "Are you sure it was my stable master? I have no camels, only horses. Why did he say he was buying this camel? Are you sure it wasn't for himself?"

The men replied, "Oh yes. He said that this unusual camel had caught your eye, and he purchased it from us to present to you at an appropriate time. We put her safely into an enclosed room in your stable. The next morning, he came looking for us, and said that the camel had been stolen in the night. He was very angry about it, and thought we had stolen it back. We had not."

He continued, "For the next few hours we looked all over the city, but found no trace of her. Then she showed up for the races, and raced in the fourth camel race. This boy was riding her, and after the race he ducked out and disappeared. We followed him to the caravanserai, but the guards refused to let us collect the animal. Then she vanished."

"When we returned with soldiers to help us secure her, she had disappeared. Your soldiers found this boy beside the northern trade route, almost to Tata. He is a thief and was clearly fleeing from justice. We ask you to return our camel to us, and to punish this boy as a common thief."

The men glared over at Samir, and sat down, waiting to hear what the judge would say.

Ibn Yasin said, "I believe there is some merit in your case, however, I am more than a little familiar with this white camel. Let us hear what the defendant has to say in his behalf. Samir ibn Jamal you have heard the charges against you. Please tell your story and say only the truth." His face remained stern and impassive as he looked at Samir.

Samir stood, and, with his voice shaking a little, said, "Your eminence, on the day after our caravan arrived in Awdaghust, I took Amuna, my white camel, out to the desert for a run. She is a racing camel, as you have seen yourself, and each day I take her out to stretch her legs. She is the prize animal in my father's small herd."

"On that day you and your men surrounded me and you asked me to give you my camel and you would spare my life. I begged you to let me return with the camel to my father and promised to bring you her first calf when it is born. My Amuna is still too young to breed."

Out of the corner of his eye, Samir saw Mansur watching him.

"You agreed, and left us to return to town. The next day was the mawlid, and my uncle and I took Amuna into the markets to find out what her value is, as my father asked us to do. After a long day of looking at other camels and having merchants look Amuna over, we went back to the caravanserai."

"A boy I didn't know invited me to come into town and locate the race track for the next day. When I returned a few hours later, Amuna was missing. My friend Ali, one of the guards, helped me to discover that she had been stolen, and we looked all over town for her after dark. "

Ibn Yasin glanced up at him occasionally, and nodded. "Continue," he said.

"I heard her voice when we were searching in the inner circle of the town, so we found the stable where she was kept. I didn't know it was your stable. She was hidden in an enclosed room where no one would see her. I let her out and rode her back to the caravanserai, and then I decided to run to the desert with her overnight so she would not be stolen again."

"The next day was the racing day, and again, you know that I rode her in the fourth race, because you kindly sponsored me when the fee taker raised his rate higher than I could pay. You and your son saw me bring the camel from the caravanserai and line up for the race."

At this point, he looked over at Mansur, who nodded in agreement, and said out loud, "Yes, it is so."

"Your eminence, after the race I was tired and afraid, so I went back to the caravanserai and packed up my belongings. People kept crowding around, wanting to see her or ask questions. Our caravan was not going to leave for two or three more days. After dark, I rode Amuna out to the desert to escape, and for four days I navigated by the stars to find Tata. I hoped to rejoin my caravan at the oasis and return home with them. My uncle is in that caravan." His voice quivered for a moment, then he got control.

"Amuna is my father's best camel, as I told you in the desert. I came here with her, and I did not sell her, and I want to go home with her. I don't know what else I can tell you. I am not a thief. She belongs to me," he said. "I have been with her since her birth."

As he had done in the desert, he looked Ibn Yasin in the eye as he said it, not as a challenge but as an assertion of truth.

The accusers had not expected this straggly camel boy to be able to tell his story so well. They looked at each other and shook their heads. It was clear they were going to lose. Now they were worried about their own right hands being cut off for stealing,

Ibn Yasin waited a moment, then asked Samir, "Do you have any witnesses who can testify that what you say is true?"

Samir shook his head. "No, your eminence. My uncle and my friend the guard are both with our caravan on its way to Fez now. All the people on that caravan know I brought Amuna here. She was the only white camel, and everyone talked about her. Besides them, only you and your son. You saw us only a few hours after we arrived. I did not want to sell her. I would never sell her."

Ibn Yasin looked to his son. "Mansur, do you have anything to say with regard to this story?"

Mansur was surprised to be asked, and knew his father was testing him in some way. He decided to stand and say the truth, because he thought Samir was in the right.

"Your eminence, I saw this boy in the desert on the day he said, and I heard his promise to you to bring you her first calf when she is old enough to breed. A man who planned to sell the camel would not have made such a promise. He refused to sell her to you when you offered a fair price. He did not seem then like he had stolen that camel, and I believe he spoke the truth. He was very frightened." He glanced over at Samir with a sympathetic twinkle.

"We don't know who sold the camel to these men," Mansur continued, "but that person had no right to sell her. He had stolen her from this boy. She belonged to this boy, and it seems he was doing all he knew how to do to keep her safe and well."

Ibn Yasin listened thoughtfully and said, "Thank you," then paused. Mansur sat again.

The room was silent as they waited for his judgment. Finally, Ibn Yasin said, "My ruling in this case is for the defendant Samir ibn Jamal. He brought his white camel from Fez, he raced her here, and there is no proof or witness to say that he sold the camel himself. Anyone else did not have the ownership rights to sell her. The defendant is innocent."

"The plaintiffs appear to have been involved in a questionable sale," he continued, "and then the theft of the animal from her correct location. The _Qur'an_ says that a man who steals from another should have his right hand cut off so that all may see and know his offense."

The two accusers were sitting very straight and hanging on every word. They had not come here expecting to lose their right hands!

"Samir ibn Jamal, is it your wish that these men who stole your camel should have their hands severed?" Ibn Yasin asked.

"No sir," Samir replied. "If they thought they had purchased Amuna, I mean, my camel, then they did no wrong. The person who was wrong was the one who took their gold and sold what was not his to sell."

Ibn Yasin turned to the men and said, "I agree with this boy. You did commit theft, but you thought you had made a legitimate purchase, so your theft is not punishable under the law. I declare you both to be innocent." The two men stood and bowed, and said "Thank you, your eminence! We are truly grateful!"

Ibn Yasin said, "In exchange for your freedom, I give you the task to find the man who sold this camel to you, and bring him to justice. We do not want such criminals wandering around in our city."

The men nodded and said, "We will do our best to find him, your eminence."

"And finally," Ibn Yasin turned to Samir, "Samir ibn Jamal, I order my guards to release your camel and your belongings to you. I encourage you to return to Fez as quickly as possible. I have not forgotten the bargain we made. See that you do not. My son Mansur can walk with you to the stable to make sure the guards do not question this ruling."

He placed his signature and seal on a document. Then he stood behind his table, nodded to the courtroom and said, "Allahu akbar. God is great," and he left the room.

CHAPTER 31

Mansur was a head taller and a year older than Samir, but they immediately began talking comfortably as boys do while they walked back through town to the barracks. Mansur was eager to learn about Fez. His father had just told him he would be going to the university soon, so he was curious about the city, the people and the university. Samir was able to provide some information, especially about the library and the madrasa and how different the city layout was. He had not yet entered the university himself, but he hoped the extra gold dinars he was bringing home for his racing prize would pay for a few years of study.

As they approached the stable, Samir focused only on Amuna. He hoped she was well cared for. It had probably been a difficult two weeks for her. He didn't know what to expect. They approached the guard, and he turned out to be someone who recognized Mansur. Mansur explained the ruling and produced a paper stating that Samir was free to go with his camel. The guard studied the paper, then with a gruff nod, gestured with his head toward where Amuna could be found.

Samir rushed to the door of her stall. She was standing quietly in a back corner. When he entered to greet her, he ran to throw his arms around her neck, but she didn't respond as usual. She turned her side to him indifferently.

"Amuna! My little moon. Are you okay? Why are you not friendly with me?"

He was very sad. He glanced at her body and saw that she was in good condition. She was apparently mad at him for being gone. He tried to rub her nose, but she pulled her head away. He continued stroking her neck, and talking to her. Little by little she seemed to forgive him, and started to respond. He went over to his saddlebags and rummaged for a treat. He only found a few figs, so he fed them to her one by one, and they became friends again.

Mansur stood by the door watching. He understood. His horse Shams could be moody at times, too. Samir told Amuna to kneel, then he put the pack frame on her back and loaded his few belongings onto it. They were ready to leave. He told her to stand. As he led her toward the door, it suddenly occurred to Samir that he had no idea where to go. He could no longer go to the caravanserai, because his group had left. He didn't want to spend money on an inn, but he needed food for his trip home and water, and Amuna would need a place to stay out of sight of people who might be curious about her. And the thief who stole her!

Samir must have had an odd look on his face, because Mansur asked, "What's the matter?"

"I don't know where to go!" Samir replied, looking at Mansur with a quizzical expression. "I just realized this minute that I don't know where to go next. Or how to arrange for a caravan heading north." He was serious and confused, and then started to smile crookedly and burst into a laugh. It was a laugh of relief, release, joy and amazement. It was contagious, and Mansur started to laugh, too. They each made the other laugh more, and they laughed for more than ten minutes. They sat down to rest, and held their sides and rubbed their aching cheeks.

Mansur said, "I have an idea. Come back home with me. We have lots of stables for Amuna and they are well guarded—except from thieves who come looking for camels in the dead of night like you did!" The boys laughed again. "I can find you a place to stay with the guards or groundskeepers, and I will make sure you get fed. It will be fun to have someone my age around who is not my relative or a slave."

Samir agreed, and they started walking toward Mansur's home, talking with great animation about whether camels were better than horses and how it had felt to ride in the big race. They were, after all, boys.

CHAPTER 32

Things were not so jolly in the caravan on the road to Fez. Uncle Moosa was beside himself when Samir didn't show up to join the caravan. Ali took him aside and told him the whole story about the boy and the camel, and how they had fled to the desert. Moosa was sick about it. He wished Samir had just waited for him to return from dinner. They could have worked something out so he didn't have to flee. He and Amuna would have been safe in the caravanserai. He would have hired bodyguards to protect them until they got on the road.

The caravan had arrived at Tata two days ago, and no one he talked to had seen a white camel. He didn't want to believe something bad had happened to Samir in the desert, but he couldn't imagine what had delayed him except something terrible that he didn't want to think about. And they were pulling out in the morning. The caravan had to continue.

Moosa was tempted to stay behind in Tata to see if Samir would show up in a day or two, but Sayyid Walid talked him out of it. "This oasis is not kind to stragglers," he had said, and he was right. Moosa knew no one here. Plus there was no guarantee that Samir would even show up. So he had decided to continue home with the caravan. Oh, how he dreaded facing his brother.

He left messages and information with three of the merchants in the village. If a white camel did appear, they would give the boy Moosa's instructions. He left five gold dinars with one of the olive merchants he knew slightly, and asked him to help the boy buy supplies and join another caravan north. The man recognized Moosa from prior trips, and agreed to help. That was about all Moosa could do. There was no point in remaining in Tata alone and full of uncertainty.

Ali didn't have to force himself to look stern these days. Since they left Awdaghust, he had been searching hard for signs of his young friend. He was a little concerned about things he had seen and heard in Awdaghust, and wondered if there might be an uprising of the slaves at some point. There were more slaves than masters in the town, and the people he talked to spoke softly about pockets of discontent with the strictness of the Almoravid rule. He hoped they would be well away from there if such an uprising did occur.

As he promised, Ali had placed strips of colored cloth in little rock pyramids on the road periodically after the caravan had passed. He didn't know what else he could do for Samir. He was kicking himself for letting the boy go on that dangerous journey alone.

It had been bad enough having to tell Moosa what had happened, but at least they had had hope that Samir would show up around Tata. Now they didn't know what to say to each other. Ali tried to avoid Moosa. They were leaving in the morning, and they certainly didn't know what to say to Jamal when they got back to Fez. Ali knew he would have to go and tell Jamal the story, and it would be a difficult, emotional conversation. He dreaded it. It would be a long, sad journey of uncertainty for the next few weeks.

Ali thought about leaving the caravan and heading back toward Awdaghust to see if he could find signs of the boy. He decided to sleep on the idea, but when he awoke he knew in his heart that he could never find him alone in the vast desert. After even a single day the dunes left no traces of passage.

Perhaps Samir had become confused and found his way back to the city, but he knew Samir a little now, and knew he would try to continue to the oasis. Ali could only pray for his safe and speedy return to Fez with another caravan. He knew the boy had some gold, so he hoped the coins would get him through any difficulties. That wouldn't comfort a father who has just lost his only son and his best camel, though. The worst part of Ali's journey was still ahead of him.

Moosa was having his own grim thoughts. He had lost his only son Mohammed a few years before to a snake bite. It had been devastating. Samir had been there to fill that hole inside of him, with his eager mind and optimistic outlook on life. The boys were nearly the same age.

Moosa had been very proud when Samir won that camel race, and now he regretted all the things he had not said to his nephew. And he dreaded from the depths of his being the day he had to tell his brother this terrible, terrible news. He also dreaded facing his conscience for his irresponsibility and lack of oversight. He should have done many things differently. He would now. If only…

Sayyid Walid tried to comfort Moosa. He reminded him that Samir was a smart and observant boy. He was smart enough to get money to race the camel. He was smart enough to win against much older and more experienced riders. He had been out into the desert alone with the camel before, even overnight, so there was reason to hope.

Perhaps he just didn't go north far enough to find the trade route in time or had ridden too slowly. Perhaps Samir had felt uncertain, and turned back to town, hoping to catch the caravan before it left. He had provisions for himself and the camel for at least a week, and it was only now a week since he had left the caravanserai.

Hearing Walid's words was somewhat comforting to Moosa, but he still didn't know how he was going to live with himself if it turned out the boy was lost or dead. His brother had relied on Moosa to keep his son safe and return him home. He had done neither. The road home stretched in front of Moosa like an executioner's blade.

CHAPTER 33

Mansur was able to find a place for Samir to stay with the stable master Azim. Azim groomed Ibn Yasin's and Mansur's mounts personally, and was partial to the young Almoravid.

"Master Azim, this boy has no place to stay, and I wonder if you would be able to find a place for him? He will also need a stall for his camel. I don't know for how long. His caravan has left without him, and he has to make other arrangements," Mansur had said.

Azim bowed to Mansur with respect and said, "Of course, excellency. I will find him a good place and care for the camel."

Azim recognized the white camel immediately. He had been the one who purchased her from the two thieves who sold her. He had seen her that night, and had put her into the enclosed room in the stable. He had also seen her race the next day, and realized that he was welcoming racing royalty, even if the boy did not yet seem to realize it. It seemed fitting that now this camel was his guest and the young "thief" who had stolen her was living in his home.

Mansur came to visit Samir every day or two, but he was busy with his normal responsibilities. That left Samir with a lot of time on his hands. He desperately wanted to find some way to send a note to his father, and let him know that he was safe and secure. Perhaps a scribe would be able to send a letter for him by messenger.

Time dragged by, and taking Amuna out for rides was not a good idea. They were famous here, and anyone who saw Amuna immediately wanted to touch her, talk about buying her, or question him about the race. He didn't like all the attention, and worried that someone would try to steal her again, so Samir walked everywhere on his own two feet, and just took Amuna out for runs after dark.

One morning he left the compound early and headed into town to look around. Instead of asking where to go, he decided to wander the city and follow his own nose. He remembered what Uncle Moosa had said about pickpockets, so he kept his few pieces of gold close to his skin, and tied a wide woolen sash around his middle to cover it. He hoped to get a lead on a caravan, or at least find a cleric who would help him send a message to his father.

Samir struck off for the markets, where he felt more at ease. He was trying to learn what he could about how he might get home, and where he should buy his supplies. He wandered the streets with no particular destination in mind, just watching and learning.

An aging physician was sitting in the shade at the front of his apothecary shop with a glint in his eye and a week's growth of beard on his chin. A few onlookers were gathered around him. With care, he weighed out half a dozen dried chameleons, wrapped them in a twist of paper, and passed the packet to a young woman dressed in black. She handed him some coins quickly, and walked away.

"She will give birth to a handsome boy child," said the physician with a wink when the woman had gone.

"How do you know? Are you sure?" Samir asked.

The man stashed the money in a pouch under his shirt. He nodded, and scanned his assortment of wares--mysterious pink and brown powders, snake skins, live turtles, bundles of aromatic argan and cedar bark, and vials of tinctures.

"Of course. We have been helping women like her for five centuries," the physician said slowly, "And never has a customer come to complain."

Samir looked unconvinced, but what did he know of women. His mother had died when he was small, so he had never had the company of women.

"Believe me, I speak the truth," the man said. "Ask anyone." He ground a mortar half-filled with dried Damascus rose petals and added a few drops of olive and argan oil. This preparation would make any woman beautiful again, he said. It certainly smelled good.

Women wearing long, loose cloaks walked past and paused to watch him work with interest. The large sleeves of their ka'ifs were fashionably rolled up at the cuff to expose inner fabrics of contrasting color or embroidery, and, more importantly, lots of gold bracelets of every size. It was important to advertise one's wealth to attract a suitable husband or claim status.

Their heads were usually covered with a light scarf and their faces were exposed, but some of the older women wore the traditional full face veil where only their eyes could be seen. Wealthier women often had elaborately fashioned disks of gold hanging on their foreheads, and long, dangling earrings of gold and beadwork decorating their veils.

The physician called out to the passersby as they walked, "Potions and compresses for every ailment and desire. Come and tell me your need. I will create something for you or your husband to cure what ails you and make your life lively again!"

The women were scandalized by his words, and pulled their scarves quickly across their lower faces. They scurried away in bunches, like clucking chickens. The old man laughed. He knew some of them would trickle back by themselves later.

Samir thanked the man for allowing him to watch, and moved off down the road. A few turns later, he found himself next to the meat market, where goats, sheep, camels and cattle were ritually slaughtered and sold. The strong smell of blood and butchered meat was a physical presence here. Occasionally a butcher would fill a bucket with water and splash it over the stony ground to wash the blood away, but the floors were soon red again. Animal corpses hung everywhere. Though slaves holding thick horsetail fly whisks stayed busy fanning the area, flies swarmed endlessly.

One of the butcher shops featured rack after rack of dark, smoke-dried and seasoned meat strips. Pink legs of lamb lay on mounds of fresh sweet mint. A slave was grinding meat to make sausages in the back. Samir bought a few different dried strips to try the flavors.

Across the square was the metal working enclave. The temperature rose about ten degrees immediately when he entered the area. Three large open stone furnaces with roaring flames stood in the center of the square. Piles of logs were stacked against the walls, and sweating men moved busily from forge to furnace to anvil.

Smiths and forgers of all kinds came from their shops to use the furnaces. The ringing sounds of hammers pounding hot iron and copper were everywhere. After a few minutes, Samir's head was ringing, too. The ringing broke every few minutes with a loud hiss as one of the smiths quenched his red hot creation by grabbing it with heavy iron tongs and dipping it quickly into a barrel of cold water.

In Fez there was much less metal work and it was across town from where he lived, so this was new to Samir. The sound here was deafening, and made his ears hurt. He was fascinated to watch the muscular, half-dressed smiths swing heavy hammers in a rhythmic dance as they pounded the metal to amazing thinness and into elaborate ornamental shapes. But the sound! He put his fingers in his ears to cut down on the noise, and watched a while longer. Sweat was pouring down his face. One man was working on a short sword, hammering and folding, hammering and folding the metal. After quenching it, he started to grind down the edge to sharpen it and see how it would hold its sharpness. Samir watched as long as he could, but finally had to leave. The heat and the noise were exhausting!

Down the way there were a dozen booths of carpet sellers who draped their colorful wares over wooden rods as high as they could reach. Piles of rugs lay on the floor to flip through with customers. Salesmen lounged on the piles when no customers were around.

This road was shady and Samir dawdled a bit to cool off there. His face was red as a pomegranate. He accepted a cup of tea from one of the merchants who had pity on him. The carpet sellers always offered hot mint tea to prospective customers to get them into the stall and spend time talking about the carpets. Mostly the rugs were hand knotted wools of many types, dyed in the nearby weavers' village. Large looms stood outside so the weavers, usually women, could talk as they worked. It was easy to recognize a weaver—their hands were usually stained from regular submersion in the dye vats.

After two weeks of watching Samir stroll around daily, some of the merchants began to recognize him, and would bid him salaam or nod. Once Mansur came for a walk with him in the market. It created quite a stir. The merchants recognized Mansur's fine dress, of course, and the streets buzzed with curiosity about how the son of their Emir could know this poor laborer's son. They didn't recognize the famous camel rider walking among them.

Walking through the streets was a nice distraction from Samir's gloomy thoughts, but he began to get discouraged. He started to think he would never find a way to return home. He couldn't get a lead on any caravans headed north. And while he was comfortable in his quarters, and Amuna was getting a little fat from all the food around her, it wasn't home. He longed to go home.

CHAPTER 34

A few days later Mansur rushed out to the stables to find Samir, who was idly brushing Amuna's back with a fine curry comb. Her coat was looking beautiful. She was very clean from being indoors all day every day, and the good food and constant brushing she received from her bored friend Samir was making her coat shine. It was dazzling in the sun now.

"Samir! Where are you? Samir!" Mansur called loudly for his friend as he ran into the stable.

"Here, in Amuna's stall. Why are you so excited?" Samir asked.

"Great news! Father just told me I am to go to university next week. Next week! In Fez!" Mansur waited for his words to sink in.

"What? In Fez? That's wonderful news. How did that happen?"

Samir tossed the curry comb toward the shelf and grabbed Mansur's arm enthusiastically. He was glad for his friend's good fortune. "That's great!" he said.

"We talked about it a few months ago, and I guess he decided that I am old enough now. He made arrangements with one of my mother's aunts for me to stay there while I attend classes. I don't know them, but it doesn't matter. I will spend all my time in my classes or studying or sleeping anyway. I'm so excited! This will be the first time I am allowed to live on my own. It will be great!"

"Maybe we will be able to study together. I am going to go back to school when I get home," Samir said. Oh. When he said the word home, it was as if a large stone had fallen in his chest. He was immediately saddened.

Mansur saw his face change and said, "What happened? Why are you sad?"

"Because I don't know how I can get home. I haven't found any news of caravans heading north. It may be months before I can leave," Samir said.

"I forgot to tell you!" Mansur jumped around and grabbed Samir's arm. "Father said that when I go, we are to take you with us. He will have a company of soldiers escort us to Fez. I will ride Shams and you will ride Amuna, and we will get there fast. The men will take care of our food and water. I will even buy you a fine map so you can make your own notations about stars and terrain. Then you will be able to come back to Awdaghust whenever you want to visit us. If you have time that is…you will probably be some famous camel racer astronomer and never get out of your own city except to race." Mansur laughed.

This unexpected good news overwhelmed Samir. He stood there without moving, like he was in shock. He couldn't believe it. He would be going home next week! The boys both jumped for joy, laughed with excitement and talked about their trip a bit longer, then Mansur headed back to his house to start planning what personal things he wanted to take with him to school.

The excitement of the impending journey was building. Samir felt relief, apprehension, joy and anxiety all at once. He was going home at last! Amuna was going home! Father would be so relieved and happy, but he would be furious that he had not stayed with Uncle Moosa and followed instructions. Uncle Moosa would be furious that he had taken such a risk, too, and would thump him on the head.

I will probably have to spend a month cleaning the camel stalls every day as punishment, he thought. But punishment is good! It means I will be with Father again. His smile was ear to ear.

He turned to Amuna, jumped up and threw his arms around her neck unexpectedly. She jerked her head back and almost hit the wall.

Samir laughed loudly and said, "'Muna, we are going home! Finally our life can be normal again. It's a good thing we are leaving soon, or you would be too fat to ride! Father is going to think I don't know how to take care of you."

He petted her cheeks and hugged her neck. She nibbled on his fingers. "You are his best camel. He will be so glad to see us."

And I will be so happy to see him, he thought. *We are going home!*

CHAPTER 35

The next few days were full of preparations and chaos. Samir couldn't rely on Mansur and his family to provide him with what he would need for the journey. He started to put together a pile of items in the corner of Amuna's stall.

He still had all of his gold in his water bag except for the four gold dinars he kept with him. That would be enough for his supplies. He really only needed to provide for himself. The soldiers would bring feed and water for the animals. Still, he remembered what Father said about filling his water bags full at every stop, so he made sure his two bags stood in the corner as full as possible and ready to load.

The day before they were to leave, Mansur came down to see him, and in an excited voice asked, "Are you ready to go? Do you need anything before we pack? They have loaded a lot of scrolls and clothing and books for me, so I can carry a few things for you if you need me to."

"No, I have everything I need. I already had what I need from my first trip, so I just replenished my food and water. I will be ready when you are!" The boys talked a few minutes more, then Mansur dashed off to check his personal things one last time.

Samir didn't need anything because he had already purchased a saddlebag full of dried meats and fruits, including some special treats for Amuna. The vendors in the market had placed more in his packages than he paid for as a kindness. He still had Uncle Moosa's two burnooses, so hot or cold he would have something to shelter or wrap in.

The water bags were ready, and he had been taking Amuna for long drinks at the water trough in the yard. Her hump seemed a bit larger to him than when they first left for Awdaghust over three months before, so she would probably make the journey without any distress. All that was left was for him to find a gift to take home for Father. And maybe one for Uncle Moosa, too. Uncle Moosa had suffered because of Samir's reckless actions.

He realized he still had one other obligation. He had not found the old camel Jabbar, and he had made a promise to him. He found his way to the saddle shop he visited his first day in Awdaghust. The merchant didn't remember him, and greeted him like a stranger.

"Salaam aleikhum, young brother. Are you in need of a nice saddle today? Or perhaps some saddle blankets?"

Samir replied, "No, thank you. I was here before the last racing day, and you recommended to me to bet on the camel Jabbar al-Takruri, your brother's camel."

The man squinted his eyes at Samir and said, "Perhaps. And did you wager on him? God is merciful, he won his race!"

"Yes, I did, and I won my bet. But his race was an accidental win. He was lucky. He was in terrible shape!"

The shopkeeper shrugged noncommittally. "Nevertheless, a win is a win. He won. So what can I do for you today?"

"I would like to visit Jabbar. Can you tell me where he is kept?" Samir asked. The shopkeeper stifled an astonished look. No one he knew of had ever asked to visit a camel. He seemed a little confused.

"You want to…what? Did I hear you right? Why would you want to visit a camel? Such a strange request!"

"Yes, well, I have business with him," Samir said mysteriously. "Soon I will be leaving town and I made a promise. I need to see him. Do you know where I can find him?" Samir asked again.

"Little brother, I tell you this with a heavy heart. Jabbar has passed into Allah's great garden. As you so wisely noted, he was an old camel, and he won his race only by God's will. My brother decided his time had come, so he was released from this world of suffering. He is dead," the merchant said.

Samir was instantly filled with conflicting feelings. He was sorry that the old camel was no more, and he hoped he met a peaceful end, but he was thrilled that he no longer had to fulfill the promise to mate Amuna with him. One less thing for Father to be angry about! A big smile started to creep over his face, but he forced himself to look solemn and expressed his sadness about the loss. The merchant looked quizzically at him, then shrugged and said, "He was only a camel. They are easily replaced."

No. Not my Amuna, Samir thought.

While he was in the shop, he decided to buy Father a brilliant orange camel harness with orange and white tassels hanging from it. It would be a special harness that he could use on his champion camels. He thought about putting it on Amuna, but she already turned a lot of heads when he took her out to run. He didn't need to call more attention to her.

Samir quickly made his purchase and left the shop with a light heart. One less obligation. He celebrated by buying a small melon from a vendor in the street, and took it back to treat Amuna.

She greeted him with enthusiasm, running up to him and bumping him. She could nearly knock him down now with her affection. He put down the melon and grabbed her around the neck, lifting his feet to swing in the air. Then he rubbed her soft nose and offered her the melon. She sniffed it curiously, her nostrils flaring. She could tell it was to eat, but wasn't quite sure what to do first. It didn't have an end or a branch. She reached out her rubbery lips cautiously and felt around on the smooth shape.

"Go head, bite it!" Samir said. She didn't understand, of course, but she was ready to try teeth. She opened her mouth wide and her long teeth clamped onto the rind. Samir held the melon tightly and helped her to rip it open. Her first bite went down quickly and she immediately reached out for more, swallowing as fast as she could. He thought for sure he could see a smile on her face.

"It looks like you like melon, girl," he said. He put the last bits in his palm and let her take it from his hand. "You certainly are a mess now. Let's go to the trough so you can wash your face!" He put a rope harness around her head and led her outside. He smiled. This was a good day.

Amuna didn't know that she had been spared the attentions of Jabbar, but she did know that Samir was happy about something from the wonderful treat he had brought. That was enough for her.

CHAPTER 36

Azim the stable master woke Samir just after midnight by bringing in a bright lantern. "Get up, boy. It is time to load up and go. You are heading home."

Samir sat up immediately and nodded, rubbing his eyes. He hadn't been asleep long anyway. He was too excited to sleep. He had a few things here in his room to gather, and his travel goods were already waiting to be loaded in the stable. He rolled and tied his bedroll and prayer rug, and went into the kitchen.

Two slaves were busy preparing some breakfast, and had already started the chopping and grinding for the midday meal. Azim was seated on a cushion on the floor with his food in front of him. Samir joined him.

"Shukran, Sayyid Azim, thank you. I am grateful to have stayed in your house these weeks. You have been a generous host."

Azim gave a brusque nod with his eyes down on his food. "You can tell your father you gave me no trouble."

Samir smiled just a little and said, "Thank you. He will be pleased. Perhaps he will not beat me for that. I'm sure I am in for beatings once I have told him my whole story. He is very worried about me now, and thinks I am dead. I'm sure of it."

Azim said, "The next time you are in Awdaghust, come by and see us. The men liked having you around." Of course, he would never admit that he was really the one who would like Samir to return.

"I will, Sayyid Azim," he answered. He tore a piece of flatbread and dipped it into some fragrant chickpea porridge. There were tomatoes and olives and halves of eggs, so he put them on top and took a large bite. He ate his fill, knowing this was the last fresh food he would have for several days or maybe weeks. When he finished, he stood and bowed formally to Azim.

"As-salaam aleikhum, Sayyid Azim. Peace be upon you. I hope we will meet again."

Azim nodded and replied, "Insh'allah." If God is willing.

Samir grabbed his belongings from his room and stopped by the door to slip on his sandals. He turned to wave and hurried over to the stable to rouse Amuna. He wanted to be ready when he was summoned.

CHAPTER 37

Samir placed a padded blanket on Amuna's back, and put the familiar wooden pack frame over it. He made sure to pull the lashings tight around her middle. Then he hung the saddlebags on either side.

There were no salt slabs or grain bag to carry this time, so he put the heavy water bags on each side for balance. He lashed them into place, and slipped his bedroll, prayer rug and the two burnooses under the lashings where he could get them out easily. Then he filled his small water bag full. He was ready to go.

Sayyid Azim sent one of his stable boys to lead him around to the courtyard where Mansur and the soldiers were finishing their loading. There were three camels to carry the heavy burden of the water and feed bags, the sleeping tents and the chests with Mansur's belongings, but the rest were horses. Mansur greeted him with a shout, but he quickly quieted at a sharp look from his father. It was still the middle of the night.

Even in his sleeping robes and without his turban Ibn Yasin was a commanding presence as he stood erectly on the stairs. His head was bare for once, and it was possible to see his dark hair and neatly trimmed beard and mustache. His blue silk robe seemed thin to wear at this chilly time of the night, but he showed no signs of discomfort. He calmly watched the preparations as if it were the most normal thing in the world to be sending his favorite son away for several years. Only a twitch in his little finger revealed his inner tension.

The goodbyes were brief and stoic. Ibn Yasin said, "Excel at your studies, my son. Never forget that you have a path to follow. Do all you can to prepare for that journey. Trust in Allah. May he keep you safe from brigands on the road."

Mansur nodded and smiled at his father. Ibn Yasin gripped his son's arm affectionately for a moment. His father was not demonstrative. It was a moment Mansur would always remember.

"I will be back for the Ramadan fast, Father. We will have many interesting things to talk about then! I will be a star gazer!"

"And you, camel boy," Ibn Yasin said, turning to Samir. "You have a safe journey as well. Do not forget our bargain. God be with you."

Samir bowed respectfully and said, "Your eminence, I cannot forget our bargain or the generosity you have shown to me here. I am in your debt in many ways. Salaam." He touched his forehead in respect.

Ibn Yasin smiled briefly. The boy was poor, but he was well-mannered. He then turned to general Malik, who was escorting the boys. He gave him a few brief instructions as he straightened his last strap and tucked the end under the saddle. Then Ibn Yasin nodded and stepped away from the riders, as if to say , You may now leave.

"It shall all be as God wills. Good journey all," Ibn Yasin said. He turned abruptly and went into the house as the party mounted, as if it were too painful for him to watch the small company ride away. It probably was.

CHAPTER 38

The band fell into a line with soldiers in the front and rear. The boys rode side by side in the middle with the pack camels behind them. Mansur was true to his word. As soon as they got to the city gate, he reached into his ha'ik and pulled out a rolled parchment. He stretched his arm out and reached up to smack Samir on the arm with it.

"Hey, camel boy!" They both laughed, and Samir knew he was going to have to get used to that nickname now. "Here is the map I promised you! It is on gazelle parchment, guaranteed to last a lifetime. Start making your marks and notes. Some day you will be glad of this gift!"

"I'm glad of it now! Thank you!" Samir said enthusiastically.

Samir was thrilled. He had forgotten Mansur's promise, and realized just now that he really did want a map. He could hardly wait for a rest stop so he could roll it all the way out and study it.

For now he had to be satisfied with only unrolling a few centimeters at a time against Amuna's hump and trying to make sense of it. They were moving too fast to read anything. Tonight he would mark the locations of Yildun and the other guiding stars he knew.

The company made good time. They rode along the main roads, so they arrived in Tata on the third day. The last time Samir was here he had been arrested. They rode into the narrow, shady canyon and came upon the wide, beautiful lake surrounded by trees. It was a vision of paradise.

They would stay overnight, just long enough to refill their water bags and barrels. They had a hard ride ahead to Todra. Malik wanted to meet with the officers here and find out what kind of road conditions they would face on the next leg of the journey.

Samir was surprised when a merchant approached him and signaled for him to come over. He walked over, wiping his wet hands on his robe, to see what the merchant wanted.

"Are you Samir ibn Jamal?" he asked.

"Yes." Samir wondered how the man knew his name.

"Salaam aleikhum. Your uncle said you might come here on your white camel. He left me some gold for you and asked me to help you find a caravan to Fez."

Samir was astonished. "My uncle did that? Where is he? He was here? When did you see him?"

The merchant replied, "He was here with a large caravan a few weeks ago. They were moving slowly. Some of the animals were making their first caravan, and were causing delays."

The man reached into his belt and handed Samir five gold dinars. "Here is the gold he left for you. He told me to be sure you get any supplies you need. What do you need?"

Samir said, "God is great, I need nothing. I am traveling with this company of soldiers, and they are providing water and feed. I have food in my saddlebags for myself."

Samir held the five gold coins in his hand, then took one and handed it to the merchant.

"Thank you for watching for me and offering to help. Take this coin for your trouble. I will tell my uncle of your kindness." The merchant happily took the gold. They bowed, and the merchant walked away.

Samir waited a minute, then smiled and tucked the remaining coins into his belt. Yes, Allah and Uncle Moosa were watching out for him. He would soon be back where he belonged.

Each night Samir and Mansur placed their bedrolls on the ground near Amuna. They stared up into the night sky and talked about the stars they knew and what they would study when they got to Fez.

Most nights the sky was a rich, velvety black and a thick carpet of stars sparkled like diamonds thrown across it. It was the new moon, and only a sliver was visible low in the sky, making the light show from the stars even more brilliant than usual.

Late at night, a wide band appeared from the horizon and arched overhead, as far as they could see. They watched the sky in silence for a while, feeling the deep wonder of lying on a small planet floating in the immensity of space.

"Mansur, do you know Mullah Baba stories?" Samir asked.

"Yes. I had a teacher at the madrasa who loved to teach us with those silly stories. Who can make sense of them?"

"Uncle Moosa told me this one. Mullah Baba was teaching astronomy at a school. One of the students asked him the number of stars. Mullah said, 'When I was younger, I was going to go to space to count them, but I did not do it for two reasons. First, I have been way too busy. Secondly, I was afraid that at night there may be not enough light there so I could see the stars.'"

They chuckled.

"I have one," Mansur countered. "A man said to Mullah Baba, 'What is more valuable to us, the sun or the moon?' Mullah answered, 'Well, the sun is out during the daytime when there is light. The moon, on the other hand, provides light during the night when it's dark. Thus, the moon is obviously much more valuable.'"

Samir said, "I heard it told this way. One day Mullah Baba entered his favorite teahouse and declared, 'The moon is more useful than the sun'. An old man asked, 'Why Mullah?' Mullah Baba replied, 'Because we need the light more during the night than during the day.'"

"I like your way better," Mansur said. He was silent for a few minutes. "I heard this path of stars over our heads is the one the Prophet, peace be upon him, rode when he rode up to heaven on his horse Buraq."

"I heard it is what remains from a huge battle in the sky from the ancient times. Allah was attacked by evil demons and blasted them to pieces with light. They are still burning," Samir said. There was a long silence.

"Oh look! There! A dying star. And another." Samir pointed to his right. Mansur leaned up on his elbow to look.

"All those pieces of demons have to die sometime," Samir said. "Allah is giving us a blessing to let us watch him triumph over evil."

Mansur shook his head, and lay back down. "That's not what I heard. I heard it was the souls of new babies coming to earth. They fly down from heaven and when they get close to earth, their wings burn off and the soul enters a newborn baby."

Samir liked that story. But he couldn't say anything, because he had already fallen asleep. That night they both dreamed of flying horses and starry roads.

CHAPTER 39

The caravan taking Moosa and Ali to Fez was still moving slowly, but the new animals were finally getting into the rhythm. They were able to travel a little faster each day than the day before.

They were almost to the Azrou oasis now, and at night the smell of cedar trees traveled toward them lightly on the breeze. The ground was already getting rocky and had started to rise up into the hills ahead, but the sun beat down on them unmercifully. The caravan leader passed back word that they should be arriving tomorrow night. They would pass through trees that lined the road on the way in, so at least the next day would not be as hot.

Ali was eager to get to a cool place, and bathe himself and Gawa. Gawa smelled like stale horse sweat and Ali smelled worse.

Earlier today they had passed another caravan coming south from Fez. He was able to talk briefly with the officer in charge, and asked him if he had any news of General Yusuf and the coastal campaigns. The man said that the battles were grim. Many lives had been lost, and

General Yusuf still had not moved much further north than where he started. It looked like the coastal barbarians were much tougher than the southern tribes had been.

Ali hoped that meant he would soon be able to join Yusuf and start being a soldier instead of an escort. His muscles ached for a good fight. With all the Almoravids focused on the western coast, there hadn't been any opportunities for skirmishing to save the caravan.

"I guess that's good," he mused. "No need for innocent people to be killed or raided. I just want a little action. I am tired of all this monotonous long string of swaying baggage day after day."

He looked up at the stars as he lay down to sleep away from the noisy camels. They grumbled and belched all night. He wondered as he watched the small sliver of moon where his friend Samir was.

"Is he seeing the same sky?" he said to himself. "God is merciful, he survived his days in the desert and either returned to Awdaghust or made it to the oasis. Perhaps he caught another caravan ahead of ours moving north, and was able to join with them. Maybe he will be in Fez before we are, and he will jump out to surprise us when we go to tell his father he is missing. I hope so." He wasn't really convinced of that scenario, but he hoped Allah had some good outcome in store.

Moosa had tied his camels behind those of Sayyid Walid, so the two didn't have as far to walk in the evening to talk or drink tea together. They usually shared a fire and their evening meal. Moosa was reflecting on a conversation they had had the night before.

Walid had asked for details about Samir and what had happened after the big camel race. Moosa told him the highlights, but something kept him from sharing the whole story. He didn't mention that the camel had been stolen or that Samir had left town after the race because he was being followed. He did mention that Ibn Yasin had helped Samir to pay the fee so he could race, which startled Walid.

"No! How can that be? He's just an ordinary boy. How did your nephew even think to ask for his help? What a strange story."

Moosa replied, "Yes, strange but true. I don't know about this boy. He seems to manage to stay one step ahead of disaster. If only he had not decided to ride out on his own! That was a stupid thing to do just to avoid the crowds chasing after him. I could have gotten some bodyguards. Now look where we are. I don't even know where he is or if I will ever see him again. He is like a son to me."

His voice broke a little. He quickly grabbed his cup and sipped some tea.

"Still, it is very odd that he chose not to remain inside the caravanserai," Walid said. "There were guards there. It almost sounds as if someone was after him or his camel. I wonder what made him feel he should run away."

Moosa shrugged and nodded. "All boys that age have brain damage. They don't know right from wrong, up from down, stupid from smart."

"Yes, that is true. I myself was that way. I once climbed a crumbling watchtower just to prove to my father that he was wrong about it being unsafe. Of course, I fell and cracked my head open." He pointed to a scar on the side of his head. "I really hope your nephew is as smart as he seems to be, and that he reached safety…even if you don't know right now where that is," Walid said kindly.

Moosa nodded again, and the two men sat in silence a while.

"I think I will sleep now," Walid said, and he stood up, brushing sand off his robes. It was getting chilly, and morning would come early for them. In fact, morning would come when it was still black dark. They said good night, and went to their bedrolls.

Lying on his back, Moosa stared at the star filled sky. The sliver of moon hung low, and the starry road was shining brightly above. Stars give the night a silvery light, and they were bright enough tonight to cast shadows.

Moosa noticed a few shooting stars and closed his eyes. His wife had believed that a shooting star is a sign from Allah to make a wish, and it would be granted. He wished earnestly for his nephew's safety, and wished a second time that Samir would make it home.

He couldn't bear the thought of telling his brother that Samir was lost. It would break him. He fell asleep to troubled thoughts and had troubled dreams.

CHAPTER 40

The *Holy Qur'an* states that there can be no compulsion in religion. No one can be forced to convert. To the Berbers of the Maghrib, Islam appeared to be freer, more personal, less oppressive, and a more powerful religious form than they had previously encountered.

Most volunteered to convert, but those who wished to resist and chose to fight gave the Muslim armies a reason to exist. They would swoop in on the heathen infidels and crush them. The fearsome force of their power preceded them, and, as a result, new villages often surrendered to the armies without any bloodshed. At least, that is how it usually worked.

The natives along the western coast of the Maghrib, however, believed powerfully in their own pagan religion, or else they thought they could defeat the Muslims. They fought back with vigor. As a result, a large force under General Yusuf had been formed to bring the area under shari'a law. It was not easy, and his troops took lots of damage.

The natives on the coast were unusually strong and well provisioned, and in several battles they defeated Yusuf.

He fell back strategically, and called in more troops. He wanted to increase his cavalry, so one of the soldiers he sent for was Ali, the young lieutenant he had left in Fez.

Yusuf's message went first to the barracks in Fez. Ali's commander dispatched a messenger, as he had promised, to carry the orders to Ali on the great trade route. It took a week for the message to catch up with Ali and the caravan at Azrou.

"Lieutenant Ali al-Harghi?" the man asked as he rode up beside Ali. He saluted.

"Yes," Ali replied and saluted back.

"This message from Fez, from the commander of the garrison, sir," the soldier said. The man handed a small scroll with a wax seal on it to Ali.

"Thank you," Ali said. His heart pounded as he opened the message.

The commander had written, "This message came from General Yusuf. You are to join him on the coast as soon as possible. A large cavalry force is forming against serious native opposition. See Captain Ibrahim for further instructions. The bearer of this note will take your place with the caravan. Good luck."

He read the note twice, and then looked at the waiting soldier. "I will introduce you to the caravan leader and some of the others. You will take my place escorting this caravan the rest of the way to Fez. Come now and have some food and water. We will stop in the oasis for three days, so your horse can rest there. I will leave in the morning for the coast."

The two men rode off to the front of the caravan where the leader was. The caravan was just arriving at the first cedar trees when they reached him. Ali would bathe that night and be on the road tomorrow. His day couldn't get much better

CHAPTER 41

The caravan pulled into Azrou a few hours later. The trees and hills cast long shadows in the western sun, and the animals seemed to regain a little life as they smelled the water and began to cool in the shade of the great trees.

The caravan leader met with the oasis guards to pay the watering fee, and all the animals began moving up to drink at the wide river. Upstream, the caravan suppliers were refilling the water barrels for the animals. A separate branch off the main river was used to fill the water bags for the humans.

Ali's mind was busy on other things. Now that he was relieved of duty, he needed to clear his head and think about how he would travel to the coast, and what he might need to take. Gawa was still holding up well to the long journey. "He has lost some fat, but is well-watered, and should be up to some hard riding, if needed," he thought.

Ali headed into the village hoping to find a cartographer. He was in luck. A tile designer had been trained in map making, and had a few map options on hand to sell. Ali selected one that marked water locations and major trade roads.

To make good time, he needed to stay on the hard packed roads as much as possible. His journey would take him first toward Errbat, a new town on the coast, and then south to Mazagan, northwest of Marrakesh, where General Yusuf's headquarters were.

Errbatt had been founded by the Banu Ifran Berbers when his father was young. He remembered his grandfather telling stories about the Banu Ifran. They were tough fighters. No wonder General Yusuf was having a difficult time.

Ali had the cartographer go over the map with him, and indicate the path he would recommend. The recommended route was not direct. It went more to the north. The Almoravids were dominant in the south, and he didn't want to run into unfriendly soldiers while he was riding alone. The cartographer indicated some landmarks for him to spot, and Ali thanked him and left.

Next he picked up some dried meat strips and fruits from the food vendors. The distances were not exact, but he calculated he would be on the road about two weeks. Unfortunately, Gawa was a horse and not a camel, so he also had to carry plenty of water and some feed for him. They would be heavily loaded the first few days.

To make their next journey easier, Ali decided to give Gawa a wash and rub down that night. He led the coffee colored gelding to the river, and they both walked in until the water was up to Gawa's belly. Ali had brought a bowl to hold water for rinsing, and a soft bristled brush. The water was almost up to his waist, and it felt very pleasant after the hot day. He wanted to hurry, though, because the nights cooled down fast, and he didn't want Gawa to become chilled.

He started by splashing his horse to get him wet all over. Gawa seemed to understand, and stood perfectly still. Next Ali used a little soap on himself, and then lathered the horse's back and sides. He used the brush to spread the soap throughout his coat and up his neck to his ears. He scooped up water with the bowl and poured it over the soap to rinse it away. He was careful to avoid Gawa's ears. Then he poured water slowly over his long bony face, avoiding his nostrils.

Gawa swished his tail in the water as if rinsing it, and suddenly dipped his head down to the water and splashed sideways to soak Ali. Ali jumped back and said playfully, "Oh, I see…it's like that, is it?"

He started scooping bowl after bowl of water at Gawa with big splashes. Gawa bobbed his head up and down and danced a little. It looked as if he had enjoyed his joke. After a moment Ali stopped splashing and wiped the horse's face to clear his eyes. He put his arm around his neck, and said, "I think that's enough for tonight, big boy. Let's go dry off and eat."

They returned to the small encampment of soldiers. He dried his horse with a saddle blanket, then laid an opened blanket across Gawa's back to prevent a chill as he dried. He quickly slipped into a clean uniform, and brought some food and tea to the communal fire to heat up. The other men were sitting around having low conversations.

The replacement seemed to be fitting in well, so Ali sat a little to the side as he ate his meal. He had things to think about, and he had formed no real attachments with these men.

A short time later, he hobbled Gawa for the night and gave him a feed bag, then he went off to say goodbye to Moosa. It had occurred to him a short while before that he had not told Moosa of his transfer, and that it would leave Moosa to face his brother alone with bad news once he got to Fez.

Moosa happened to be eating by himself this night. He had been to the hammam and bathed, and looked as if he would sleep soon.

"Salaam, brother," Ali said as he approached.

"Welcome, Ali. Come and sit. Have you eaten?" Moosa asked.

"Yes, thank you. I just finished eating with the men, and bathing my horse. I wanted to see you tonight, because I have to leave in the morning." He waited a moment to let the words sink in.

"What? Leave? Where are you going?" Moosa stopped in mid-chew, a startled look on his face.

"I have received orders that I am to join General Yusuf on the coast as soon as possible. A new man arrived today to replace me," Ali replied. "I must leave in the morning."

"Well, I suppose that is good news to you. A soldier likes to be soldiering, and not babysitting a bunch of old ladies like us in a caravan," Moosa said. "But I will be very sorry to lose your company. I had hoped that you would be with me to talk to my brother about Samir. You are the one who knows all the details."

Ali replied, "Yes, that is true, although I believe I have told you everything I know. Do you have any last questions for me tonight? I hope you will convey my deepest sorrow to your brother. Tell him that I will pray every day to hear word that Samir has made it safely home again. I feel in my heart that he will. He is a smart boy, and can turn bad situations into good ones for himself."

Moosa nodded. "It is so," he said. The two men talked for another hour, going over the details of what had happened in Awdaghust once more, and then Moosa asked about Ali's travel plans. He was a little concerned that the young man was heading out into the desert on his own, with no backup and no sure direction of where he was supposed to go, but Moosa encouraged him.

When Ali stood up to leave, Moosa shook his hand with both of his own and wished Ali a safe trip and good fortune. He invited Ali to come to visit them when he returned to Fez, and hopefully, he said, he would take Ali to see Samir and Amuna. Ali agreed, and they parted as friends.

When the first rays of the sun broke over the horizon, Ali was already well on his way.

CHAPTER 42

The caravan journey was uneventful the rest of the way to Fez. From Azrou, it took them just over a week more. They camped a few miles south of the walls of Fez on their last night, even though everyone was anxious to get into town or get home. They could see the Kairowiyyan minaret clearly from their camp.

The camel leader had learned that entering the city late in the day creates great confusion and noise that disturbs the city residents. Especially a caravan this large. The maze city was difficult enough to navigate during the day, but at night, with no lamps in some parts of the city and the narrow, twisting lanes, it was a nightmare. Everyone would have to be patient for one more night.

As they made camp, the caravan leader and his assistant rode down the long curving line and collected their fees from the merchants. This was a good night for the caravan leader. They were unlikely to be attacked tomorrow this close to Fez, and the anxious merchants were grateful to be home and willing to pay their fees for the safe journey.

It took the caravan leader nearly three hours to work his way down the long line. Finally, he reached the end and the men who handled the water and animal feed for the travelers. He congratulated them on doing a good job, and told them where to find him in Fez to collect their pay. Everyone was going to sleep that night with a sense of completion. Except Moosa.

Moosa had kept hoping every day that somehow Samir would show up on that white camel, and then their story would just be an adventure they would share with Jamal. Unfortunately, Samir was still nowhere to be found.

Moosa started to dread the next day. He knew Jamal would come to the caravan looking for them as soon as he heard it had arrived. After all, they had been gone almost four months, and Jamal's future rested on what Moosa and Samir would bring to him from Awdaghust. At least he would have a good amount of gold. That wouldn't begin to make the story any easier for his brother, though.

The next morning, Moosa woke with resignation and prepared his animals for the last leg of the trip. At the first light, the long line started swaying slowly toward the city gate.

Moosa's camels passed through just before midday, and when he got to the part of town he had started from, he turned off with some other merchants. They stopped in a local square and started to unload their animals. As he had expected and dreaded, Jamal came hurriedly around the corner of a building and rushed toward him.

"Brother! Marhaba! Welcome." Jamal exclaimed. He ran toward Moosa with open arms and they grabbed each other's shoulders with glad greetings.

"How was your journey home?" Jamal asked. "No, wait. Tell me everything when we get home. Come to my house for your meal. I want to hear everything!"

Moosa was a little surprised by the warm greeting, but nodded. He was glad to put off telling Jamal the bad news a few minutes longer. Besides, it was not right to tell him about Samir in a public place where he might display his grief openly. He hoped that Jamal would forget for a little longer that Samir was not there.

Moosa tied his camels to a post, and he and Jamal took the most valuable of the trade goods with them to Jamal's house. The rest should be safe until he returned. The caravan guard was still there. They walked down two alleys and the wall of the great library rose up on the left. After two more turns, they arrived at Jamal's front door.

They put down the bundles they were carrying. Just as they removed their shoes to enter, Moosa heard, "Amo!"

He looked up in surprise and then disbelief. There was Samir with a huge grin on his face. Moosa stood there in shock for a moment, and then he grabbed his nephew and spun him around off the ground.

"Samir! I thought you were dead! You terrible, terrible foolish boy. I am so glad to see you." He set Samir down with his arm locked around Samir's neck, and with his middle finger he thumped Samir sharply twice on the back of the head.

"I have been so worried about you!" Moosa exclaimed. "Why did you do such a foolish thing as run away to the desert? Ali told me the whole story about your adventures, and I had to come all this way back alone, dreading this moment when I had to tell my dear and only brother that I had lost his son. I want to hear everything about what happened. How did you get here before me? Where is Amuna? You have a lot of explaining to do, young man!"

"I have a very interesting tale to tell, Amo. And I want to hear about you and Ali. You won't believe what happened to me. I don't believe it myself. God is great, we have come through it all and we are all here. Home. At last!" Samir said.

Moosa could not hold back his joy, and hugged his nephew again with teary eyes. It was good to be back in Fez after all.

.

CHAPTER 43

Hours passed as the three finished with their questions and answers. Only Jamal's life had been normal for the past four months. One of his other camels had given birth, but they were pack animals, so it was scheduled for sale as soon as the calf reached its adult size in a year or so.

Moosa was delighted to produce the thirty-nine gold for the two salt slabs, and Jamal was just as pleased. This was a great fortune, and he decided that he would quit his job in the salt mine the next day. Samir waited until the excitement died down, and then he pulled out the small purse in his belt with Ibn Yasin's seal on it. It contained eleven gold dinars. Four from the olive merchant in Azrou oasis, four from the ones he had taken out of his race winnings, and five from his bet, minus two gold he had spent on food for the trip and his gift for his father.

"Father, when I left you gave me three silver shekels. I cannot lie. I wagered on a race and won five dinars so I could enter Amuna in the race. I spent a little to have food for my trip home. Here are seven more dinars." His father's face showed his great joy to have his financial burdens lifted.

"And uncle, you very kindly left gold dinars for me with an olive merchant in Azrou. I paid him one for being honest, and doing as you asked. Here are the four dinars that are left." Samir was glad to clear his debts. Now the biggest surprise of all.

"But father, when I won the race with Amuna, I won a prize purse from Emir Ibn Yasin himself. It was fifty gold dinars!" Moosa was astonished. This was the first he had heard of the prize winnings.

"Well, now I certainly don't feel like I have to share my winnings from my bet on this white ghost of a camel," Moosa said. "I felt so sad that I was going to split all my winnings and earnings with my poor, sad brother."

They all laughed. It felt good to be able to laugh again.

Jamal was overjoyed with all this good fortune and with the prospects for a good future.

"Where are the coins, my son?" Jamal asked.

"I didn't know how to keep them safe in case I was captured, so I...finally I put them in my half-empty water bag," he said with a very proud and goofy look on his face. Both men burst out laughing at his cleverness, and congratulated him on being so smart.

Samir had arrived home a full day before the caravan. "I will bring the bag here when I go to feed Amuna tonight so we can liberate the gold," Samir said. His father could say nothing. He just sat shaking his head in disbelief.

Finally he said, "Allahu akbar. God is great. Tell your uncle about your new friend, Samir".

"Oh Amo, you just won't believe this part." He told of his last weeks in Awdaghust, of his trial and of his friendship with Mansur. He described the fast trip he made home with the soldiers. They had not paused long in any place, and it turned out that it was night at the time the soldiers would have passed Moosa's caravan, so they swung wide to avoid creating a disturbance. Moosa never knew how close his nephew had been.

Another hour passed in happy conversation, and finally Moosa said to his brother, "Well, Jamal, what is next for you now that you have become so rich?"

Jamal nodded, and said, "Yes, I am very rich, thanks be to God, but not from gold. I have a good son who keeps his father's interests in mind and works hard. I have a brother I can rely on. Those two are above the highest value. Financially, it will now be possible to build my camel business. Amuna will be old enough to breed in a year and a half, and we will find a very good partner for her since she won a big race. In a few months, I will breed Alama again, even though she is a terrible mother, and see if she can produce another baby like Amuna. Perhaps we have the start of our racing camel herd after all."

Samir was waiting for father to mention his school, but so far he had only talked about business.

Jamal continued, "I imagine there will be a race or two in the nearby areas or here in Fez in the next year. The city is building a racetrack in the new arena. Samir can race Amuna and give her some local visibility. If she wins, it will add greatly to the fees we can charge for her calves. And perhaps this year we will be able to find a better home in a better part of town, away from the terrible air from the tannery!" Everyone nodded.

Then he said, "I think, God willing, it is also time for Samir to return to school and his education. If he wishes." He turned to his son and smiled. "You thought I had forgotten, yes? No. You have helped me achieve my dream, my son, and now I will help you to achieve yours. Whatever that may be."

Samir grinned again, ear to ear. "Thank you, father. I want to study astronomy. I spent a lot of time looking at the stars and talking about them in the desert. I will show you my map that Mansur gave me. I will turn it into a great travel map that can be copied and sold so anyone can find their way in the desert. And maybe when I am older I will use it myself to navigate to other distant and new places, if God is willing." It felt good for him to tell his family what was in his heart.

It was after dark now, and Moosa stood up to leave. The muezzin was singing the adnaan for the night prayers. He still had to tend to his camels and take his goods to his home. Jamal volunteered to walk with him after the prayer, and Samir said he would go and settle Amuna in her stall for the night. As they knelt down to pray together, there were no three happier men in Fez.

CHAPTER 44

A few weeks after he returned home, Samir was enrolled in the university. Father had prepaid for two years, so there would be no question of Samir having to drop out because they couldn't pay. He managed to get into two classes with Mansur, basic astronomy and philosophy. They both had religious studies as well, but not at the same time.

Samir was set on becoming a navigator. He decided that, whether he chose to go by camel or by ship or on foot, the ability to navigate by the stars would be priceless. And if he could make star maps, so much the better.

After having seen his father work so hard all of his life just to bring home food for them, he liked the idea of working with maps and calculations and measuring devices. They were quiet, didn't require physical labor, and didn't involve the need to be licked clean by camels at the end of the day.

A year passed, and one day he saw a notice pinned on the library wall that a big race day was planned in the city. The grand opening of the new arena on the east side of town outside the wall would feature races in the new racetrack. The city commander of Fez was offering a large prize of 100 gold dinars each to the winners of the horse and camel races. The large prize would attract many racers who were not normally in Fez.

Samir and Mansur had decided to go together to exercise Amuna that day. Samir showed Mansur the notice. It would be Amuna's first big race in Fez, and Samir was anxious for her to do well and help his father establish a good name for his racing camel business.

Mansur brought Shams to the house, and the boys rode double to the stable. Samir slipped off Shams' rear. It was much closer to the ground than Amuna's back, so it was easy to get on and off.

Amuna was waiting and eager. Samir had remembered to bring her two dates, and she greeted him enthusiastically with a snort and a half bray. He didn't get to spend as much time with her now as he used to, but he tried to run her every day. He rubbed her nose and cheeks, and tugged on her tiny ears until she pushed him away.

"Kneel, Amuna," he said, and with a gurgling grunt she did. He put his hand grip around her middle. Then he got his saddle blanket and put it against the back of her hump and climbed on. "Up Amuna," he said with enthusiasm as they rode to the city gate. "Let's see how far we can go today. We will outrun our friend Mansur for sure. Let's make this a real race!"

Mansur nodded. The boys stopped at the wall. "I will count three, and then we go," said Mansur. "Ready? One…two…THREE!" Both animals leaped forward, startled by the sudden kicking of heels in their bellies. Shams was away first, his long dark tail streaming out behind his sand colored coat.

Mansur shouted over his shoulder, "Come on, camel boy! Where is your big talk now?"

Samir shouted back, "You just watch. We will run right past you!" He kept encouraging Amuna to go faster, and she did. A moment later Amuna and Shams were nose and nose. Then Amuna started to pull ahead. She was not breathing hard yet, but neither was Shams. The boys shouted, "Faster, faster!" The animals understood and leaned into it. They were going full speed now, stretching their legs out in strides of impossible length.

Samir realized they had not set a finish line, so he shouted "First one back to the gate!" and Mansur nodded. His hair had come loose and was whipping around his face and stinging his eyes. They turned their animals back and Amuna started to really stretch out her legs. She was very strong now, and could push hard off the packed ground. The city wall was approaching fast. Amuna gave another burst of speed and managed to beat Shams by a length.

Both boys were amazed with Amuna's speed and second wind. Shams was bred from solid Arabian stock, and could almost dance on his feet. But Amuna could run so fast that she seemed to fly at times.

"Wow, she is fast now," Mansur said. "Shams is out of practice, but he should have won easily. I wonder how she will do in the race? It's only two weeks away."

"Yes, she is almost an adult now, and has her full muscle development. She weighs more, but she has much more power. I don't know any camel in Fez that could beat her, but we don't know who might come from the outside," Samir replied. Mansur smoothed his hair back into a pony tail and stuffed it back under his turban. They went to groom their animals.

Mansur was up early most days because he was eager to get to his classes. The great library closed at dusk, and he usually prayed next door in the mosque before dark, then headed home for a light dinner.

His great-aunt and uncle were often out with friends in the evenings, and on other nights Mansur met with his university friends to go out and study the night sky. Sometimes, Samir joined them. Mansur was rarely home before midnight. His relatives didn't see him much at all, which suited everyone.

As the months passed, Mansur became consumed with the idea that the stars were somehow connected to each other, and that they were immensely further away than tradition held. The latest theories from Baghdad and Damascus held that the earth and other planets circled the sun, and that there might be other planets circling other stars.

This was very controversial, because most people believed the earth was the center of the universe, and all planets and the sun circled the earth. There were teachers and students in his classes, though, who were developing mathematical theories to help to prove this new concept.

Mansur loved to sit all afternoon debating theoretical concepts, and then spend the nights on a hillside outside the city noting the positions and movements of the stars. Mansur felt a special peace there. His childhood belief that the stars engaged in a celestial dance with each other seemed more and more true.

Samir often invited Mansur to his home for the evening meal. Mansur would usually stop at a street vendor on the way and buy a piece of lamb, some tea or some ripe tomatoes and aubergine to contribute to the dinner. He enjoyed coming to visit them, and didn't want to be a burden.

Jamal had found a new house, this time with three rooms and a small rooftop garden. The flowers Jamal had planted there bloomed with a sweet fragrance at night. The new house was along the northern wall of the great mosque and away from the acrid tannery smells.

Jamal had not yet found a stable to purchase, so each day Samir had to walk a long distance to Amuna's stall and then get back to the university in time for classes. His father was negotiating with an elderly horse breeder to buy a nearby stable and practice yard when the man retired. It looked like that deal would go through in a few weeks. Jamal's plans seemed to be on track. He had just confirmed that his camel Alama, the mother of Amuna, was pregnant again. They were hoping for another racer in about nine months.

Seeing the happy relationship between Samir and his father made Mansur homesick. He missed his father, but knew that Ibn Yasin was now away on a military campaign with his generals. Mansur had been home twice in the past year to see his family. He received letters from his father from time to time when messengers would come to Fez.

There was really no reason to go back to Awdaghust right now. Since he wasn't close to his great-aunt and uncle, he more or less adopted Samir and Jamal as his family. They welcomed him easily, and he spent a lot of time with them. They often forgot that he was the son of Ibn Yasin. To them he was just like another son or brother.

Most times Mansur would walk with Samir after dinner to visit Amuna, and then when Samir took her to run, Mansur would head back to his aunt and uncle's home, or go out and meet some other friends for some stargazing. For him the universe, the earth and all of creation was a part of the infinite being of Allah. This universal, mystical view of the universe was not widely held in the more traditional circles of government and society, but younger voices rising up across the Muslim world were starting to reach the same belief.

CHAPTER 45

The race day in Fez came quickly. Samir spent all of his spare time exercising Amuna and balancing her diet to be sure she was well-fed but not over-fed. He still brought her a daily treat, though. She wouldn't have listened to him if he didn't.

The next day was the start of the festivities. There would be all kinds of entertainments and activities throughout the city. All the town squares had put up colorful banners and signs celebrating the new arena, and merchants and hucksters were busy setting up their tables and carts for the grand event. Two large caravans had come into town, so money was flowing freely.

Samir wanted to get out and see the sights, so he groomed Amuna early. He hoped to sneak a look at the racing camels that had come for the next day's events, and get an idea of what Amuna's competition looked like. He took a long walk around the perimeter of the city, and casually stopped by each of the caravanserais.

Even though there was widespread fighting on the western coast and a lot of Almohad men were there, somehow the caravanserais were all full. That probably meant that many attending this festival were from the east or north, where there was no fighting. Samir didn't know about racing in that part of the world, so he practiced looking invisible and listened to conversations at the caravanserais. Camel handlers always knew rumors.

He heard a rumor that several companies of soldiers had arrived from Egypt and were camped on the south side of the city, near the main gate. He wondered where they were headed. Most likely to help General Yusuf against the Berbers. He would skip that caravanserai. Soldiers wouldn't have any racing camels.

Finally, he found a caravanserai where several racing camels were stabled. He wandered in when the guard wasn't looking, and went to look them over.

There were two males. One was magnificent--tan with black fur on his head and down his back and a beautiful body shape. The other was ordinary brown. He didn't look especially good. His feet were very wide, as if he had walked many caravans, and his winter coat still grew in unsightly tufts on his body. A good camel handler would have already trimmed those down so the camel would look better.

He turned back to the tan and black camel. He was a beauty. His hump was higher than Samir could reach. The callouses on his knees and elbows were clean, which meant that this camel was kept stabled. He was probably a valuable racer. Samir wondered where he was from, and what his name was? He didn't have to wonder long.

A gruff looking man hurried over to him, and said, "Hey! You boy! What are you doing around my camels?"

Samir put on his innocent face and said, "I was just admiring them. This one with black fur is very tall! Is he a racer?"

The man decided there was nothing to fear from this poorly dressed boy-man, and said, "Yes, we are here for the race tomorrow."

Samir persisted. "What is he called, this big one?"

The man squinted his eyes and said, "Qadr. Divine Power. He is a champion, and has overpowered all the camels he has raced against. I brought him from Tlemcen, where he won grand champion. If your father is a gambler, tell him to wager on him tomorrow. He will certainly beat them all."

Samir nodded, and pretended to study the camel more intently. "He seems well cared for. I will remember your suggestion and tell my father. What happened to this other one?"

The man shrugged. "He is a second son. Allah doesn't make all brothers the same. Qadr was first and got all the gifts. This one came second and cannot follow his brother. I have been using him to carry loads to market. He is no racer. I had hoped for better, but this is what I got."

Samir said, "Thank you for letting me see them. I will tell my friends that Qadr is a fine animal and he would be a good bet." The man wasn't very excited by that comment.

What could this boy know about who has money? And how much money would they have? Not much, he surmised.

Samir could hardly wait to get home and tell father. Amuna would have her work cut out tomorrow in the race against this big camel! He could only hope that Amuna's courage and heart would move her legs faster than Qadr's.

He stopped off at Amuna's stable on the way home. It always relaxed him to be with her. Today she seemed restless and like she didn't want to be penned up. She growled a lot and paced. Samir was sympathetic, but told her he didn't have time to go for a run and groom her just now.

He fished in his pouch and found that he still had a dried fig there, so he gave it to her. Then he told her to kneel, and he sat down beside her with his head leaning against her back.

She still seemed anxious. She kept twitching her tail nervously, as if there were flies, but there were no flies. Now and then she would throw her head back and slap him, and make gurgling noises.

"What is going on with you, girl? Are you nervous about the race? Maybe my excitement is making you anxious. Settle down. Maybe you smell that other camel on me. He was a beauty, alright. You will see him up close tomorrow. I hope you can beat him. If you can win this race, father will have a lot of money, and you will be famous." He sat calmly against her belly, talking about what he had seen and what they would do tomorrow. His voice seemed to soothe her.

After a while, he jumped up to leave. "I have to go home now, 'Muna. I have to talk over this race with father. Maybe Mansur will come tonight. We will come back to see you after dinner."

Samir walked away full of energy and excitement. The next day was going to be a big day, and there was no way to prepare. He had only to wait, and waiting is hard!

CHAPTER 46

The next morning, Samir and Jamal were up early. Jamal had never raced a camel before, and he wanted Samir to explain once again what would happen and what Jamal should do.

Samir had told him about the tan and black camel Qadr, and Jamal decided to have a conversation with his owner some time during the day. He thought Qadr would be a perfect mate for Amuna, and hoped to negotiate a fee he could afford to pay. It was getting near the time for her to mate for the first time, and this male sounded better than any others he knew of in Fez. He didn't mention it to Samir.

They had a quick breakfast of cold porridge, tomatoes, olives and dried lamb, then Jamal went to his secret hiding place behind a brick in his sleeping room and took out some gold dinars. He would pay Amuna's racing fee, and he had some extra to bet. It didn't matter to him who was racing.

Even though the *Qur'an* says not to wager, Jamal would bet on his son and his camel. He had great hope for their success, and believed Allah would want him to try to make their life better in any way he could. At least, that was his justification. He would pray about it later.

The walk to the new racing arena took them by Amuna's stable. They decided to take her with them and put her in a stall at the track so they would not have to come back all this way for her. It was a pretty long walk.

Samir had kept his present for his father secret until now, and when his father started to put the normal harness on Amuna, he told him to wait. He went into a back corner of the stall and returned with the orange harness in his hand.

"This is for you, Father. Every racing camel in the big races wears a colored harness and tassels. Some have matching blankets or saddles. This is for Amuna. You can lead her in style to the racetrack." He was very proud to give his father the gift.

Jamal took the brightly colored harness with delight, and slipped it over Amuna's head. He stood back and shook his head with a "tsk,tsk" sound. The big tassels hung down from the straps on either side of her head between her cheek and neck. Her coat was in beautiful condition, and was as white as the white yarn in the orange and white tassels. It was a perfect decoration for her.

Father looked very pleased. He said, "There. Now I look like a man who races camels." They started for the track. All that was left to do now was win!

They arrived at the arena, and father made a big show of paying their entrance fees and the five gold dinars racing fee for Amuna. Samir had been around people with money now, and had seen things at a track that his father had not. It was amusing to watch him. This was the most money Father had ever had, and he was enjoying to spend it. Samir enjoyed watching his enjoyment.

They found a guarded stall where they could leave Amuna, and walked around the arena, looking at all the people and camels. The park was like colored confetti. People were celebrating today, so they wore their colorful robes and turbans and veils.

Here and there he could see the Egyptian soldiers in their long white robes with belts crossed over both shoulders and fastened at the waist. There were also Almohad guards, and a few Almoravids here and there. Mostly the soldiers kept to their own units and avoided any confrontations.

The camels all had colored harnesses and blankets, and they were being walked all over the track. Since it was a new track, none of the riders or camels had been on it before. The riders were walking the track to notice any rough spots in the packed sand or areas where their camels might shy. They were also eying each other, sizing up the competition.

As in Awdaghust, the boxes for the wealthy families and the city commander was by the start/finish line. Workers had just rolled out the long silk runners that created a sunscreen above the seats. It brought back memories to Samir. It was already more than a year ago when he had seen his first race track, and Uncle Moosa was in the stands.

Just then a familiar booming voice shouted out, "Brother! Nephew!" and they turned together. It was Uncle Moosa. He had been looking for them, but expected to see Amuna. He was glad to find them.

Moosa asked, "Brother, are you going to wager on your camel? I have seen her run. There are some fine camels here, but I have faith that this is her destiny."

Jamal smiled and confessed that he had planned to bet. The two men went off to find a bookie they liked.

Samir was left on his own to wander, look and listen. Just around the curve of the track, he spotted the tan and black camel Qadr. He was hard to miss. He was very tall, and his owner had dressed him in bright turquoise blue harness and saddle. Even his rider had a silk shirt of the same color.

Samir wandered over to him. His head came only to the top of Qadr's legs. He was thinking about his strategy for beating this giant, when the owner saw him and came over.

Samir greeted him politely. "Salaam aleikhum."

The man replied, "Aleikhum salaam. You have come back, I see. You want to check on your wager?"

Samir smiled a half-smile, and said, "Yes, I have a lot riding on this race." Not a word he said was untrue. "He is a beautiful camel. Very hard to miss! Do you still think he will win?"

The man replied, "Insh'allah. He looks like the best animal here, and he is very fast. We shall see."

Other people approached him to look at Qadr and compliment him, so he turned to them. Samir took the opportunity to slip away. He would find father and send him over to see this animal. Maybe they could work out a deal with the owner to breed camels together. He smiled imagining how fast a calf from Qadr and Amuna would be. It was an exciting thought. But first he wanted to see the big male run. His future depended upon this big camel.

CHAPTER 47

The sun was out in full fury now amid the banners and tents. It was mid-morning, and everyone was wrapped in layers of loose sheer cotton or silk. Movement or slight breezes fluttered the clothing to carry away heat and keep them cool.

Tea peddlers were everywhere with their large urns of hot mint or sour hibiscus karkady tea strapped to their backs, pouring drinks for a small fee. Everyone living in the desert knew that drinking hot tea on a hot day fools the body into perspiring more, and the evaporation and loose clothing cool the body down. It was a trick known for centuries.

There were slaves in Fez, but not as many as in Awdaghust. Rich people walked around with slaves carrying their valuables, waving bundles of horsehair around their owners to keep away flies, or holding umbrellas above them to make shade. Umbrellas had arrived from China hundreds of years before along the Silk Road, and they caught on fast in North Africa.

The races would not start for another hour, so children were on the track racing each other and cheering.

Some camels from the first race were being led around the inner ring to settle them and make them familiar with the surroundings.

Samir decided he should probably do the same thing, but once he started walking back toward the stable to get Amuna, he decided against it. She wasn't easily frightened or distracted by crowds or new places as long as he was there talking to her, and something in Samir made him want to keep her presence a secret until he had to reveal her.

Samir didn't want to break his concentration now by having to answer questions from curious strangers. He wanted to think about his race, and how to defeat Qadr. He didn't know if they would race in the elimination races together, but he knew they would race in the final race for the grand prize. Samir badly wanted that prize for his father.

Samir found a bench near the entrance and sat down to wait. He didn't know where father and Uncle Moosa had gone, but he knew they would enjoy the day off together whether he was with them or not. He enjoyed just watching the people mill around with their happy, expectant faces. Festival days were always fun, for young and old.

The next thing he knew, Mansur threw a leg over the bench and slid into the seat beside him. "Hey, camel boy," he said, "Did you think you could race Amuna without me? Who will pay your fee?" They laughed.

Samir pulled the racing papers from his belt. "I am already registered, as you can see. But thank you very much for your kind offer. We will be in the third race, and God willing, in the last one! I want to win that prize money for father."

"Insh'allah," Mansur nodded. They sat there silently for a few minutes, remembering the last camel race in Awdaghust. It had been eventful, and had changed both of their lives dramatically.

"Hey, I walked around the caravanserais last night to look for the racing camels," Samir said. "I found one. His name is Qadr. I think he is the one to beat. I had a chance to see him up close before his owner spotted me and came to push me out. Can you see on the far side of the track over there...that turquoise dot?" Mansur had trouble spotting it with all the people and colors milling around.

"Not really," he answered.

"Come on then. I want you to see him and tell me what you think. I believe he and Amuna are the two best racers here, and I have to find a way to beat him. He is much bigger than she is. I couldn't even touch the top of his hump!"

"Yes, but then you are notoriously short in the arms, my friend," Mansur teased him.

The boys wandered in the direction of Qadr, and Samir hung back. He didn't want to seem too eager to keep seeing this camel. His owner might get suspicious. Mansur went closer, though, and when he saw how tall Qadr really was, he was amazed. He turned and made big, wide eyes at

Samir. Mansur was pretty tall, but he couldn't reach the top of Qadr's back without jumping either. He walked back over to join Samir.

"Wow, that is some camel! I have never seen such a big one. What do we do now? Will Amuna be able to beat him, or should I go and place a big wager on him instead?" Mansur grinned at Samir's scowl. "I'm just kidding, camel boy."

They talked strategy for a while, and it was clear that Amuna could never just outrace Qadr. He would be able to match her speed with his long stride. The only hope was for Amuna to get on the inside track quickly, and then somehow stay there. Qadr was probably used to running on the inside track, and perhaps moving him out would take him just a little off stride, enough to slow him so Amuna would win.

They also talked about dirty tricks. In Awdaghust, the two leaders had tried to squeeze Amuna out or bump her off her rhythm. If she was on the inside lane, she would not be able to move left at all. If Qadr pinned her against the rail tightly, the only way she would be able to hold up to his squeezing would be to pull forward, if she could.

Samir had not yet seen Qadr race, so he didn't know if that would even be feasible. He hoped that she didn't get trapped between two large males again and pushed out, because then she would not qualify for the final race.

It was time for the first heat. A horn sounded from the stands, and the first group of twenty camels began walking out to the track. Qadr was not among them. Samir knew he only had time to watch one race, and then he would have to run to get Amuna and bring her to the ready area. Mansur left to go sit with Jamal and Moosa.

Samir squeezed in past larger men and managed to get to the rail. He was about one hundred yards down the track from the starting line. His goal was to watch the lead camels come off the line, and then see who managed to take the rail position. Places were not assigned at the start. All the animals just squeezed in together and tried to be ready to bolt when the starting shot rang out. It was a game of brute force and intimidation.

Everyone held their breath as the camels lined up. Suddenly the shot fired, and the camels leaped forward. Long legs grabbed at the air, and about six of them seemed to pull forward at the same time.

The one on the inside rail was one of the leaders. He was a big male, and had clearly forced his way into that position behind the starting line. It might be that Qadr's rider would do the same. Amuna needed to be there first— or be able to slide into the hole if he moved even five centimeters from the rail. Samir knew she was not going to like a physical fight like that. His best bet was always going to be to get her off the line first, and out in front of those bigger camels. Samir would concentrate on that.

When the first race ended, the camel on the rail had managed to hold his lead all the way around the track. He and the second place runner would go into the final race.

Now Samir had to run over to the stall and bring Amuna out. He would have just enough time to take a few deep breaths and calm himself, and then ride her to the ready area. He still had to paint her number on her neck and check all her lashings. He didn't want anything pulling loose in the race!

Luckily, the muezzin started the call to prayer just at that moment. It was midday and all action in the arena would stop while people prayed. He ran as fast as he could until it became obvious that everyone nearby had kneeled down, so he did the same. He went through the ritual ablutions with sand since he had no water, and prayed as quickly as permitted. He got to Amuna's stall just as most of the people stood again.

She greeted him with her usual head bump. She was standing, which meant she was getting restless and needed to stretch.

Samir put his arms around her neck, and said earnestly, "Amuna, this is an important race. You have always done what I asked you to do. You are the best camel that was ever born. God willing, I need you to run two more races today. The first one is important, but the last one is the most important of all. I want everyone to see you for the amazing and graceful runner that you are. I know you don't understand my words, but I hope you can feel from my heart how important this is to father and me. Just do your best. Run your heart out. I know you can win. You are the best camel ever."

He reached up to pull her tiny ears and then slid his

hand down her long face to her soft nose. He stroked her nose and then kissed it, and said, "Let's go and show our city what a beautiful girl you are." He did a final check on the hand grip and her blanket.

Samir hadn't decided whether he would ride bareback or not. In some ways it was easier, but the little extra padding helped to protect his tender places. He would decide in the ready area. His father would meet him there.

For now he chose the blanket. Samir laid it in place behind her hump and climbed on. "Up girl," he said. She made some normal grunting noises as she stood, back legs first, then front.

They rode out into the sun. In the time they paused to adjust their eyes to the brilliant glare, Samir became aware that everyone within sight had turned and was staring at them. It pleased him. He knew she was in beautiful condition, with her white fur shining, and her orange and white pompoms dancing on her harness. No one had ever seen a camel like this one, and one by one they stepped back in silence back to let her sway past. After today, she would no longer be a secret.

CHAPTER 48

Amuna made it uneventfully to the ready area just as the horn blew signaling the second heat. Samir showed the guard at the entrance his papers and went in to find an empty spot to wait. He was happy to see that Qadr was not in the ready pen with them. Maybe he would get back out to the track in time to watch the big camel run. But that was for later. For now all his concentration was needed on the camels in this pen. Amuna had to be better than eighteen of them. Unfortunately, Samir didn't know which ones he should be worried about.

Jamal and Mansur entered at that moment, and walked over to find him. "How are you, son? Are you ready?" his father asked. He squeezed Samir's shoulder, trying to appear casual and relaxed. Samir knew he was tense and very excited. Jamal was looking around at all the competitors, assessing their qualities and their riders.

Mansur looked at Amuna and said, "Samir, you forgot her number."

Samir jumped quickly to grab the small paint pot and brush. He double checked his entry form and wrote eleven on both sides of Amuna's neck. He believed eleven would be lucky for them. It was the sign of the narrow road that leads straight to the goal. He said a silent prayer that this omen would be true, and handed all the papers and paint to Mansur to hold.

Just then, the crowd roared and cheered. The second race had ended. In about fifteen minutes, his group would file out to the starting line.

"What do you think, father? Who is the biggest competition here?" Samir asked. Jamal was quick to point out one beautiful male off in the corner on the far side—number seventeen.

"That one for sure. He is calm and his rider is confident. They are ignoring all the other racers. They will race according to their own plan. Watch for him. Also, watch for number three. He seems aggressive, and may be unpleasant to run beside. He looks like he is a bully, and his rider has the crooked face of a man who forgets to tell the truth and will try to run over you."

Father had never raced an animal, but he could judge people, and Samir respected his judgment. Number seventeen was wearing red and yellow colors, and number three was wearing dark blue and white. He made a mental note of that, because during the race he wouldn't have time to look for numbers.

Jamal and Mansur decided to leave and go get a good place near the finish. Moosa was already there trying to save spots for them. Jamal hugged his son and said, "Whatever happens in this race, Samir, everything will be okay. Pay attention, take care of Amuna first, and you will win if God wills. We will be cheering for you!" They turned and walked out of the pen.

Now that Samir was alone, he sat down next to Amuna and leaned against her. This was the way they communicated best with each other. When he was relaxed, she relaxed. He made every effort to show her that this was a normal day and being around these camels was nothing special. It seemed to work. She put her ears back and snorted. Then she twisted her head around to the side to knock Samir's arm with a few gurgles. She was showing affection. Samir knew they would be okay, whatever happened on the track.

Just as he thought that, the horn calling his group sounded. He stood and pulled Amuna's reins so she would stand. Then he remembered he needed to ride, so he had her kneel again, and laughed to himself as he climbed on and told her to stand again. He had decided to ride without the blanket. One less thing to think about.

They got into the line, and the procession moved out to the starting area. Samir's senses were suddenly alert and he was aware of everything around him, as if it were all in slow motion.

The race organizer opened the gate onto the track and the animals walked to the line. The race would be two laps of the track. Samir looked quickly to see where the red and yellow camel and blue and white camel were. Neither were near him. He knew he was causing a stir in the crowd with his white camel, and some of the riders just now realized that he was racing against them. Samir took advantage of that moment to slip in toward the rail. He managed to slip inside three camels, which put him in the fourth position. Suddenly, the starting shot rang out and Amuna leaped forward in a burst of fear and began to run. She came out in first place, a neck ahead of the other camels, and he forced her hard to the left. She managed to cut them off and find the rail. The rest of the field were close behind.

Their large feet and long legs and necks stretched out and occasionally touched Samir's back and legs. They were literally breathing down his neck. As they rounded the first curve, one of the big males made a move to push him from behind, hoping to dislodge him from Amuna's back. He kicked her harder and she pulled a little forward. He glanced back and saw the blue and white camel's colors. He gripped his strap even harder.

As they rounded the second turn and approached the starting line again, Samir became aware of red and yellow on his right. The big male had worked his way up to the lead, and was going to try to force Amuna off the rail. He was matching her stride for stride, and may have been pulling away a little, because his gait was longer than hers.

Samir caught the eye of the other rider for a moment, and realized that he didn't have to worry about this man. He would race fair. His camel was a winner, and all he could see was the race between the two camels. Samir nodded once, and focused his eyes on the track again.

Amuna was holding up well. She was not winded, and the red and yellow camel had not gotten ahead of her. They were pretty evenly matched. The blue and white camel rider behind tried again to knock him off his seat. This time he forced his camel's head between Amuna and the red and yellow camel. He pushed forward to come between them, squeezing Amuna against the rail. The camel's head was bumping against Samir's knee.

Samir did not use a whip or prod and only had his hand. He whacked the camel on the nose with his hand, and it startled the animal so that it pulled back for a second. That was enough to close up the gap again.

The pack rounded the last curve with Amuna in the lead by a tiny sliver. Samir assumed that the red and yellow camel had saved a burst of energy for the final straight, and he had. He suddenly shouted to his camel, and kicked him hard. The animal bolted forward nearly half a length.

Samir called to Amuna. He saw her ears turn back to catch his voice, so he said over and over to her, "Run, Amuna. Run! Run!" With an unexpected burst of speed Amuna surged forward and managed to nose out the other camel just at the finish line.

Samir was thrilled! This time he had kept his eyes open, and crossing under the finish line banner as the winner was the most exciting thing he had ever done.

He shouted and whooped at the top of his voice, as the camels gradually slowed to a trot and then a walk. He was still beside the red and yellow camel, so he moved closer to him and held out his hand.

"You ran a good race. He is a beautiful animal." The other rider acknowledged Samir's hand with a nod, saying, "Your camel is good, too."

Then he turned away. They would meet each other again in the final race.

CHAPTER 49

For the next thirty minutes, Samir was surrounded by well-wishers and the curious, as well as some of his friends from school who had recognized him. He hadn't thought about what it meant for him to be racing at home. He forgot that people would know him. It was hard to pull away from them, but he finally did, and managed to get Amuna back into the guarded stall uneventfully. He gave her water and wiped her down quickly, and then headed back to the track, hoping to see Qadr run.

He heard the horn calling the third heat riders, but he couldn't get near the track fast enough to watch the lineup. Just as he got within eye distance, the gun went off and the camels leaped forward. He would miss the first lap.

He hurried to the rail to see if Qadr was running. He was. He was easily three lengths ahead of all the other racers. Clearly he had no competition in this round. As Samir had thought, he seemed to like to hug the rail, even without other runners around him. He easily won his race, and as soon as he had rounded the track again, he vanished. His owner pulled him off the track to avoid mixing with other riders and took him to a secret place. It was clearly all business with that man.

Samir found his family and Mansur, and they all watched the remaining heat together. No other camels were outstanding to them, and they believed the final race would be between Amuna and Qadr and the red and yellow bridled male from Samir's earlier race.

There would be a break in the races now, to allow the camels to rest, and to let people eat and drink, stretch their legs, and buy more festival items. The final race would be after the afternoon prayers, to give the animals a chance to recover.

Moosa and father called Samir and Mansur over to a shady spot behind the stands. They wanted to talk strategy. The two men talked several minutes with determination and strong instructions about what to do and how to do it.

Samir listened quietly, but he knew that only he and Amuna could run this race, so he didn't take a lot of what they said to heart. He just nodded silently. Mansur made an important observation.

"Don't you think that those two big camels will try to do what those other camels in Awdaghust did? They forced you to take Amuna to the outside to get around them. It is in their common interest to hold her back. In third place she will win no prize. They will prefer to race against each other, and not you. You are unknown and unpredictable to them. That means they will be a little distracted, and you may be able to use that in some way," Mansur said.

It made sense. Father and Moosa nodded. Samir wanted to go drink and make sure Amuna was ready for the final race. It would come in about half an hour. He slipped away and went back to her stall to sit and think. He wanted to visualize what might happen and how Amuna might react. That was really all that mattered. He lay down by her and put his head on her neck.

The call to prayer came a short time later, and he bowed down outside the stall. He knew he wasn't supposed to ask for anything for himself in prayers, so he prayed for his father's future and for Amuna's safety. Allah would understand, and whatever happened was His will.

Samir suddenly felt very calm, as if he were going for a ride in the desert. He walked over to Amuna and tugged on the curly fur on top of her head. He stroked her cheeks and nose and said a few soft words to her. He led her to the water trough and let her drink, but this time he pulled her away before she had her fill. He didn't want water sloshing around in her stomach. Samir simply didn't know which small thing might be the one that would cause her to win— or lose. He was taking no chances.

Samir had her kneel one more time and got up onto her back. He had decided to ride bareback again. He felt more in contact with her that way.

"Up, 'Muna," he said, and she grumbled to her feet. They left the stall and headed toward the ready area. Soon the horn summoning them to the starting line would blow. Samir wanted to have a few minutes to watch how Qadr's rider prepared his camel for the race. He already knew about the camel in red and yellow harness.

Amuna was not the first camel in the holding area, but the two big opponents had not yet appeared. Finally the red and yellow harness flashed at the entrance, and the rider took his camel to the same spot he had waited in before.

A moment later the resplendent Qadr in his turquoise trappings came through the entrance as if he owned it. He walked to a spot in the center of the pen, and kneeled down there. He was truly a magnificent camel. Samir thought to himself, *If we lose to Qadr, I will not be ashamed.*

Qadr's rider was a small man, but he looked as if he were the age of Samir's father. His weathered face had seen many summers. The jockey's face was impassive. He clearly didn't smile often, but his face wasn't cruel. He inspected his saddle and harness professionally, adjusted the straps around his camel's face, and stood ready to mount. He was all business.

Samir knew that Qadr's rider had probably seen Amuna race, and his strategy would be to squeeze her out before she could pull up into the lead. Qadr was big enough to squeeze her for sure.

Suddenly, Samir had an inspiration. It was a gamble, really. He knew the logical plan for the two larger camels was to hug each other and the rail to hold back the rest of the pack. He was going to change his strategy, and ignore what Father and Uncle Moosa had said.

Mansur's words rang true to him. Samir decided to line up in the middle instead of fighting for the inside at the start. Perhaps if Amuna got off the line fast, he could confuse the two big males as to what he was planning, and in the split seconds that the riders wavered, Amuna could gain ground and get around them. Samir was going to take Amuna outside and around to the right immediately at the start. It was their best chance.

CHAPTER 50

The race organizer entered the pen and checked all the animals to be sure they were the right ones. He nodded, and said loudly, "This is the field for the final race. The horn will be in five minutes." He left the area.

All the riders were silent now. They were thinking of their strategies or praying. An occasional camel snorted or gurgled. They all knew something big was about to happen. Samir's palms were sweating and his heart beat thundered in his ears.

The horn blared loudly, and he jumped. The riders all mounted their camels and kicked them to stand. Many had the high racing saddle that left both hands free, but Amuna and Qadr's riders both rode behind the hump. Samir briefly wondered how Qadr's rider could see from behind that big hump, but he realized that was a distraction and focused again on Amuna. He needed to pay attention to her. White curly fur on her head. Tiny ears. The feel of his heels in her soft belly. The way she was breathing.

The racers filed out to the starting area and entered the track. A roar of appreciation went up from the crowd. Each camel had its own supporters.

The usual shoving match occurred at the starting line as the animals pushed into position. Samir managed to get Amuna into the sixth spot from the rail. He could feel the fur and straps of the camels on either side scraping against his knees as the animals struggled to maintain their spots. All around him camels were snorting and breathing loudly.

He noticed the red and yellow camel's rider glancing over at him, so he feigned a frustrated expression and pretended to try and move Amuna closer to the rail. He was actually exactly where he wanted to be. Magically, for one moment all the camels were motionless behind the line, and the starting shot fired.

Samir kicked Amuna hard and startled her into jumping forward off the line. She managed to get ahead of the camels on either side of her, and hit her running stride very fast. Legs and necks and arms and legs were flying everywhere. Samir kept his head down near Amuna's hump to avoid getting hit.

Amuna pulled away into the lead of the animals around her, and was racing with the red and yellow camel and Qadr. She was half a length behind them, but exactly where Samir wanted her to be. The riders of the other two camels would have to turn around and look back over their shoulders to see her. Each time they did it cost them a little of the lead.

Amuna was running effortlessly. Samir believed she had a little extra speed in her, and he would call on it after they rounded the second turn. For now he liked his position, and just crept up on the leaders slowly.

As they rounded the second turn, the other two camels seemed to become aware of each other, and started to race for first place. They didn't ignore Amuna, but they were focused on each other. They thought Amuna was running at top speed, and there was no way she would catch up with the long strides of their bigger mounts. That was their mistake.

Samir licked his dry lips and tightened his grip. As soon as they straightened out of the curve, Samir threw up a brief prayer to heaven and made his move. He started talking to Amuna, and saw her ears turn back toward him. He said, "Run, Amuna. Run, girl. Run! Run!" She knew those words. She ran straight ahead and pulled even with the leaders, then started to creep ahead. The other riders were shocked. They began to whip their camels harder, but Amuna had the momentum.

As soon as her tail was even with the head of the red and yellow camel, Samir turned Amuna sharply in toward the rail. Both of the leaders lost a step as their camels instinctively pulled back to avoid colliding with Amuna.

She got to the rail just as they entered the final turn. Samir's heart was pounding. His strategy had worked! He knew the big camels would pour on the pressure for the last half kilometer. He gripped his strap tightly with both hands and shouted again, "Run, Amuna, run, run!"

Qadr nose was breathing on Samir's back. The hot breath was annoying. His rider was trying to bully his way past Amuna on the inside, so Samir held Amuna tightly by the rail. He could see the finish line ahead, and he kept kicking Amuna in his excitement. He heard her snort, and realized she knew what to do. He stopped kicking and said another prayer.

Both of the big camels were closing on her now. Their heads were even with her shoulder. The foamy lather from their panting mouths flew back and covered his legs. Samir ignored everything but the feel of Amuna's body under him and the position of his heels locking him onto her back.

Samir hoped she could just hold on a few more meters. She did. The race was so close he saw all three camel's heads in front of him at the end. Samir had no idea which of the other two camels had come in second, but he knew Amuna had won. He threw back his head and shouted at the top of his voice, shaking his hands in the air, as they continued around the track one more time, gradually slowing their pace.

The crowd was going crazy! People were yelling and jumping and waving scarves, turbans and arms in the air. It had been a thrilling race for everyone.

Samir put his head down on Amuna's hump and patted her sides. "Thank you, girl," he said repeatedly. "This is what I always knew you could do. You are the best camel. You are the queen of all camels."

He glanced back toward his competitors. The riders looked annoyed, but he could also see admiration for Amuna. He wanted to drop back and congratulate them, but decided they would think he was gloating.

Instead, Samir rode toward the covered box seats. The race organizer took Amuna's harness and led her to the winner's position of honor in the front.

"Ladies and gentlemen, visitors, guests, and citizens of Fez. Here is your grand champion," he shouted. The crowd roared again. The man asked the camel's name and her owner. "The winner of the race of champions is Amuna from the stable of Jamal ibn Walid of Fez."

Father came running over at that moment and stood beside Samir and Amuna. The City Commander stepped forward and handed Jamal the leather purse with the prize of one hundred gold dinars. Jamal bowed to the Commander and raised the purse high in the air to show it to the audience. Everyone cheered. They were glad a local camel had won.

The events of the rest of the day were kind of a blur for Samir. Crowds of people surged forward to touch Amuna and ask questions.

"Mabruk! Mabruk! Congratulations!" he heard over and over. "Where did she come from? How old is she? How long has she lived here?"

Most of them had never seen Amuna, since she ran out in the desert during quiet times, and they were amazed to see a solid white camel. Everyone wanted to touch her. She was on her way to becoming a legend.

After a few minutes, Samir began working his way toward the exit, hoping to get Amuna into her stall quietly.

He needed to groom and water her after this big day. She had done everything he had asked, and he felt deep gratitude.

When the crowd pushed down from the stands to see Amuna, Father quietly slipped away, giving Samir his moment of glory. What Jamal really wanted to do, however, was talk to Qadr's owner. The big male camel was not hard to find. Jamal walked up and introduced himself, and the two men shared a cup of tea as they negotiated the possibilities of breeding.

They reached an agreement that Qadr would remain in Fez in Jamal's stable for the next two weeks. This would be a long term arrangement. As the owner of the female, Jamal was entitled to the first calf. If it survived its birth, then two years later, Amuna and Qadr would breed again, and this time the calf would belong to Qadr's owner.

In addition, Jamal agreed to pay thirty gold dinars, a very high stud fee, and all the expenses of caring for Qadr as long as he was in his stable. This was a fairly routine sort of arrangement, and both men shook hands to seal the deal.

Although Samir had missed the signs, Jamal knew that Amuna was ready to breed. He hoped that having Qadr in the stable would speed up her hormones and give them a few chances to try. Jamal arranged with Qadr's owner for them to come to the stable the next day and settle the big male in his new quarters. His owner would remain in town for the next two weeks. Jamal would tell Samir tonight. For now, Samir was full of his race, and his father was content to have it so.

CHAPTER 51

After a long and tiring day, Samir returned home with Amuna. He put her into her normal stall, and removed her fancy harness. He put her usual harness over her head, and led her to the water trough. She had earned a big drink, and it took her ten minutes to drink her fill.

After that, he fed her a few handfuls of grain with his hands, telling her repeatedly what a beautiful and wonderful camel she was. She made happy gurgles a few times and nudged his shoulder with her nose as if to say, "We did it!"

He got the grooming tools and began to comb her coat. He didn't want to wash her just yet. That was a messy prospect, and he was anxious to get home to celebrate.

A few people walked by the stables to try and get a look at Amuna in her stall. He walked out and thanked them for their interest, but said she had to rest now, and he closed the big wooden doors. He realized that they were going to have to hire a guard for the stable. Amuna had become a very valuable property.

He put some fresh sand and straw in Amuna's pen, and left her to sit in peace and ruminate. He checked to be sure all the onlookers were gone, and he slipped out the side door to run home.

Mansur, Moosa and Father were all there to welcome him. Everyone talked at once and the conversation was very animated. His shoulders were soon sore from all the affectionate slaps on the back they gave him. He understood bits and pieces of the conversation. Moosa had won one hundred gold dinars on his wager. Father had won one hundred gold dinars on his wager, in addition to the one hundred in the winner's purse. Financially, they were all set for life now.

Mansur had roamed around and listened to all the comments people made about the camels, and especially about Amuna. Some people still felt she was a bad omen, but more than most thought she had a special gift from Allah. Samir agreed. She did have a special gift.

As the conversation died down, Father decided to tell his own news. "I had another piece of luck myself today," he said. "I went to talk to Qadr's owner, and we have reached a deal to breed the big male with Amuna. He will come to our stable tomorrow and remain for two weeks."

Samir's eyes got wide. "Really, father? He is a beautiful animal, but he is very large! Do you think he is too big for Amuna? Will she be able to hold such a large calf?"

"Of course," father said. "Amuna's body will adapt to the size of her baby. It will be born a normal size just like every other camel. If God is willing, the calf will be a male and grow up to be a big racer like his father, with the beautiful heart of his mother. Whatever is born, it belongs to us. We will breed Amuna with Qadr again when she is in season, and that second calf will belong to Qadr's owner."

"But why is he coming tomorrow? That seems too soon," Samir said. "She is not three years old yet."

"No, but she is close, and she is showing signs of readiness. Haven't you noticed her restlessness and distraction? And she is off her food. Perhaps being in the same stable with the big male will encourage her. We shall see. Tomorrow we will greet our guest at the stable, and let them get acquainted."

The next morning, Qadr's owner led his big camel into the stall next to Amuna. The camels greeted each other over the fence by throwing back their heads and bellowing to the sky. They settled down right away, though. Perhaps having raced together the day before, they already recognized each other's scents. The next day, father would open the gate between them and let them begin their courtship.

For the next two weeks, someone had to sleep at the stable every night. It was important to know when the camels mated, so they could calculate the due date of the calf.

Samir slept there the first two nights to be sure Amuna would be safe from the big male. The two camels entered the pens on one side or the other and seemed to be absorbed in their courtship, but nothing happened. The next two nights father slept there, along with Qadr's owner.

The fourth day they reported success. They left the animals alone together for the next three days, and since everything seemed to have gone well, Qadr's owner took him away a week earlier than expected.

Now all they had to do was wait. Insh'allah, in thirteen months they would greet Amuna's baby. It would be four months, though, before they knew for sure from her physical signs if she was pregnant.

CHAPTER 52

For the next few months, life continued as normal. Mansur continued his religious studies at the university. His father insisted, of course, that he should fully understand shari'a law and the teachings of the *Qur'an* and the hadiths. About half of Mansur's school time was spent in discussing and debating the commentaries of famous Muslim teachers. He enjoyed it.

Mansur had also discovered the writings of the young Persian mystic and philosopher Abdallah Ansari, and he was reading the manuscripts of Ansari's contemporaries, the metaphysical physician Ibn Sina and the Sufi poet Abul-Khayr.

Central to Ibn Sina's philosophy was his concept of reality and reasoning. He believed that the ultimate object of all knowledge is God, the pure intellect. Ibn Sina said that the soul is eternal and cannot be destroyed, and this belief colored the way he treated his medical patients. Abul-Khayr referred to himself as nobody, son of nobody. His belief was that his life was subsumed in the Divine--that God is all things and all things are God.

Such ideas were outside traditional religious teachings, but they represented a philosophical shift in Islam that was occurring. It had started to gather a following that included many Almohads, as well as Mansur, son of Ibn Yasin.

One day Mansur's religious teacher mentioned that a well-known desert sheikh Taqi al-Madyani would be coming to lecture at the university the following week. He knew of Mansur's religious beliefs, and thought Mansur would be interested in what the man had to say. Some were calling Sheikh Taqi a sufi or mystic. Sufis typically wore robes of wool or *suf*, and often wandered without a home.

On the appointed day, Mansur was sitting in the front row when a small, modest man walked into the lecture hall in simple woolen robes. Sheikh Taqi surveyed the students before him silently, one by one, for several minutes, and then opened with words that would change Mansur's life.

"We begin in the name of Allah, the merciful and compassionate. My teacher, peace be upon him, said, 'Whatever is inferior to God is an obstacle that separates us from Him.' Can you understand that statement? "

He paused to let his words sink in.

"Does this contradict the teachings of the *Qur'an*?" He waited.

Silence. None of the boys felt brave enough to answer.

"No, it does not. Nothing can be inferior to God, because there is no duality. God is all things, all beings, therefore nothing can be inferior to God because everything is God. Neither can there be separation. Neither is there an 'us' or a 'Him'. All that is seen and unseen is one.

There is only the Divine Unity." He leaned forward and looked at them intently.

"When we look through these eyes," he touched his eye, "we are God seeing through God's eyes. When we hear with these ears," he pinched his earlobe, "we are God hearing with God's ears. When we breathe in, we are breathing God's life into these bodies, and when we breathe out the One absorbs our human experience. To achieve the highest state of being, our sense of self must pass away into the ocean that is the One. Do you understand?"

He paused. Silence.

"We are the ripples on the water that all can see. But we are more. We are also the ocean itself."

He paused again.

"The One flows through us, even when our thoughts are limited to our bodies and life around us. We are blind to our unity. To realize the immensity of the ocean of being that supports us and flows through us, we must die to our small concept of self and resurrect in the consciousness of unity with all. We must die before death that we may live. Do you understand?"

He paused again.

"Each one of us must search within our hearts for the truth that has been placed there from before time. Let your journey to the Oneness begin. Always remember when you have doubts that That which you seek is also seeking you."

Perfect silence filled the room. Mansur was in shock. His heart was quivering. He had never heard words like these before. No one had. He simply knew in that moment that whatever this teacher knew, he wanted to know it, too.

The rest of the lecture lasted a short time, but Mansur remained deep in thought and heard nothing. He had heard what he needed to hear. He felt as if his life had been upended. All he could do was stare at the small, simple man before him and think, *Who is this man? I want to know what he knows.*

When the lecture ended, most of the boys filed out of the room with quizzical looks after bowing to the visitor. Mansur stood rooted in his place. He didn't know what to do next. He wanted to go up to the teacher, but he knew he couldn't say one word. Instead, the sheikh came over to him.

Sheikh Taqi glanced at Mansur intently for a brief moment that felt like eternity. His eyes were nearly black and sparkled with light. They seemed as deep as the night sky swallowing Mansur up.

The sheikh put his hand on Mansur's heart and said, "Oh Abdallah, praise be to God. What a light he has put into your heart!"

Mansur would have fallen to the ground if someone had touched him with a feather. He clasped his hands together and made a kind of half bow. "Thank you, Mawlawi, for this wonderful instruction."

It seemed a completely inadequate thing to say, but it was enough. The small man reached up and put both hands on Mansur's shoulders. He said quietly but firmly, "Your path is opening before you, my son. You may come when the time is right."

Then he turned and walked out of the room, leaving Mansur in a state of wonderment and confusion. He only knew that every word this man had said was burned into his heart.

Why did he call me Abdallah? Does he confuse me with my father, he wondered. He couldn't wait to tell Samir.

CHAPTER 53

Ali al-Harghi's hands were covered with blood, so he wiped his eyes as best he could on his arm. His chain mail was caked with dirt and dried blood. He had never felt so dirty. He had never felt the price of war so strongly. The battles along the coast had been fierce. Six of his closest comrades lay dead on the sand before him. They had stood together against an onslaught to protect him. Corpses of the enemy were piled everywhere. The smell of blood was thick.

He glanced around to see if he was safe. For the moment there were no enemies nearby, so he quickly checked each man for any tiny sign of life. There was none. Three had had their throats cut, two had been stabbed and hacked with sabers, and the last one, Rashid, who was only a boy of eighteen, still had a spear in his heart. Both of his hands had been severed.

Ali wanted to throw up. The *Qur'an* forbids mutilation of enemies, but as Ali knew well, the Berbers held different views.

He took something from the bodies of each of the fallen soldiers—a ring, a token of office, or any small item he could find in their belts. He gently closed their eyes and recited a prayer for the dead, asking God to take them all into Paradise. He would make sure that the tokens were returned to their mothers or wives. It was the least he could do. He paused for a moment to recite another prayer, then mounted Gawa and rode back to join his company with a heavy heart.

General Yusuf had been pleased to welcome Ali when he arrived more than a year ago. They seemed to complement each other. Ali was quiet, steady and got things done. Yusuf was inspiring, impulsive and insightful. He was good at motivating men and creating devotion in his army, but it was officers like Ali who won his battles and gained Yusuf his reputation. Yusuf started to rely on the young man who was so solid and unshakeable. Three months after he arrived, he had promoted Ali to Captain in the cavalry.

Now almost a year later, Ali was a malakh, or leader of more than five thousand horsemen, and one of Yusuf's favored advisors. Ali's cavalry had just suffered heavy losses, and he was on his way back to Mazagan to report the bad news to Yusuf.

Something in their strategy needed to change. The Banu-Ifan Berbers they were fighting were too entrenched and had too much local support. For two years, Yusuf's army had gained little ground.

Ali hoped Yusuf would make time to discuss what they could do to change the balance. If not, they would lose many more men, and Ali could not get accustomed to that aspect of war. The men were not tokens on a game board.

They were real human beings. He knew their names. He drank and ate and fought with them.

Ali rode into Yusuf's headquarters the next day and went straight to the general's command center. He saluted, and was greeted warmly by Yusuf.

"Ali, you are here just in time. What news? Let's be seated. Lieutenant, bring this man some tea."

Ali remained standing. "General, we have suffered a terrible defeat. I believe we have lost over four hundred men, two hundred in the cavalry unit alone. The Berbers seemed to be waiting for us, as if they knew when and where we would attack. They blindsided us, just as we came over the eastern ridge, and forced us into disarray. By the time our formations regrouped, the field was littered with corpses, and those Berber scum were riding away into the hills."

General Yusuf listened to the report in silence. He, too, grieved the loss of life. "I'm sorry, my friend," he said. "We cannot sustain such heavy losses. You are right. We are losing here, and need a new strategy. Go and clean up. We will have dinner tonight with my top officers, and discuss what can be done. I need you to be there. Your ideas are always sound."

The Lieutenant returned and handed the tea to Ali with a salute.

"Yes, General," Ali said. "I hoped you would say that. I have been giving our situation some thought as I rode, and I may have a suggestion or two that could help." He drank the tea quickly and put down the cup.

"Good. Meet back here before evening prayers, and we will see what tactics we can come up with." Yusuf turned back to his campaign table and studied the placement of all of his men. Ali knew he was dismissed. He saluted to Yusuf's back and left the tent.

The army's camp was on a broad wadi, and a pool had been diverted for the officers to use for bathing. Ali watered Gawa and hobbled him near a feeding area. He took a clean uniform from his pack and went down to the pool.

Ali sank into the water with relief, and put his head completely under. The muffled silence was peaceful. He wished he could have stayed there for a long time, but he had to breathe, so he came up. He lathered quickly and rinsed the dirt and blood off his skin. He had a few new cuts, but nothing serious, so he decided to ignore them. *What are a few scars for a soldier?* he thought. *Just memories or badges of honor.*

Ali took his pack and went to lie down in an officers' tent for a few minutes. The bath had been good for his body and spirit. His appetite was back, and he was ready for the evening. He didn't realize he had fallen asleep until the Lieutenant came to wake him.

"Sir. Sir?" The soldier thought for a moment about where to touch Ali to waken him. It is dangerous to wake a sleeping soldier. If they mistake you for an enemy, they can kill you. He decided to tap him on the forearm and step back. "Sir."

Ali sat up immediately, fully awake.

"It is almost time for evening prayers, sir. General Yusuf asked for you."

Ali nodded. "Thank you, Lieutenant. I am awake now. I will come," Ali said.

The Lieutenant saluted and left the tent.

CHAPTER 54

Despite the challenges of the field campaign, Yusuf fed his officers well. After evening prayers, they shared lamb stew with onions, garlic and tomatoes. There was also steamed kuskus, fresh, hot flat bread, thick slices of fried aubergine coated in yoghurt and lemon, and small smoked sardines marinated in vinegar and oil with black olives. Large glasses of pomegranate or grape juice finished the meal.

Yusuf knew that an army rides on its stomach, and his officers thought better when they were fed. They relaxed and told a few jokes as they ate, and finally the environment was right for him to speak.

"My friends, we are in a difficult situation," Yusuf began. "We cannot keep up the pressure on these Berbers. They are hitting us too hard, and then vanishing into the hills before we can regroup. We cannot replace our losses as fast as they come. Let us have a candid conversation here. What is it we are failing to see or do? Where is our error? How can we win the day decisively so the people in this region can get back about their lives, and we can move on with ours?"

General Yusuf was candid. That was an unusual feature in a commanding officer, and it was one reason why his officers were devoted to him.

"If any of you have ideas or observations to share, please, I welcome them. We are all fighting this war together, and we can win it if we share our ideas freely. Who will start?"

Three hours passed in heavy discussion and a few heated exchanges. Gradually it dawned on Yusuf that they had been missing something very important. The Berbers were getting help, and that help was coming from the Almoravids.

They had completely missed the obvious. Ibn Yasin was supplying the Berbers with both information and supplies to damage the Almohads.

That changed everything. They needed to find a way to weaken and sow distrust in that alliance somehow. That would change the current situation dramatically.

For the next four weeks, Yusuf pulled back his troops. He clustered them around the coastal city of Mazagan. Meanwhile, he sent scouts and spies north into the Berber strongholds and east toward Marrakesh, where Ibn Yasin was reported to be running his operations.

Ali had lived in Marrakesh a few years as a boy, so he volunteered to investigate what was happening in the city. His Berber looks and dark skin would help him to blend in. Perhaps he could befriend someone in Ibn Yasin's camp.

Ali had no experience as a spy, but he was intrigued with returning to Marrakesh and discovering if there was a secret supply line that he could uncover. He borrowed some Berber clothing and armor from a recent recruit, and headed out on his own. He left Gawa in the care of a young cavalry officer, and struck off riding a non-descript horse with a Berber saddle. It was definitely not his elegant Gawa.

It was a good thing he had to ride for two days, because it took that long for him to adjust to the untrained antics of his mount so he looked natural riding him.

Ali's preparations paid off. He entered Marrakesh virtually unnoticed. There were always Berbers in town from the Sous Valley, where Ali had been born, and in the past year an increasing number of northern Berber tribes flowed in as well. They were mostly converts to Islam, and he blended in. No one seemed to take notice of him.

He asked around discreetly for an inn where he might find Berber kin, and was directed to the Rose of Baghdad, a long-established inn that had fallen on hard times. The rooms were cheap, the tea was weak, and the mattresses were filled with straw, but the coffee was strong and food was edible. Ali took up a spot in a corner where he could listen and watch without being obvious.

The men who flowed in and out spoke Maghribi Arabic, but late at night when all the transients had gone to bed, the men reverted to their Berber dialects.

Ali felt like he was in a time warp. He remembered sitting with his father in groups of men like these, listening to them tell stories of warriors, famous stallions and the old gods late at night when he should have been in bed himself.

These men were no different, and when Ali was asked to do so, he managed to come up with a tale or two from his memory that he hadn't recalled for twenty years. These men understood without asking what it meant to be a second son and have to find his own way. He blended in.

One night after the evening meal, he noticed that many of the regulars were missing and the room was not as full. He nursed a cup of thick coffee, and asked casually where everyone had gone.

He had become friendly with a young mercenary named Rahim, and Rahim shrugged and said, "to deliver supplies." Nothing else. Ali had to learn more without raising suspicion.

"Supplies? Then there is work? Do you think I could get work delivering these supplies? I could use some silver," he said casually.

"Perhaps," Rahim said. "You are strong, and that is what they want. There are lots of bags and crates to lift. I went a few weeks ago, but they sent me away. They told me I was too much of a boy, and to go build up my muscles. Usual barbary kindness." He rolled his eyes. "Go down to the stables near the south gate. They can guide you from there."

Ali thanked his friend, and after a few minutes he stood up and said, "In that case, I think I will go see about getting some work, so I can afford to stay here and keep the company of you fine people. Salaam." He bowed to the room with a swagger and headed out the door. This was the first real lead he had had, and he worked hard to maintain his composure. He didn't want to tip his hand.

When Ali got to the stable, and asked for work, the stable master eyed him up and down carefully, then spoke in the Berber dialect of Ali's tribe. "Where are you from and who sent you?"

Ali replied in kind, saying "I learned in the Rose of Baghdad that you might need strong men to help loading supplies. I am in need of silver. Perhaps we can make a deal."

The man studied him again and asked, "Where is your home?" He chewed on a piece of straw.

Ali gestured to the south and said, "I come from the Sous Valley. My family is al-Harghi."

The man nodded and said, "You have the accent. There are many second sons in the al-Harghi."

Ali nodded and replied, "Yes, and one is here looking at you. My brother took over our father's flocks, and I am trying to find what I can do. Do you have work, or not?"

The man went to a table inside a stall and wrote out a small paper that he handed to Ali. "Take this east of the city about two kilometers in the hills. Talk to Abadi. He will put you to work." Ali took the paper, stuffed it into his sash, and nodded his thanks.

He didn't return to the Rose of Baghdad. He rode through town on a winding trek to be sure he wasn't followed, then left through the east gate. "I will sleep under the stars tonight, and find this Abadi in the morning," he decided.

CHAPTER 55

The next three days went by in a blur for Ali. He found the supply camp, and presented his paper to the overseer Abadi. He was put to work immediately. He saw a couple of men he recognized from the Rose of Baghdad, and worked his way over to be near them. Perhaps they would loosen their tongues about what they knew.

All the supervisor told him was what to lift and where to put it. Ali wasn't there to learn about the operation, as they told him none too kindly--he was there to move supplies as quickly as possible.

Soon Ali was indistinguishable from the other laborers. They were all sweaty and grimy and hot. He stripped down to his undershirt to try and cool himself. Every hour a man would pass through with a water barrel and the workers were allowed to stop for five minutes and drink.

Ali joined his fellow workers in moaning about the heavy work, and asked where all these supplies were headed. One of the men said, "North. We supply our brothers in their fight against the Almohad." Now Ali had to walk delicately.

"That is a long way to carry vegetables. Surely they have food there," Ali said.

"Yes, but they don't have food made from metal and hardened leather."

Ali's surprise didn't show in his face. He nodded wisely and said nothing. This was the connection he needed. Armor and weapons were being transported in food caravans from Marrakesh to Errbat right down the main trade road. It was a brilliant idea. The supplies were passing right under the noses of the Almohad.

"Do you think I can get work guarding the caravan when we finish here? I would like to move north and see if I can find some steady work there," Ali said.

"The only steady work there is fighting," the man replied, "But you go if you wish. The Almoravids who run the caravans never have enough Berber guards. They all turn into soldiers when they reach Errbat."

Another man joined in. "My cousin is guarding the next caravan. It will leave tomorrow. He said the army of Ibn Yasin is moving north to support the Berbers against General Yusuf. They will need all these supplies and more for all the extra men who will need to eat."

Ali didn't want to appear too interested. "What those bigshots do doesn't interest me," he said. "I just need some silver in my belt, and I don't care much whose silver it is." The other men nodded in agreement, and they got back to work.

On their next break, Ali moved up to the front of the supply line and asked the head man if there was a place for an additional guard. He told him he had experience fighting and guarding caravans, plus he had his own horse.

The man took a look at Ali's muscles and scars. "Yes," he said, "I think I can find a spot for you. Bring your horse."

The next morning, Ali rode out with the caravan. It would take them five days to reach the Berber supply base. Ali had to think carefully now. Should he break off from the caravan before Errbat and take what he knew to General Yusuf, or should he ride to the end point and find the supply location first? He had not been able to send word to Yusuf for three weeks now.

Both options had merit. He decided to sleep on it overnight. He found his thoughts drifting back to his last caravan ride. He wondered if Samir had made it to safety. He was a nice boy, and Ali hoped he had survived. He wondered if Moosa had had a difficult time talking with Samir's father Jamal. He vowed that the next time he was near Fez he would go by to see Moosa and Jamal. He didn't realize how soon that day would come.

CHAPTER 56

Ali decided to wait until he got to the supply point before slipping back to General Yusuf's camp. The night before they arrived, one of the other guards shared a rumor that Emir Ibn Yasin and his two main generals Malik and Umar were heading north with a large army of men. The army was traveling to the east of the supply caravan, off the main trade route, and would arrive about two days after they did.

This was big news. Ali started watching carefully for signs of their destination.

As soon as he knew where the supply point was, he would find a way to slip off in the night and alert the Almohads. They were about a day's ride south along the coast and would need a day to prepare. Perhaps they could strike the supply post and catch Ibn Yasin and his men off guard. It might be the decisive victory they needed.

Ali studied the men around him carefully, and kept his eyes on the landscape. He needed to be able to tell his men about the terrain and create an attack plan. To others, he looked like a bored caravan guard, but his brain was spinning.

Toward the end of the day, they came up over a rise and Ali saw what he needed. A road far ahead forked off the trade route to the northeast, and he could see some hills where a supply center could be hidden in the valley between. He was sure that was the destination. Ibn Yasin's troops would likely enter from the east. It appeared as if a road went off that way.

Now he only had to disappear without being caught and get to his army. This was an important chance they couldn't afford to miss. It might mean a crushing loss for General Yusuf otherwise.

The day dragged on. Finally they reached the turnoff, and the leading camels struck off to the northeast, just as he had surmised. Ali made small talk with the nearby camel handlers and guards, commenting on how tired he was. He told two of them that he felt unwell, so he would get to sleep early that night and just eat a little dried meat and fruit. He had made it a habit to sleep somewhat apart from the other guards, so they would think nothing of it if they went to bed and didn't see Ali there. So far, so good.

As soon as the camp started to settle for the night, Ali hobbled his horse and pretended to sleep. Soon the area was silent. He unhobbled his horse and cautiously led him about a kilometer west toward the coast. Then he mounted and rode west across the dune tops until he found the hard packed trade route again. He checked the sky for the star Yildun, then turned south and ran his horse as fast as he dared for the next five hours. He began to recognize some landmarks, and got to Yusuf's camp as the sun rose.

The guards apprehended him at once. To them he was an unknown Berber racing into their camp unannounced. At first they didn't recognize or believe him. He was dirty and sun baked, riding an unfamiliar animal and clothed in Berber leather armor and chain. He kept insisting they take him to General Yusuf, and eventually the disturbance brought an officer who recognized him. They woke Yusuf immediately, and Ali told his story.

The general wasted no time. He roused his officers and readied the army. They would leave by noon, and surround the supply post that night. With luck, they would catch Ibn Yasin and his army off guard and defeat them. It was not easy to ready an army of ten thousand men in a few hours, but they were disciplined soldiers and did what they needed to do. The army paused for the midday prayers before heading out, and General Yusuf addressed them. He said that this might be the telling battle of their long campaign, and bid them all to make a difference.

He never said, "Do this for me." He always inspired his men to do their best, because they always did more than they thought they could do when they believed they had made the decision to fight for themselves. This day they would need that inspiration.

The army was well-rested, and set out rapidly. Despite the crushing heat, they wanted to be within an hour's march of the supply center before dark. They would rest and wait until dark to move the last few kilometers and surround the location. General Yusuf and Ali had made a plan for how to surround Ibn Yasin's army if they were not already in the supply camp. They were uncertain how large a force they would face.

Ali would take his cavalry and move quietly to the rear of Ibn Yasin's guards and remain out of sight. Yusuf would station two units of infantrymen to the north and south of the Almoravids. On Yusuf's signal just before dawn, the two infantry units would attack at once. When the Almoravids were fully engaged on two fronts, Ali's cavalry units would ride in from the east and defeat them.

It was a good plan, and Yusuf's army executed it with ruthless precision. Ali's cavalry poured over the eastern hills and all but wiped out the Almoravid army and the supply camp. As Ali pressed forward with his men, he saw the Almoravid command camp off to his right and veered that way. He arrived just in time to see one of his officers run a sword through Ibn Yasin. He recognized the Emir from the racetrack in Awdaghust, a tall slim man with a dark, pointed beard. He jumped off his horse and rushed to them. It was too late. The greatest leader of the Almoravids lay dead at his feet. His army had been defeated.

As he had done before for his own men, Ali closed Ibn Yasin's eyes and whispered a death prayer, asking Allah to take this man to Paradise if it was His will. He noticed a small chain around Ibn Yasin's neck. A crescent moon medallion hung on it. He removed the medallion and put it into his sash. He knew what he had to do now. He had to go to Fez. Fast.

Ali found General Yusuf on the battlefield, and rode up to salute him. "Sir, Allahu akbar. God is great, it is a tremendous victory. Ibn Yasin is dead. I saw him fall myself. His general Malik died with him on the hill, but we believe that General Ibn Umar escaped. I sent riders to track him."

Yusuf slapped Ali on the shoulder and said, "Well done, malakh. You have my gratitude for your excellent spy work. I was starting to despair that you had been captured. Instead, you have given us this victory. We will celebrate tonight!"

Ali said, "Sir, may I have permission to ride to Fez? I would tell my old commander this news myself before the rumors arrive."

Yusuf looked at him thoughtfully for a moment, then he grinned and said, "I suppose you could ask me for just about anything at this moment and I would grant it. If the reward you seek is only to return to Fez, then be gone."

He extended his hand to Ali, and they shook. "Well done, Malakh Ali. I will await your return, God willing."

Yusuf turned and rode off to join his other officers in celebration. Ali rode into what was left of the nearby supply camp and loaded up Gawa with water and food for the long journey east.

CHAPTER 57

The ride from Errbat to Fez was new to Ali, but the roads were well traveled all the way. Errbat was a large seaport, and most of its cargo went east to Fez or south to Marrakesh.

Gawa was well rested from his long absence, and seemed happy to stretch out his legs and run on the hard packed sand. A caravan would take two weeks to cover the distance, but it took Ali only five days riding hard. He didn't think any messengers could have made better time than he did.

He stopped on the fourth day in the oasis at Meknes, southwest of Fez, and spent the night there to rest both Gawa and himself. There was a small hammam, and he arrived in time to bathe before the evening prayers. They would be on the road again before the sun, and would arrive in Fez twenty-four hours later. At least he would sleep clean tonight.

The next evening he saw the minaret of the Kairowiyyan mosque on the eastern horizon. It seemed many years since he had last seen that tower. He rode until well after dark, and was within a two hour ride of the city when he camped for the night. He hobbled Gawa and brushed him. The dust had quickly coated them again, and he wiped it off as best he could. Ali's lips were parched from the sun, and he drank a lot from his water bag. Perhaps tomorrow he could bathe again at the barracks. That depended upon how his day went.

Ali rode into Fez without being challenged the next morning. From the winding alleys he heard the sounds of life. The narrow side-streets were packed with hundreds of one-room workshops where master craftsmen labored from morning to night.

There were sounds of artisans beating patterns into sheets of burnished copper, forming cauldrons, platters and kettles. He heard the snapping of wooden looms weaving and hand turned lathes grinding pieces of scented argan wood into ornate shapes.

Everywhere the city smelled faintly of the tanneries and fresh green vegetables piled high on wooden carts. Perfumes mixed with the fragrant spices. It was all familiar, and yet it was not familiar at all.

Ali looked like a military messenger, and there were many of those coming and going each day these days. No one took notice of him. He rode straight to the barracks. His commander didn't recognize him at first. Ali's dark skin was even darker from the sun, and he was coated in sand. Even his horse was unrecognizable. The commander was walking across the yard as he arrived. Ali dismounted and greeted him with a salute, and then approached him as an equal.

"I think I should recognize you," the commander said. "You seem familiar, but there is something unfamiliar here."

"Sir, I am Ali al-Harghi," Ali said. He gave the commander a moment to remember his old recruit. "I went to join General Yusuf when I was guarding a camel caravan from Awdaghust over a year ago."

"Ali? I remember now. The Lieutenant who always trained," he said. He stepped back and then leaned in closely to look at the designations on Ali's very dirty uniform. "I see that you have achieved some success in your posting, Malakh! Congratulations. Very impressive. What news do you bring from the coast? I heard there have been terrible battles there, and we are losing. Come, let's get you some refreshment." They went inside the commander's office.

"Indeed, the battles have been terrible," Ali said. "We have lost a great many men. But I am here to report good news to you. The northern Berbers have been defeated at last. We discovered that Ibn Yasin and the Almoravids were supplying them with men and weapons. God is merciful, we managed to launch a stealth attack against them just a week ago near Errbat. The Almoravid army there was wiped out, although it appears that General Umar may have escaped. Emir Ibn Yasin and his general Malik were both killed. I saw them with my own eyes," he said.

"This is great news!" the commander said, and slapped his hands down on his knees. "I will call the men together now, and you can tell them. They will all be glad for some good news."

"No, commander, you can tell them. I have an urgent errand to run before I can relax this night. Perhaps I will return in time for the evening meal. I remember the excellent quality of the meals in this barracks," Ali said, with the twinkle of a shared joke in his eye.

"Malakh Ali, we would be honored to have you join us for our meal. It will be the same high quality as meals have ever been here." He paused, then said with a wry smile, "You may find better fare in the city."

They saluted each other, and then shook hands. Ali left Gawa to be stabled and groomed, and he set off on foot for the great library. All he remembered was that Samir had told him he lived in the shadow of the east wall. Surely it would not be that hard to find. He wanted to pay his respects to Samir's father.

The buildings were all made from the same, uniform brown mud bricks, but none of them looked the same. The entrances were narrow or wide, and every house had a door that was different and unique. Most were painted in bright colors of red, gold, turquoise blue or green, and had colorful tile decorations surrounding them. Some doors were iron or had copper decorations on them. Even the most meager houses found a spot on a wall for a design from broken tiles or rock chips.

A frustrating hour later, Ali finally offered a boy a silver shekel if he would lead him to the house of Jamal the camel breeder. He had forgotten everything he ever knew about the tangled streets of Fez. The boy didn't hesitate. Everyone knew Jamal's name now since the camel races. He led Ali on a confusing journey through a maze of winding streets, and they ended up on the north side of the mosque. Ali said, "No this is the wrong place. I need the east wall of the library."

"No sir, this is the home of Jamal the camel breeder," the boy said confidently, and he darted away.

The house was a simple peasant's house, with no courtyard or gate. A few green plants showed from the top of the roof. Ali approached the door with doubt, but knocked on the opened door. No one answered. He knocked again, and was turning around to leave, when a voice behind him called, "As-salaam aleikhum."

He turned, and couldn't believe his eyes. Samir stood before him. He was hardly changed, just a little taller, and it looked like he had the start of a mustache coming in. "Aleikhum salaam, little brother! You are no longer little." He waited for Samir to recognize him.

"Sir. I'm afraid…" he paused for a moment, and squinted his eyes. "Is that you, Ali? It is you!" He rushed forward and grabbed his shoulders. "I didn't know what happened to you! Where have you been? Come in, come in."

Ali couldn't believe this good fortune. He had never heard whether Samir had died in the desert. He wanted to know everything about Samir from his capture to his university studies to his racing experiences. And, of course, about Amuna.

They talked solidly for more than an hour. When Samir mentioned Mansur and Ibn Yasin, Ali sat up alertly.

"You say Mansur is here? In Fez?"

"Yes, I see him almost every day. We share classes, and have become like brothers. He will be here later," Samir said.

"I'm afraid I have some news that will distress you," Ali said. He then told Samir about his experiences at Marrakesh and Errbat, and of the death of Ibn Yasin at Errbat just a week before.

Samir was very upset. For him, Ibn Yasin was not a soldier. He was a man of kindness who had returned his life to him. He was a man he owed ten gold and the debt of a camel calf to. He was also the father of his best friend.

"Mansur will be here soon, and my father will come also," Samir said. "You must stay and tell them both the story. I'm sure Mansur will have questions. You are a famous warrior now, Ali! A malakh? Ali the caravan guard is a malakh for the famous General Yusuf? And Gawa carries the backside of a malakh in his saddle? Well, I can believe it of Gawa, but not of you!" he teased Ali.

"Could you have imagined this story? You are going to be famous. They will tell all the little children about you," Samir said. "You will have your choice of any wife."

"Truthfully, brother, no, I could not have imagined this. But I'm afraid the only stories they will be telling will be about Amuna and her rider. That is a real legend in the making. When they talk of me, it will be like Mullah Baba stories." They laughed.

"Come up to the garden on the roof, Ali. There is water for washing up there. It would be good to see your actual face at dinner instead of the dusty mask you wear now. And you should wash before prayers. Would you like some clean clothes?"

"I would, but I had best keep on my uniform. There is likely to be a lot of uncertainty in the city once the word of Ibn Yasin's death gets out. I don't know what I might have to do. I left Gawa at the barracks, but you will have to lead me there if I have to go suddenly. I have no idea how you find your way around in this twisting maze of a city!"

Samir left him to his cleanup, and went down to start the dinner.

Ali washed and brushed himself off as best he could. He was just climbing down from the roof when Jamal and Mansur arrived from different directions. Samir heard their greetings and came out to introduce Ali. Jamal was very glad to meet the soldier who had helped Samir find Amuna and escape from the thieves.

"Let me send for Moosa," he said. "My brother will not want to miss seeing you. You will only need to tell your story once that way."

Samir went down the road to a neighbor's boy and promised him a silver shekel if he would go to find Moosa and bring him back immediately. The boy ran off at top speed, and while they waited, Samir and his father finished preparing the dinner. As usual, Mansur had brought food, so they spread out a generous meal and waited. They didn't have to wait long.

Moosa knocked on the door frame and entered panting. "What is so urgent that I must run here immediately? Is someone dead? Was there an accident?"

Everyone in the house was silent. Moosa looked around the room and spotted an unknown soldier. Suddenly, his face beamed as he recognized Ali, and he walked over to him with open arms. "Ali! My brother, so good to see you. Marhaba! Welcome. God is great! You have made it back to Fez at last!"

Ali was pleased to be welcomed with such enthusiasm by everyone. It made all of the difficulties of the past two years melt away. He felt himself among real friends, and it had been a long time since he had had that feeling.

CHAPTER 58

Ali regaled the men with stories of his war exploits and how challenging it was to lead men who all considered themselves to be more respectable than a much younger Berber chieftain's grandson. He was working himself up to the most difficult part of the conversation. He was going to have to tell Mansur about his father's death. He liked Mansur, and he knew that as soon as he told his story everything in the room would change.

Finally, he decided he could not and should not keep the news from Mansur any longer. He told of the last battle. All he left out was the part where he had watched Ibn Yasin die. That was too vivid for a son to hear. So he said that he rode up to the Emir's command post only to find him and Malik already dead.

Mansur remained impassive. He was listening, but a kind of shock had set in. His life had just changed in a way he had never dreamed it could.

"I saw the men had charged the command post, and I raced over, because I wanted to try to capture your father alive. I was too late," Ali said in a soft voice. The others in the room were silent.

"When I got to him, I closed his eyes and recited the prayer for closing the eyes. I did that for general Malik as well. Then I said the prayer for the dead, and asked Allah to find them a place in Paradise if it is His will," he continued. Mansur nodded, probably in thanks, but no one really noticed.

"Your father was buried south of Errbat. I left a guard to be sure no one disturbed his grave. Maybe one day you can go to visit it." The room was silent. Everyone was in their own thoughts, in the way that happens when someone discusses a recent death.

Ali reached into his sash with his fingers, and fumbled for a moment. He withdrew the medallion with the crescent moon and handed it to Mansur. "Your father had this around his neck, and I took it to send to his family. I see now that Allah intended it to be for you."

Mansur stared long at the medallion, then closed his fingers around it and held it to his heart. Tears fell from his eyes, but he didn't notice.

He looked at Ali and said, "Thank you for bringing this to me. It is the one item I remember from my father more than any other. When I was a boy and he would play with me, sometimes I would pull on his medallion, and he would always take my hand away, saying 'One day when you are older, I will give you one just like this.' I guess he forgot, but I never did."

He stopped speaking and swallowed hard. "Thank you."

Jamal and Moosa were sitting on either side of Mansur. Jamal put his arm around Mansur's shoulders, and said, "God's hand is in this memento, Mansur. I believe he is letting you know that it was His will to take your father as he did. This is the way He is letting you know that you should not grieve too hard. Your father's work here was done."

Samir just sat in silence. He already knew of Ibn Yasin's death, but hearing Ali's tale again drove it home for him. He had a bitter taste in his mouth. He suddenly wondered how he would feel if it were his father who had died. It made the moment very heavy for him.

Mansur nodded at Jamal's words, but wasn't really sure anyone ever knew why another's time had come. He didn't feel like debating, though. He felt as if the life had been sucked out of him. To everyone, it was clear the boy needed some time to be alone with his grief. Unfortunately, Ali had more to say.

"Brother Mansur, I am very sad to be the one to bring you this terrible news of your father. But we have other things to consider now that cannot wait long," he said gently. Ali began to discuss the political impact of Ibn Yasin's death, and how Mansur's life was now in danger.

"I think you need to leave Fez as soon as possible. Your father's enemies will come looking for you once the word gets out that he is gone. They will be afraid that the Almoravids will want to raise you up as the new leader, and there are factions for whom that is unacceptable. Your father's general Ibn Umar escaped the battle, and most likely he will assume command of the Almoravids. He is from a different tribe. You will be in his way."

Jamal and Moosa glanced quickly at each other. They had given no thought to what would happen next, and realized that Ali was right. They needed to find a plan to help Mansur escape to safety. But where? How? Samir might also be in danger.

"What can we do to help?" Jamal asked. "He will not be safe here, and he cannot go back to Awdaghust. He cannot remain in the university. People will go there first looking for him. He could live with us, but I'm afraid even that is unsafe. Everyone has seen Samir and Mansur together."

Samir said, "Will he be safe with his aunt and uncle? They have a big house and guards."

Ali said, "I doubt it. His aunt and uncle will be in danger, too. They should leave. Everyone associated with Ibn Yasin will be on shaky ground until the politicians have a chance to sort everything out and make any changes they will make. And no, he will not be safe in this house, either."

He turned to Mansur and asked, "Do you know of any safe place you could go? Do you have relatives in other cities?"

Mansur took a deep breath and rubbed the medallion in his hand absently with his thumb. He looked at Samir and nodded. Samir would understand what he had to say. "Yes." He paused. "I know where I will be safe, and it is a place I want to go. I will go to study with Sheikh Taqi al-Madyani in the desert."

The older men were surprised. They had never heard anything about this sheikh, but Samir knew the sheikh had had a profound impact on his friend. He realized instantly that this was a good solution. The only question was where in the desert they would find Sheikh Taqi. They had no idea.

CHAPTER 59

For another hour, everyone discussed the option of taking Mansur to study with the sheikh, and grudgingly agreed with him. It was a safe place to be for the next few years, if they could figure out how to get Mansur there. The sheikh had implied that he wanted Mansur to come and study with him.

Samir was chosen to do some discreet questioning at the university. Perhaps one of the professors or students knew where to find the sheikh. Samir asking would raise fewer questions than Jamal or Moosa.

Mansur suddenly realized that he would not be able to return to school to say goodbye to his friends. That made him sad, but it was necessary. Samir would have to be his messenger. One thing was certain, though—he had no intention of leaving Shams behind. Shams would go with him to the desert.

It was already very late, but Ali suggested that Mansur go night to bring his horse and any important belongings he needed from his aunt's house that night. No telling when the enemies of Ibn Yasin would get the news of his death and start rounding up his family. Samir would go with him.

Mansur insisted on writing a brief note to his aunt and uncle to thank them and tell them he was going to a safe place. He also wrote a note that Samir could show to Mansur's friends, explaining why he had to leave suddenly. That was the best he could do. He needed to leave soon, and as few people as possible should know where he was going or when he left.

The boys walked in silence to Mansur's house. The guard at the gate let them in at once with a comment that they were out very late. They tried to look normal, and said, "We are going out to the hills to look at stars tonight. There is a special lunar alignment later that we want to record." The guard knew they often went star gazing, so he nodded indifferently and let them pass.

Mansur slipped into the house and came out a short time later with a small bundle. They went to the stable quickly and saddled Shams. They tied the bundle on his back, and led him out the gate.

As they passed the guard, Mansur said, "If my aunt is looking for me, tell her I may not be home before tomorrow night. We will go straight to our classes in the morning." The guard nodded. He wasn't really interested in the comings and goings of the boys.

"Did you get everything you needed?" Samir whispered when they got down the street.

"Yes. I left the note on my bed where someone will find it. I brought my small telescope, a bedroll and some extra clothes for the road. I didn't bring food or water. That would have looked suspicious," Mansur said. "I brought my knife, some gold dinars and some writing tools. I also stopped to put this on a chain." He lifted his father's medallion out of his shirt, and let it slide back in.

Samir nodded. "Good. Don't worry, we have water skins and we can get food. Ali can go buy what we need in the morning. It will look less suspicious if he does it."

Mansur stopped suddenly in the road and turned to look at Samir. "You are saying 'we.'"

"Well, you didn't think I would let you go off alone in the desert on an adventure without me and my map, did you? What kind of a friend do you think I am?" Samir replied.

"A good one!" Mansur said. He was suddenly energized. "Come on. Let's get to the stables and go figure out what happens next."

They put Shams out of sight in a stall in Jamal's new camel stable. Mansur gave him feed and water while Samir went over to greet Amuna. He had completely forgotten to come see her today in all the excitement. She bellowed and squawked a few times, as if to reprimand him, then nuzzled his shoulder.

"We are going back to the desert, Amuna!" he said as he rubbed her neck. "Drink a lot. We have no idea where we are going!" Amuna didn't care. As long as Samir was nearby, she would be happy anywhere.

The boys went back to Samir's house. Moosa had already left to go home, saying he would be back the next day. Ali and Jamal were half dozing when the boys came in. They quickly decided on a plan. Mansur would stay out of sight in the house tomorrow. Samir would go to school early and see what he could find out about Sheikh Taqi's location. Ali would go to the market and buy supplies for a four-week trip for three.

Ali had decided to accompany Samir and Mansur. He was needed by General Yusuf, but he decided they would be riding more or less west, so he would make a diversion and go with them. He would help Samir to arrange for a way back to Fez, and then he would continue riding to the coast and get back to his military duties.

All that remained to do now was sleep and try to look normal for one more day. The boys would leave after dark the next night. Samir gave Ali his bed, and he and Mansur took bedrolls up to the roof to sleep under the stars.

CHAPTER 60

The next morning, Samir got lucky. He found one of the senior students from his philosophy class in the library. Samir dropped down cross legged on the red and gold wool carpet beside him. Samir asked if he had heard the lecture from Sheikh Taqi a few months before. The boy said he had, and he had gone to hear him speak again in another class.

"Do you know where he is from?" Samir asked innocently. "Someone said he lives out beyond Meknes oasis, and someone else said he lives in the cedar mountains near Azrou. It must be hard to live out in the middle of nowhere."

The boy said, "He is far west of Azrou. He mentioned that his students in the desert had helped him build a zawiyah where they hold their classes and sleep. It didn't sound like they lived anywhere near any oasis. It sounded like the middle of the emptiness. Maybe he found a spring or something out there. I sure wouldn't want to live like that."

Samir nodded. "Me either. I wonder how long it took him to get here for his lecture. Did someone from the university go to get him, or did they just ask him to stop by the next time he came to town?" The boys both laughed. No one just dropped by in these desert towns. They always had a purpose and a plan.

"I think it took him over a month. He mentioned starting the trip in one month and finishing it in the next. Why are you so interested? Are you planning to go visit him?" the boy asked.

"No, just thinking about my map making. I thought if we knew where he lived, I could put that spot as a point of interest on my map. But I don't want to spoil my map with mistakes if no one really knows," Samir dodged. At least he had more information now than the night before.

Meanwhile, Ali had found a guide to take him back to the barracks. He went to bathe and changed into a clean uniform. It felt really good to be clean. It would probably be at least two more months before he felt clean again. He slipped into the mess hall and managed to get some breakfast just as the last soldiers were finishing. They took no notice of him.

As a courtesy, he needed to inform the commander that he was leaving. He went to his office, and was offered some thick coffee.

"You are leaving us so soon, Malakh? You have only just arrived," the commander said.

"Yes, unfortunately, with the big news about Ibn Yasin, I must get back on the road as soon as possible.

There is likely to be a lot of unrest until the government stabilizes again. I need to get back to the coast," Ali replied.

"That is true. I am preparing my men to start guard duty at the residences of all the important families here, as well as the gates. With our crazy roads and alleys, I don't worry about being invaded, but there is likely to be some civil unrest here. I will do what I can to keep things calm."

"General Yusuf will appreciate your efforts, Commander. I will let him know. Thank you for your hospitality. Perhaps I will be back in Fez again soon and I will come by," Ali said, as he stood to leave. The men shook hands and saluted.

Ali went out to the stable and saddled Gawa. He rode toward the mosque, and followed the west wall north. The muezzin sang the adnaan, so he stopped and prayed in the street where he was.

He mounted again, and at the next corner, he found a busy market. He took the opportunity to buy the supplies they would need for their journey. No one paid much attention to a soldier buying food and stacking it onto his horse. He was obviously a messenger about to head out into the desert.

Gawa was piled high with goods, so Ali walked him to Jamal's stable. It was actually easy to find coming from this direction. Jamal was busy tending his camels, and put Gawa into an empty stall next to Shams. They unloaded the horse, then walked back to the house together, and joined Mansur, who had been restlessly trying to stay out of sight.

Ali informed them of his plan to escort the boys to Sheikh Taqi's place, and Jamal was relieved. Ali had rank, and he seemed to know his way around in the desert. The boys would not be on their own. It would be odd for an Almohad to be escorting the son of the dead Almoravid leader, and that would help even more to disguise them. Mansur seemed relieved, too. He had only traveled with escorts before, and had had all morning to think about the dangers in what he and Samir were about to do on their own. This eased some of the anxiety.

Samir came home to find his house full again. Moosa had come by. He took Samir aside and handed him ten gold dinars.

"Put this in your water bag," Moosa said with a wink. "You shouldn't be in the desert without a way to buy water or bribe a soldier." Samir thanked him and tucked the coins into his sash.

Father and Ali were busy talking about timing and logistics. Mansur was sitting alone for the moment, so Samir joined him. "I have a little news," he told his friend.

Mansur perked up and asked, "What?"

"You remember that know-it-all Egyptian boy Mahmud in philosophy class? He had some information about Sheikh Taqi's zawiyah."

"Great! Where is it? I have been going over everything he said in the lecture and what he said to me again and again. He gave no clues at all, and yet I had the strong feeling he was telling me to come to find him. Maybe part of the training is the finding." Mansur said.

"It could be. But Mahmud was more helpful. He said the zawiyah is west of Azrou oasis, about halfway to the coast. Outside the cedars. He said the sheikh may have found a hidden spring and built his school there. Now we just have to ask people in Azrou if there is water on the way to the coast. At least it is the start of a plan. And we know how to get to Azrou, thanks be to God!" Samir was feeling jolly.

"I guess now we will have a chance to see if you were paying attention in astronomy," Mansur said. "We are about to test that map you keep scratching on."

Mansur smiled. "Father would be pleased that we are taking this 'character building' challenge. I don't think he would be pleased that I will study with Sheikh Taqi, though. Father's conservative Islam is good for imposing order and law on a people, but I believe Allah wants us to go beyond the law and understand the unity of creation. This is what I hope to learn from Sheikh Taqi anyway, insh'allah."

"Whatever you learn, you should be safe out there in the middle of the emptiness," Samir said. "By the time you are ready to leave Sheikh Taqi, the world will be changed, and you will find your place in it again."

Mansur nodded, and both boys fell into deep thought. They would be leaving everything familiar that night.

CHAPTER 61

The boys and Ali ate a big dinner. They had adequate food for the journey, but the unexpected can always happen. Father had gone to the stables twice today to feed and water the animals. He had filled six large water bags, and they were waiting to be loaded. He and Ali had discussed what might be needed for traveling with two horses, since they need food and water every day.

In the end, they decided to take one of the pack camels along. He would be strong enough to carry two barrels of water for the horses, plus some of the other heavy items.

As the sun set, the muezzin sang the call to prayer. They all bowed down in the room where they were. They each had their own prayers in their hearts, and they did not rush the moment. When they stood, each one said simply, Thank you, and gripped the shoulders of the others. There was nothing else to be said.

Ali took charge. "Okay, this is how we will go," he said. "We must try not to draw attention to ourselves. Mansur, you will take Shams and only a small pack and water bag. That way you will look absolutely ordinary. Ride out the east gate with your hood up, and go about two kilometers down the road. Wait for us off to the side."

"Samir, you will load some of our travel items on Amuna, and I will put some on Gawa. You and I will ride out the north gate. If anyone sees us, it will seem as if we are going to the hills for the night to look at stars. We will double back to the east and join Mansur on the east road, God willing."

"Jamal and Moosa, load what is left on the pack camel, and lead him to the south gate by midnight. Go to the caravanserai there. I will bring Samir and Mansur around to the south side, somewhere off the main road. Then I will come to the caravanserai alone and take the pack camel. By breaking up into small units, we will draw less attention to ourselves. No one will think anything of two brothers walking a camel out to a caravanserai at night. Or of a messenger soldier setting off on a long ride with a loaded camel," Ali said.

"It should be days at least before anyone realizes that Mansur has gone. By the time they come looking for Samir and find he is gone, too, we will be almost to the first oasis. As far as you know, the boys had said they were going north to the hills for two nights to study a new constellation. That will misdirect any searchers to look in the north."

Ali gave the plan a moment to sink in, then said, "We will ride fast until we get near Azrou. I plan to avoid entering the oasis. Amuna is very visible, so traveling at night is our best bet. We will turn west before we reach the cedars, and stay out of sight as much as possible. Any questions?" Ali asked.

There were none. Now all the moving pieces just had to come together on the south side of town around midnight.

CHAPTER 62

Mansur and Ali set off to the stable about an hour later. Samir followed a few minutes behind. He had to turn around after a block and go back, because he had forgotten a treat for Amuna. He knew she would be noisy if he didn't have something. The two horses were already loaded, so Samir went to her pen and greeted her with two dates. She was restless and wanted a run, so she was glad to see him.

He had her kneel, and placed the wooden pack frame over a blanket on her back. He loaded one water bag and some saddlebags of food. His bedroll was in the corner, so he tucked it under a strap. He was almost ready. Just then, Moosa and father came hurrying around the corner into the stable. This was unexpected.

Moosa came up to Samir and said, "I almost forgot something very important. Something you need when you are riding this snowflake of a camel in the desert."

He lifted a sack he was carrying and handed it to Samir. "It is four of my big, brown burnooses," he said. "They will be good cover for her and might help to disguise you."

Samir was pleased. He had just been thinking that the last time he packed Amuna's frame, he had tucked Uncle Moosa's burnooses under a strap. He gave one each to Mansur and Ali, and tucked the other two onto Amuna's back. Now he was ready to go. He thanked his uncle.

Father and Moosa bid them all good journey one more time, and went back to the house. The boys waited half an hour more for any neighbors to settle down. Then Ali told Mansur it was time to go. Mansur nodded and mounted up. He knew his way around town after a year and a half of living there, so waved at his friends silently and headed toward the east gate in an indirect way, trying to avoid any squares or large open places where he might be spotted.

All went as planned. Mansur trotted out of the east gate and galloped Shams for about two kilometers. He spotted some large rocks ahead to the right, and pulled off behind them. The moon was almost full. He hid the horse, and crouched down where he could watch the road.

Half an hour later, Ali and Samir rode Amuna and Gawa to the north gate. They both had water bags and bundles, as if they were going to be out for a day or two. They rode north for about fifteen minutes, then paused to see if they could hear or spot anyone else. The desert was silent. They got off the road to the right and rode about half an hour through low dunes, keeping the walls of Fez on their right in the distance.

When they hit the main eastern road, Ali stopped and studied the terrain. They were not quite two kilometers out of town, so they got onto the trade route and trotted east.

In a few minutes, Ali spotted rocks off to the right, and thought that might be a good spot. As they rode up, Mansur revealed himself, and mounted. The three of them widened the distance between the city and themselves, and veered around toward the south. The deep dunes were tricky to navigate in that area, and it slowed them down a bit.

A while later, they hit the southern trade route, and they rode across it. The sand dunes were heavy off to the other side as well, but the road itself was flat. Anyone coming along at night would be on the road.

The boys would hide in a valley between two dunes and wait for Ali to return. He cautioned them not to talk and to keep the animals still, then he rode back toward the trade route and turned toward Fez. He neared the gate without passing anyone, and turned toward the caravanserai.

Jamal greeted him at the entrance. The caravanserai was empty except for the pack camel. This was a piece of luck. There would be fewer people to notice them.

Moosa had come with Jamal to the gate, but they had been stopped by a soldier who wanted to know why they were out so late with a loaded camel.

Moosa always had a way of befriending people, so he immediately turned on his charm, and complained that he had to get out of bed to help his half-wit brother bring this camel over. Some messenger was riding through that night and he had been promised a double fee if they met the rider at the gate. He managed to get the soldier to walk back into town with him, freeing Jamal to meet Ali.

The men didn't waste any time. The soldier might come back. Ali leaned down and gripped the wrist of Jamal for a moment in friendship. Jamal handed him the reins of the camel, and said, "Take care of my boy." Ali nodded. Then he turned and rode away. Jamal wondered if he would ever see his son or his friends again.

CHAPTER 63

The ride to Azrou oasis was uneventful. They were a small group on good animals, and made good time. Ali left the boys outside the first small water stop chewing on dried cheese and fruit. He led the pack camel in and refilled the water barrels without raising any suspicions.

A lot of soldiers were on the roads these days, so no one even asked his business. He would have loved to bathe, but decided that would unfair to the boys, since they couldn't, so he rode out as dirty as he had ridden in.

Each time they stopped to rest, Samir pulled out one of uncle Moosa's burnooses and spread it over Amuna. She was the most likely to be spotted. Any time they stopped, he busily marked on his map. He noted any patches of scrub trees he spotted. Not only were trees good for shade and fires, but they indicated water in the area. A desperate man might be able to dig for some and save his life. At least, that was his thinking.

The closer they got to Azrou, the quieter Mansur had become. Samir tried to tell him Mullah Baba stories and make him laugh, but it didn't work.

"Hey, Mansur, here's one for you. Mullah Baba was wandering in a graveyard. He stumbled and fell into an old grave. He began to visualize how it would feel if he were dead, and he heard a noise. He thought that the Angel of Reckoning was coming for him, but it was just a camel caravan passing by. The Mullah jumped up and fell over a wall, stampeding several camels. The camel handlers beat him with sticks.

"He ran home in a distressed state. His wife asked him, 'What is the matter? Why are you late and why are you covered with dirt?' He said, 'I have been dead.' Interested in spite of herself, she asked what it was like to be dead. 'Not bad at all,' said the Mullah, 'unless you disturb the camels. Then they beat you!'"

Ali smiled, but Mansur just kept staring at the road. The ride was fatiguing, and Mansur was dealing with the loss of his father, the potential dangers of the journey, and the uncertainty of what awaited him ahead. His mind was clearly somewhere else.

On the sixth day, when they stopped to rest from the midday heat, Ali said, "It is likely that anyone we meet from here on will know that Ibn Yasin has died. We need to be very careful. If anyone approaches, let me talk. I will say that the turmoil and uncertainty has caused your parents living south of Marrakesh to want you back home. They hired me to bring you as quickly as possible."

The boys nodded. It seemed to be a good story. Ali knew the area around Marrakesh, and would be able to talk convincingly about it. Ali also took the extra step of rewrapping Mansur's turban in the Almohad style, just to avoid any questions. To Mansur this was a violation of his father's memory, but he realized it was necessary.

The next morning, they spotted the beginning of the cedar forest around Azrou. It was like a small island in a big sea of endless sand with mountains in the far distance. Both boys wished they could enter the oasis and swim, or camp in the shade of the big cedars, but they knew this was the riskiest part of the journey. Ali found them a safe spot to rest on the northwest side in the dunes There was a little grass there, which kept Shams busy.

Like before, Ali rode into the oasis alone to refill their supplies. As the animals drank, he managed to overhear a few conversations. He went back to the boys, carrying a delicious surprise—some fresh bread, tomatoes, stewed lamb with olives and honey cakes. That would cheer them.

As they ate, Ali said, "I was right. Word got around very fast about Ibn Yasin. The oasis was full of talk about what would happen next. They believe General Ibn Umar is now in control, and he is regrouping his army in the desert east of Marrakesh. There is a lot of traffic heading that direction. We will need to stay off the main roads except at night. From this point on, we aren't sure where we are going. Allah will have to guide us," he said simply.

"I believe we will ride a day and a half along the western road out of Azrou, trying to stay out of sight. Then we will head southwest for half a day. I have an old map I bought in Azrou last time I was here that marked water spots. There isn't much marked in the area where we are going, but it looks like there may be a spring somewhere out there. If the information you got was right, Samir, it points to the same general area. Perhaps the sheikh will meet us on the road and guide us to his zawiyah himself!" he laughed.

No one joined in the laughter. He realized the boys were really feeling the stress of the journey, so he decided to slow the pace a bit and give them a chance to relax.

"Let's rest until evening. After night prayers, we will start again."

The sun was still high. They each made their own little tent from their robes and riding sticks to block the sun. Samir took his usual position, lying on Amuna's neck.

After the good food, they all managed to sleep well, alone with their own thoughts. Mansur had a dream that he met Sheikh Taqi. He was saying, "You will come when the time is right, Abdallah," and his eyes were like the dark, velvety night sky. The call to prayer ringing in the distance finally woke them after dark. After the rest and the prayers, they set off in better spirits.

CHAPTER 64

The next two days sped by. They managed to avoid nearly all traffic on the main road in the night, and when they veered off to the southwest, the dunes were flatter and there was more vegetation. Now they would look for signs of other travelers or nomads. Perhaps someone would know a place with a well or the place they were seeking.

The next morning they came over a rise and saw spread below them distinct patches of green. It was a pleasing shock to eyes accustomed to darkness and sand. Someone was farming the little hidden valley below. They decided to approach to see if they could get any information. As they got closer, they could make out a small, conical house of mud brick in the center. Two wooden sheds were on either side, and there was a small pen holding one donkey. He was probably used to plow the fields.

They swung wide to approach the circular building from the front. Ali said, "Unless I heard wrong, this style of building is a zawiyah."

There were four tiny windows near the top, and some cedar branches extended out of the opening at the peak where smoke could escape. The front door was made of wood, and filled a rounded arch. It was open. As they rode toward the door, a small man walked out toward them and opened his arms.

"Welcome, travelers. Marhaba. May I offer you some tea?" he asked.

Mansur's stomach was in a knot. It was Sheikh Taqi. They dismounted. Mansur was drawn toward him like a magnet, and found his feet walking on their own. The small man turned and his face lit up like a thousand suns pouring light over Mansur. He extended his arms, and said, "I knew you would come, my son. The Divine light in you is great, Abdallah."

He didn't know why, but for the first time in his life Mansur felt like he was home. All the pain, sorrow, fatigue and tension drained out of him. He dropped his head and burst into tears. They were healing tears.

The afternoon passed in small talk and ordinary things, but under the surface it felt like something exceptional was happening that no one could quite put their finger on. No one mentioned Mansur's emotional outburst. There was no question that Sheikh Taqi would accept Mansur, or that Mansur wanted to stay. The sheikh had four other students who lived at the zawiyah, and they would return the next day from running errands.

Ali and Samir had questions. They didn't understand Mansur's reaction at all. They were a little stirred up by it.

Ali asked, "Sheikh Taqi, why do you live out here where no one can hear your words? Wouldn't it be better for you to teach in the university or the mosque? You would have many students."

The sheikh replied, "My teacher Abu Madyani, peace be upon him, taught that we are to reject the world and study the Divine law. What better place than here? My students find me. We live here with quiet self-discipline and submission to the will of God. We are walis, the friends of God. In the *Qur'an* it says 'the walis of God need neither fear nor grieve.' God provides."

Samir asked the sheikh, "It seems you knew that Mansur would one day come to live here with you. How did you know? And how does he know that this is the right thing for him to do? Shouldn't he follow in the shoes of his father?"

The sheikh closed his eyes to think about the question behind the questions.

"The friend asks what his friend cannot," he said finally, and opened his eyes. "When the Almighty sends down souls to earth, they each have a unique purpose or vision to fulfill. If we are wise and pay attention, there are moments when we receive clear guidance that we are on our path or we have left it. To be on our path brings joy and peace of mind. To be off of it, causes pain, heartache and disappointment. No man's path is like any other's path. No man can judge any other's life. We can only observe that when a person's heart is joyful, it is a sign of a pure spirit attuned to their purpose. When a person's heart is heavy, they are burdened with things they were not meant to carry. Truth that sets one back on his life's path hits the heart as a flash of powerful insight. Our brother's tears are tears of joy," he said, and glanced at Mansur, "though he has yet to understand."

The sheikh was silent for a few minutes to let his words sink in.

"There are two paths in this life," he continued. "The path of the sacred warrior goes down from the All to the creation. Emir Ibn Yasin was a sacred warrior, bringing down the law and the teachings of the Prophet, peace be upon him. The path of the saint goes up, bringing all of creation with it toward the All. That is the path I follow. We all have one path or the other."

Mansur had been silent since they arrived. He coughed, and said, "Sheikh Taqi, why do you call me Abdallah? My name is Mansur."

The sheikh gave a sideways glance to Mansur and said, "Your father named your infant body Mansur, but the name of your spirit is Abdallah, the servant of Allah. I see no Mansur before me, only Abdallah. You have found your path that was lost."

The sheikh then turned to Ali and said, "My son, you are a warrior, and you are on your path. You know where your destiny leads you. Follow your heart." Ali nodded thoughtfully.

"And you," he turned to Samir. "You have yet to touch your destiny. You have barely begun your journey, and you have obligations to fulfill before you discover your road at last."

All of the boys were silent as they reflected on what the teacher had said.

After a time, Sheikh Taqi stood and showed the boys where they could wash up. He went to prepare dinner for them. After a delicious meal of chickpeas with chopped onions, tomatoes and garlic, salted goat cheese, and fresh bread spread with ground olives, they sat in the cool shadows outside.

It was extremely peaceful there. The only sounds were an occasional gust of wind brushing sand along the ground, or of the camels chewing. They all slept that night thinking of the sheikh's words and what the new day would bring. The dark night sky spread its blanket of stars over them.

As the next day unfolded, Mansur already seemed at ease in this new location. The other students returned from their errands before dinner. Sheikh Taqi introduced Mansur to them, and he was welcomed warmly. Mansur was pleased to feel like he would fit in, and even joined two of the students in their chores.

By evening it was clear that Ali and Samir should leave that night. It would be a difficult parting. Mansur would remain in his chosen place with Shams. Ali was restless to get back to his army, and instead of waiting another day, planned to ride west with Gawa before sunrise and locate General Yusuf. That left Samir entirely alone.

Ali and Samir had a long talk in the afternoon about whether he thought he could make it back to Fez alone. He would take both camels, and could fill his water bags here. He believed he could do it. He split the feed they carried with Ali, so the two camels would have one good meal in a few days. That should see them home in good shape. Ali would take the rest for Gawa.

Samir had felt safe riding off the roads with Ali and Mansur along, but he knew it would be different when he was alone. It still would not be safe for him to approach the oases on his widely known white camel. But he did have his map and three long journeys across the desert under his belt. He felt like he could make the trip alone. There might also be a caravan he could join once he got north of Azrou. As long as he had Amuna, he felt like he was the master of the desert.

CHAPTER 65

The decision made, Ali departed just after evening prayers. He hugged his two young friends, gripped their shoulders and wished them well.

Samir departed the zawiyah around midnight. He was becoming familiar with the night sky, and riding was always cooler at night, so to him it made sense to ride at night and stop for the day. He sat for an hour or so with Mansur in the deep quiet under the thick blanket of stars before he left. They reminisced about some of their adventures together, and acknowledged that they didn't know when they might see each other again

Samir could tell that Mansur would be fine here. It was a place of peace and reflection, and it would be healing to Mansur's grief, as well as suited to his thoughtful nature. Samir was amused to think of this rich son of a former emir growing his own vegetables and shoveling out horse stalls, but he also knew a person can get used to anything.

Finally, he stood up to go. It was time. Staying would not make his journey any shorter, and having Amuna so visible in this place was probably not good for the sheikh. He went into the zawiyah, and bowed to Sheikh Taqi.

"I will leave now, Sayyid. Thank you for your hospitality and for taking in my good friend. I know he will be happy here and learn a lot from you," Samir said.

The sheikh looked up from his reading, stood up, and came over to take Samir's hands in his. The candle flickered, casting shadows around the room.

"You are a khalil'ullah, Samir--a friend of Allah, like the prophet Ibrahim. You are attuned to His bidding. We shall see you again here, if God is willing. Your friend is in the right place, so don't worry about him. God be with you on your journey."

Something about the sheikh's presence was exhilarating, and Samir was suddenly ready to go and wide awake. He walked out and gripped Mansur's shoulders affectionately. "Don't give the old man a lot of trouble. And watch where you step in the animal pens." He laughed.

Then, more seriously, he said, "He said we will meet again, Mansur. Goodbye until then. Be well and stay safe." Mansur nodded and gripped Samir's shoulders back. He was going to miss this true friend.

"Ride safely, camel boy," Mansur said. "Do you have your map?"

Samir nodded and patted his belt with a smile. He had tied the pack camel's harness to Amuna's frame. Amuna was kneeling and waiting for him. He climbed onto her back and said, "Up, Muna. Up." She lumbered to her feet with some gravely noises, and they turned to face Mansur.

"Go with God," Mansur said, and the boys waved goodbye. They were both starting new adventures. Mansur turned to go into the zawiyah. Samir kicked Amuna and took off riding to the northwest. The north star Yildun was visible off to the right of Amuna's shoulder and the pack camel trailed behind.

Unlike other trips through the desert, this one was fairly easy. Since he rode at his own speed and at night, he was able to use the hard packed trade routes most of the time. The pack camel kept up well. As they got closer to Azrou, the ground became hillier and rocky, giving him many options for safe hiding during the day, especially with Amuna draped in Uncle Moosa's cloak. He made it back to Fez in eight days, almost two days ahead of schedule.

CHAPTER 66

After he returned home, Samir entered his normal routine again. He went back to his classes and studied astronomy intently. He was learning about the variations that occur in the skies at different seasons of the year, and found it challenging. Samir and his father missed Mansur's company. He had become like part of the family.

Alama was due to give birth within a few days. It was her first calf since Amuna, and Samir reflected on how much their fortunes had changed in three short years.

Both he and Jamal were very interested to see what kind of a baby she would produce this time. And whether she would mother it. He said a little prayer of hope that she would, because he didn't see how he could take time from his studies to milk Alama and feed a calf around the clock.

Three nights later, Alama delivered a little brown male calf. The baby stood up quickly on his shaky legs and tried to walk. Alama sniffed him a few times and walked away. But this time when Samir led the baby over to nurse, she allowed him. Father and son were both very relieved not to have to nurse another baby for six months.

Amuna was in the next pen, and leaned her head over the fence rail with great interest to watch the birth and the new calf. They still didn't know whether she was pregnant or not, but if so, a year from now they would be helping her with her own baby.

The next year passed quickly. Samir had decided not to give Mansur's note to his friends to read. He had been too revealing. Instead, Samir met the boys one by one and told them that Mansur had to go to a safe place, and no one knew where that was. They all seemed to understand. He had lost his father in a very dramatic way, and everyone speculated that Mansur might have been in danger.

Being boys, they sat and whispered all kinds of stories about where he probably had gone and the kind of grizzly death he would probably face wandering alone out in the desert. None of them were even close to the truth.

One day some Almoravid soldiers came to Jamal's house, and Samir was questioned about Mansur, but he looked them in the eye and said that they had said goodbye one evening and he had not seen Mansur since then. It was true; he only let them believe it happened on the night Mansur supposedly left town. The soldiers said to contact them if he heard from Mansur, and then left.

Amuna showed signs of pregnancy a month after they returned from the desert. Father was thrilled. Soon she became so round and fat that Samir didn't ride her at all. Some days she seemed to want to go to run, but she was in no shape for it.

When she got really restless and shoved him around with her nose, Samir would take her for a walk. Usually that was enough. By the time they had gone a kilometer or so and walked back, she was happy to be home. She was round like a giant ball, and could barely find a comfortable way to sit on the ground. Samir was worried that Qadr's baby would get too big for Amuna to deliver.

Finally father said her time was up, and she should be delivering any day. Samir took up residence in the stable so he could be with her. He hoped she would be a good mother, and not like Alama had been. The afternoon her contractions started, he was with her. The first ones caught her off guard, and she bellowed in surprise and pain. Samir ran home to tell father, but he was not there. Samir took a bowl of butter and returned to the stall. It would be a long evening. He expected her labor to last for 6-8 hours.

Father finally came to the stable about five hours later, and checked her to see how she was doing. It looked like the baby would emerge soon. A short time later, Amuna knelt on her front legs and spread her back legs wide. The baby was coming.

Minutes later two little feet and spindly legs emerged and then a brown nose. Jamal wiped the baby's face so it could breathe, and then the rest of the body came pouring out in a rush onto the straw. It was a little brown male, and he started to breathe right away. Father cut the umbilical cord.

Amuna turned to nuzzle him, and tried to lick him a little, but she was distracted or didn't know what to do next.

Samir helped the baby to stand and wobble over to his mother's teats. She refused him.

"Oh no," said father. "Don't tell me she is going to do this like her mother did!" Father tried to bring the baby to his mother once more, but she turned away. This time she bellowed again.

Father and Samir looked with confusion at each other, and Jamal went to check what was going on with her. He couldn't believe what he saw. Two more little feet were emerging!

"Samir! We have twins! I never saw such a thing. Here comes another one!" father said. "I will take the calf over here, and you help Amuna."

Twins are so rare in camels that neither of them had ever heard of a twin birth before. Yet here it was, happening right in front of their eyes. Samir talked softly to Amuna, and patted her back and neck. She was working very hard. A few minutes later a little white nose poked out on top of the spindly legs. The head followed and then a minute later the whole calf fell to the ground. Samir cut the umbilical cord. Amuna was panting as if she had run very hard, and making soft growling noises.

The second baby was a girl. At first, Samir thought they had another white camel, but the baby had brown spots on her belly and back legs. She was still beautiful.

Amuna turned around and looked for both of her babies. She began to lick the little girl and nudge it to stand.

She seemed to know what was needed. Father had been putting butter on his finger and feeding the little male to teach him to nurse. He brought the baby over and he immediately latched on to his mother. Amuna didn't flinch or kick. Father and son looked at each other with big smiles.

"Oh, that is a relief!" Jamal said. "I was starting to get worried. Now if we can just get the little girl to do it, too."

Samir fed her butter on his fingers, and within a few minutes she was strong enough to stand and nurse. Samir put her on the opposite side from her brother, and she attached herself right away. He walked around to Amuna's face and stroked her cheeks and nose. She kept making soft growling noises, as if she were singing to her babies, and occasionally turned around to lick one calf or the other.

This was a momentous night. The fastest camel in the Maghrib now had two calves by another great racer. They could hardly wait to see what would come of these babies. Tomorrow Jamal would send a note to Qadr's owner to tell him the news.

Jamal and Samir sat against the fence rail to rest. Alama and her calf had walked over and peered over the fence at Amuna's babies for a few minutes. Alama then turned back to her own, who was now nine months old. Father asked, "What shall we call them?"

Samir had been thinking the baby might be a boy. The little male was the first calf. He said, "I would like to name the boy Yasin."

Father looked a little surprised. "But why name him after a dead man?"

"Because Ibn Yasin had a powerful exterior, but a kind heart. He wasn't my enemy. The other day when I was thinking of names, I looked in the *Qur'an* for the surah 'Ya Sin'. It describes one who has a strong personality, but is fair and has a loving nature. Naming this calf Yasin would be a gesture of respect, and yet many people will see the name and think we are ridiculing a dead enemy. It will be our secret. Only we will know the truth."

Jamal was a little confused by the explanation, but it did seem like Samir had put some thought into it, so he went along. "Yasin it will be, then. And the little female? Did you have a girl's name in mind, too?"

Samir said, "No, but one came to me just now. The baby can be Noor Amuna, Light from the Moon. She is mostly white, so we can call her Noor. What do you think?"

Father nodded thoughtfully, and said, "I like it. Yasin and Noor Amuna. Our herd has increased by twenty per cent this night, thanks be to God. Now let's get some sleep. It's going to be hectic around here with all these calves!"

Father left to return home. Samir yawned. He went over to pat Amuna and the babies, who were lying together on the straw in the far corner of the pen. He laid down in the corner of the pen to sleep. He would stay there with Amuna and the babies overnight. He was starting to doze off, then he remembered something. He had promised Ibn Yasin Amuna's first calf. It was on his conscience. He stood up to freshen the straw in the pen and patted Amuna affectionately one more time. He would wait another day or two to remind his father that they had to give baby Yasin away.

CHAPTER 67

From the day of their birth, the twin camels grew rapidly. Both of them had the distinctive bodies of racing camels with long slender legs, low humps and sleek bodies-- even with plump little newborn bodies. Amuna was feeding them well.

Samir finished his second year at the university, and as he had done with Amuna, he hurried home each day to play with and train the little camels. Because he had ridden Amuna in three races and won, he was the family expert on raising racing camels. Father let him do as he wished with them.

One thing Samir had learned from their mother was that Amuna could understand many more words than he had first thought. He enjoyed teaching the babies to lift their individual legs on command by just saying a word, and to hold their heads pointed up to the sky. It wouldn't help them to be better racers, but it kept them entertained as the twins grew and it taught them to follow commands.

By the time a year had passed, Samir knew he had to have a serious talk with father. One afternoon as he walked home from the university, he decided to do it at dinner.

"Father, we need to talk about Noor and Yasin," he said, as they were eating.

Father nodded and dipped some flatbread into the stew. They talked often about the babies and the camel business. One day it would belong to Samir, and his father wanted him to know all he could know.

"Do you remember when I told you the story of when I first saw Emir Ibn Yasin and Mansur in the desert outside of Awdaghust?"

Jamal nodded.

"Ibn Yasin was going to take Amuna from me, but we made a deal. I promised him I would bring him her first calf. He said to me that if I didn't do it in a reasonable time, he would come to Fez himself and take Amuna away," Samir said. "Of course, some would say that since he died, my obligation ended."

Jamal paused to look intently at his son for a moment, then kept chewing. He knew where this conversation was going. "What do you say, my son?"

Samir said, "I think I made a promise, and I have to keep it. I made an intention before God that I would do something, and it remains undone. Now I have the means to keep my word, but you need to agree with me. These camels are yours, so I would be taking your camel."

"They are our camels," Father said graciously. "I knew we would have this conversation one day, Samir. Before you struggle more with explaining, let me tell how I see this situation."

"First, since God blessed us with two calves, He clearly intended one for each of us," he continued. "He knew of your promise, and He provided you with a means to fulfill that promise. And He gave us another one to race. It was an answer to both our prayers," Father said.

"Thank you, father. I hoped you would see it the same way. I have been thinking about what I should do, and I believe the right answer is to take Noor and give her to Mansur," Samir replied.

"Why Noor?" Father asked with genuine surprise. "She would be a good breeding animal, whether she wins any races or not. She has a good pedigree."

"To me it is obvious that Yasin will be the better racer," Samir said. "He is already bigger than Noor, like his father, and he is very smart. You should keep him. I think he will be faster than his mother or his father."

"Noor is gentle, and might not have the heart of a racer," he continued. "Mansur could breed her and sell the calves to help his life in the desert. She could also give milk for the zawiyah. We will still have Amuna. She has a long life ahead of her, and will deliver more females, insh'allah."

Samir had had months to think up his arguments. Father appeared to think hard about the problem, but he already knew his answer.

"Yes, I agree with you that taking Noor to Mansur is the right decision. You made your promise, and I agree that you should keep it. I also owe a debt of thanks to Mansur and his family for bringing you safely home. He was like a second son to me when he was here. Noor will be our gift."

The young camels were still in the awkward stage, with long gangly legs and voices that croaked unexpectedly when they tried to communicate. They would be weaned soon, so Jamal and Samir decided that it would be a good time to go in about two months.

Samir began to train the calves differently, because their lives would be different. He couldn't yet ride Yasin, but he put saddles on him and taught him voice commands that would help him during a race. He let Yasin follow along when he took Amuna out to the desert to run.

He trained Noor to carry loads. He placed small pack frames on Noor's back with light loads and taught her caravan commands.

Amuna watched all this activity placidly. She still greeted Samir affectionately each day when he came, and he still brought her treats. Now he also brought treats for the babies.

Lately he had started to feed the camels their treats standing outside the pen, because having three big animals charging at him wanting their treats when he arrived was intimidating. They would not hurt him, but he had been knocked down a few times and stepped on, so he decided to be kind to himself and let the young ones get better control of their bodies.

Two months later, Samir was between seasons in his studies, so he talked with his father about the trip to see Mansur. The babies were eating grass and grain and were weaned, and he wanted to plan his journey.

Samir had been thinking of what he could take for a gift in addition to Noor. He had decided to give Mansur a copy of his map. He purchased a gazelle skin parchment, and had spent hours every morning for a month meticulously redrawing the ground map and the overlay of stars. When he finished, he signed his name in the corner.

Yes, this will be a very good gift, he thought. Samir rolled up the map carefully, and put it into the bedroll that he would take on the journey.

As the departure day drew closer, Father helped him to buy supplies for the trip, as well as a crate of dried food and some fabrics that he thought might be useful to the zawiyah.

Amuna would carry Samir's belongings and the supplies for the journey, and Noor would carry the gifts plus two water bags.

He didn't know how fast he would be able to travel with Noor. When he had taken Amuna on her first long journey, it had been in the slow paced caravan. She had had time to build up her muscles and stamina over time. He would have to monitor Noor's fatigue and remember to check her pads.

At least they didn't have to go through any gravel pans or rocky areas like on the way to Awdaghust. The only rocky stretch of any size would be near Azrou, when he detoured around the oasis to avoid being seen.

It seemed odd to be planning to set off on such a long trip entirely alone. Samir knew it would be hard to travel without anyone to talk to for weeks, but he had his map to update, and Amuna and Noor would be with him. The political unrest had calmed in the past year as General Ibn Umar gained control over the Almoravids, so travel felt reasonably safe again. Especially for someone traveling fast.

The day before he was to leave, Jamal and Moosa prepared a big, hearty dinner for Samir. They went over his plans one more time until everyone was satisfied.

Samir woke before dawn the next morning and set off for the stable. Father walked with him, and helped him to load the animals. As he liked to do, father reached into his belt and pulled out some gold coins for Samir.

"It is always good to have money when you travel," he said, and handed him the coins. "Give Mansur my good wishes, and tell him he is welcome here any time."

Then he counted out ten more dinars and gave them to Samir. "These are to repay our debt," Jamal said. "Emir Ibn Yasin paid your entry fee in Awdaghust, and we never repaid him. Give this to Mansur, too."

Samir smiled and thanked his father. "I will, Father. If Noor travels well, I believe I will be back in about a month."

"Be safe, my son," Father said. "God be with you on your journey. I will be waiting for your return. Remember to pray." A good father always has to remind his son of something, no matter how old they are.

Samir smiled and put the coins into his belt. He still had the gold Uncle Moosa had given him in his water bag. "Thank you, father, I will," he said as he mounted Amuna. Then he said, "Up, 'Muna."

She snorted as her back legs and then her front unfolded. Noor followed suit with a rumbling gurgle, and watched Samir expectantly with big brown eyes. Both camels were ready to run.

CHAPTER 68

Samir rode out of his father's stable and guided the camels through the winding alleys of Fez to the south side of town. Several people waved as he passed. Amuna was well known in Fez now for her racing successes. As he approached the main gate, he could see the sand dunes in the distance amid some nearby scraggly trees growing from the rocky landscape. A few merchants had set up stalls near the gate for travelers.

The main trade route led straight south for a distance, and the scene looked like a painting framed in the peacock blue tiles that surrounded the arched opening. He loved the beginning of long trips. The moment was pregnant with the unknown.

It seemed strange to be riding through the gate on Amuna, heading out to the desert to see Mansur, in broad daylight. He rarely traveled by day, preferring the cool of night and the ceiling of stars to the heat and pale blue dome of day. But today was the first day of the journey, and Noor had just been weaned. It was her first trip. Samir wanted to gauge her stamina on an easy road before he started pressing her through the big dunes and rocky patches further ahead. The callouses on her feet, knees and belly were still forming, and her small hump had not developed enough yet to store reserves for a long journey. He was uncertain how long this journey would take, and she was the reason why.

When he and Amuna had come back from Sheikh Taqi's zawiyah almost two years ago, they had made excellent time. Traveling at night they didn't have to rest as often. Amuna could easily travel thirty-two kilometers per stage.

Instead of the eight days it took him before, though, this trip to the emptiness might take fourteen days with a young camel in tow. He had stocked up on water just in case, because he didn't think it would be wise to enter the oasis at Azrou to refill the water bags and water the animals. The camels were valuable. Amuna was easy to spot and Noor was so distinctively marked that it would be easy for anyone who wanted to follow them to do so. They would not be able to hide. It was better to travel off the main trade routes, even if it was a little riskier and took longer.

Samir had trained young Noor to obey basic caravan commands, so she understood up, down, stop, forward, left, right and slow. She also understood no, yes and treat. Like her mother, Noor expected her daily treats of dates or figs. They moved at a moderate pace, and didn't pass much traffic on the road that first day. Noor was holding up well, so he decided to go on for a few hours more in the cool of the night. That would get them through the worst part of the big dunes before they got off the road and found a safe place to rest.

Twice Samir stopped Amuna on the road for a short time to give Noor a bit of a rest. Each time Noor had been

starting to grumble and let him know she was
uncomfortable. It looked like four hours at a time on a
good road was her limit for now. That meant when they hit
the rocky patches he would probably need to stop every
two hours for a breather. He had hoped for more, but he
didn't want to damage the young camel.

The moon came up about two hours after sunset. It
had been a glorious, red sunset and he had enjoyed
watching the colors spread and then darken. Now the sky
was pitch black with a blanket of twinkling stars overhead.
The moon was near full, so the camels cast dark shadows as
they moved along. Every now and then Noor would
squawk and jump because she would notice her shadow
from the corner of her eye and it startled her. Samir would
chuckle, then tug a little on her lead rope and say a few
words to settle her down. That was all she needed.

Finally they turned off the road to the right and went
about a kilometer into the low dunes. He found some small
acacia trees and looked around carefully for hidden snakes
and scorpions. He dispatched the few he found, and made a
resting place for the camels that was more or less hidden.

Samir carefully untied and unwrapped the leather straps
that bound the heavy water bags to the pack frames and set
them aside. He removed his bedroll and the saddle bag
kilims. The straps holding the pack frames were pulled
tighter, and took some work to loosen, but finally they
came free and he could life the frames easily off the camels.

Next he hobbled them and had them kneel. The intense
heat of the day was out of the sand, but it was still warm to
touch. It would be at least two or three more days before he

would give Noor water. Amuna could wait longer, but he needed to drink often himself, so he did. Then he took out the two brown burnooses that Uncle Moosa had given him on his last trip, and draped one over each camel to dull their whiteness against the sand. He wanted no inquisitive visitors. Amuna was a very valuable and widely recognized animal now, and the wrong people would be tempted to steal her.

Noor was happy to rest close to her mother, and started chewing her cud. Samir reached into his saddlebag and pulled out some bread and cheese for his dinner. He also produced two dates and two figs for the camels.

Noor was very alert as he took out the dried fruits, so he gave her the treats first, and spent some extra time petting her and telling her what a good girl she was. Then he went around to Amuna's head and fed her the treats. He rubbed her smooth cheeks and nose like he always did, and said, "You are the best camel, Amuna. You only want to do what I want to do. And you have taught Noor to be patient. You are a good girl, too."

He tugged on the curly fur on top of her head and squeezed both of her tiny ears. She rumbled back at him in a low, happy voice.

He spread his prayer rug near her as he usually did on the road, and then checked the star positions to find the east. He bowed for the night prayer. Then he put his head on the smooth fur of Amuna's neck for a pillow, and watched the stars in their imaginary dance until he fell asleep.

CHAPTER 69

On the fourth day they neared Azrou oasis. Samir could see it in the south as a dark smear on the horizon where the sand dunes began rising up into rocky hills and mountains in the distance. The big cedar trees made tiny spikes on the dark place. They were traveling primarily by night now, and he was tempted to slip in in the dark and let the camels drink their fill of water at Azrou.

Amuna was already making little signs that she wanted to go that way. She remembered. Camels always remember places where they have found water.

The dark green cedar trees provided a deep, cool shade during the day and Samir would be able to wash. Living in a thick coat of dust was one of the hardest parts of any trip, though the dust layer did shield his skin from the worst of the sun's rays. He studied Noor. She looked a little depleted. Her head seemed lower, and her steps didn't have as much bounce. He might have been pushing her too hard. They had been off the main trade route for over a day now and travel was more challenging. He decided to find some shade and give her the rest of the day to restore her energy.

Samir remembered the last trip he had made to Azrou with Ali and Mansur. *Ali knew what to do, and he really did take good care of us*, Samir thought. *I could do with some of that delicious food he brought back to us from Azrou! Mmmm...honey cakes. That would be so good now. I wonder how Ali is doing? I hope he has celebrated more victories. There are fewer soldiers on the roads now, so perhaps life has returned to normal for the merchants and soldiers. It would be great to see him.*

Luckily they didn't have to go far before Samir found a natural resting spot in the low point between two dunes. Two scrubby trees were growing there, and there were no rocks. There was just a large enough space for the two camels to sit and rest in shade.

Samir carried an extra prayer rug, and he put it on the sand under Noor's belly as she kneeled down. That would help to cut some of the heat from the sand and let her rest better. He decided to unload the packs, since they would be there a while. He removed the heavy water bags from each frame, then loosened the strong leather straps that held the frames in place. Unstrapping and restrapping the pack frames was the worst part of the journey.

With a groan, he shifted them off to the side. He was hot and sweating now from the effort, and drank from the small water bag he carried at his waist. *Perhaps I should give Noor water now,* he thought. *No, I will water her before we leave tonight. That way the temptation of Azrou will be easier to avoid.* He pulled out the brown burnooses and draped one loosely over each animal.

Samir spread his own rug beside Amuna and used a stick to hold up his cotton ka'if robe as a makeshift tent over his head and body. It was too hot to sleep on Amuna's furry neck right now. Sweat trickled down his forehead as he folded his arm under his head, and fell asleep trying to remember the feel of the cool, light breeze through the screened window in the inn in Awdaghust where he had first slept in a soft bed.

CHAPTER 70

When Samir woke, it was after dark. The moon was rising on the horizon. Both camels were awake and chewing side to side in unison. Loud rumbles came from Amuna's empty belly, and he decided to feed them while they were here. They didn't really need to eat yet, but it seemed a good place and time. One never knew what to expect just down the road in the desert.

He stood and stretched. He decided to pray before preparing the camels to move. He was grateful that they were making good time, and that Noor was not too stressed from the pace. He was excited to see Mansur again, and learn how he was adjusting to life on a small farm in the middle of nowhere. He assumed Mansur was still safe there. No news had come to Fez about the capture of Ibn Yasin's son. Samir chose to believe that everything was well until he found out otherwise.

The camels were nudging his shoulders looking for treats, since he had appeared on two legs again, so he honored their silent requests. Then he filled a small bucket with grain and put it on the ground in front of Noor. She happily gobbled it up. Amuna had more fat reserves since she was fully grown, so he fed her a few double handfuls of grain from his hands just to be friendly. He had done that with her since she was a baby, so she knew how to eat it without wasting any.

"You girls appear to be hungry," he said. "Don't worry. It will only be about three or four more days and then you can eat and drink all you want. Noor will be going to her new home," he said, and he rubbed her head and neck affectionately. Noor snorted at him and shook her harness.

After Noor finished her feed, he dragged one of the big water bags over to her. He pulled it up onto his shoulder. It was nearly as big as he was, and very heavy. He had created a long leather spout on one corner like a nipple, and after a few tries, he got Noor to accept it and take a long drink.

She was enthusiastic once she realized there was water in the bag. Her vigorous sucking almost knocked him over. She was thirsty. It wouldn't fill her reserves, but she would travel easier.

Samir let her drink most of the bag, and then took what was left to Amuna. He didn't want her to feel left out. For her it was only a few swallows, but it was enough. He even took a good, long drink from his own water bag, then retied the pack frames and loaded them. Noor's load was now lighter by the weight of one water bag. He threw the floppy leather bag across the top of her load to let it dry in the air as they walked.

They by-passed Azrou and the temptation of honey cakes with regret. *Maybe we will stop there on the way back*, he thought, but the camels seemed okay for now, and he was cautious by nature. Within only a kilometer they were walking at a comfortable pace again, with both camels in synch, swaying right to left with their low energy stride.

The stars were bright, as they were every night unless a dust storm was rolling through. Samir had checked his map before sleeping, and knew that Yildun should be shining behind Amuna's right hip when they walked in the right direction. If they continued that line all night, by the next night they should intersect the western trade route coming out of Azrou toward the ocean.

Two nights after that, he calculated, they should be getting close to Sheikh Taqi's zawiyah. They would travel in the heat of the day on the last day to enable him to spot the green fields in the valley. He shifted his body a bit, and, for now, settled in for a long ride.

CHAPTER 71

There were no diversions or delays. Perhaps he was just lucky, but Samir's route had been mostly on sand. Closer to Azrou the ground was rocky and, in some places, hard and painful for camels. His path had protected Noor's tender feet better. They crossed the western trade route out of Azrou only a few hours later than Samir had expected. They continued on by walking at night for two more days.

He could feel the land was rising up slightly, so he decided to camp. If his memory was right, when they got to the top of this rise tomorrow, they would see the green from the zawiyah in the valley below. He said a special prayer that night that he was right.

Samir was anxious as they ascended the rise the next morning. He wanted to know if his map was correct. If there was no zawiyah ahead, he would need to spend a day recalculating where they were and where to go next. This was a dangerous moment. Getting lost in the empty desert was life threatening.

At midday, they crested the rise. In the distance he could see a small patch of green. It was further to the right than he expected, so he would have to adjust his map slightly, but they were on the right path. The camels seemed to sense the end of the journey ahead, and walked faster. The sun was just setting as they arrived at Sheikh Taqi's door.

Once again, the sheikh seemed to have been waiting for them. He walked out just as they came up to the door and welcomed Samir with opened arms. His small turban was coming loose and sat at a jaunty angle on his head. "Ah, Samir the khalil-ullah! Salaam aleikhum! Mabruk! Welcome! Come into this house and rest." The small man disarmed him with his welcome, and Samir found himself grinning ear to ear, glad to see the sheikh again.

"Aleikhum salaam, Sheikh Taqi," Samir said with a half bow as he jumped down from Amuna's back. The sheikh grabbed his shoulders and scrutinized him for a moment. His dark eyes bored into Samir.

"You have arrived just in time for the evening meal, my son," the sheikh said. "Why don't you settle your camels in the pen and wash your face? Then come in and eat."

"Is Mansur…I mean, Abdallah…here?" Samir asked.

"Not now," the sheikh replied. "I sent him on a quest, and he will not return for a few days. But we will talk of that in a few minutes when you are settled." He turned and walked back into the strange, conical shaped zawiyah. His baggy trousers were faded and worn as if they had endured a few too many washings, even in this dry place.

Samir was disappointed. He noticed now that Shams was also gone. He had been eager to see his friend and give him the camel. But he did as the sheikh suggested. He led the camels to the water trough and pumped it full from the

well. Both animals drank with enthusiasm, and he stayed
with them about fifteen minutes until they were satisfied.

Samir took a long drink from the well, too. The water
was cool and clear. It was coming from a spring deep
below, and was very refreshing. He pumped water over his
head and washed his face and hands. It felt good to feel
water on his skin again, and the slight breeze that had come
up at sunset cooled him down in a short time.

He led the camels into the small pen where the donkey
lived. There was a shed on one end where the animals could
rest out of the sun, so he unpacked their loads and left
them unhobbled to walk around and adjust to their
surroundings. Noor stayed close to Amuna. He brushed
and slapped the sand off of his clothes and sandals as best
he could, and entered the zawiyah on bare feet with a bow,
leaving his sandals by the door.

CHAPTER 72

There was still some light outside, but Sheikh Taqi had lit three candles in the dark room, and they cast many shadows in the small building. It was all as he remembered from two years before. In the back was a screen that hid the area where the sheikh and his students slept. Their beds were neat and they each had a chest for their personal belongings. The cooking area was off to the left behind another screen. The actual cooking was done on a small fire outside during the hot months, but there was a fire pit in the cooking area to use during the winter.

The sheikh did all the cooking himself. According to his tradition, the cook had immense impact on the residents of a place, because his energy, blessings and love was added to the food as he made it. He liked to feed his students the food from his hands to nourish their bodies and their souls. Samir could believe that to be true—the food he had had in this place had been ordinary, but also somehow memorable.

Sheikh Taqi gestured for Samir to join him for his meal. "Shall we pray first?" the sheikh asked. Samir agreed, and they knelt for the evening prayers together.

Soon they were dipping fresh cooked flatbread into delicious lamb stew with carrots and onions. There was sharp goat cheese with honey, dried figs and some bitter green olives. After more than a week of chewing only dried foods, the hot meal was wonderful to Samir. He ate with enthusiasm, and Sheikh Taqi beamed his approval. A cook likes to see his food enjoyed.

While they ate, Samir asked again about Mansur.

Sheikh Taqi replied, "His studies of astronomy are going well. He uses his telescope every night, and even though it is small, he manages to find new information to record. You will see that he has come to a point of balance where the death of his father is concerned. He accepts the will of God, and finally understood that his father's love and gifts will always live in his heart. That is a big obstacle for a grieving child to get past."

Samir was glad to hear that. It reminded him to tell Sheikh Taqi about Noor. "Sheikh Taqi, when I was in Awdaghust I promised Mansur's father that I would bring him the first calf of my white camel when it was weaned. After Ibn Yasin died, I struggled with what to do about my obligation, since he was no longer there. Allah blessed Amuna with twin calves."

Sheikh Taqi raised his bushy eyebrows and looked surprised. His dark eyes sparkled.

"Yes, twins! We couldn't believe it. A male and a female. I decided after much reflection that I should bring the calf to Mansur to honor my obligation. Father and I discussed it, and we decided I would bring the female.

Mansur will not be racing camels, I think, so I have trained Noor…her name is Noor Amuna, the light of the moon…to obey pack camel commands. I believe he can breed her and produce good babies to sell, or to help you here. She will also be a good source for camel milk for the zawiyah. It seemed to be the right solution," Samir said.

"That is very generous of you and your father, Samir," Sheikh Taqi said. "I know Mansur will appreciate the gift, and we will all appreciate the bounty that having Noor here will bring us."

"Oh, and I almost forgot!" Samir jumped up. "Just a minute," he said, as he hurried toward the door.

He went out to the shed where the camels were. Of course, they came to greet him as if he had been gone for weeks, and he had to dig into his saddlebag while they nudged at him to give them their treats. He gave them each dried dates, and a little affection, then turned back to his supplies.

Samir took the two crates his father had prepared, and with an effort, managed to get out of the pen and back to the zawiyah with both of them.

He placed the boxes near Sheikh Taqi and said, "These are a gift from my father to you. He thought they might be helpful. He thinks of Mansur as his other son, and is glad he is in the place where he wants to be."

Sheikh Taqi accepted the gifts by folding his hands over his heart and bowing to Samir. "I am grateful to be in your father's memory," he said. "Please thank him for his thoughtfulness and give him my blessing."

The sheikh pried up the top of the first box and was thrilled to see it full of cloth of all colors and sizes. "Oh, what a blessing for us!" he said. "We are always wearing out our garments with the work in the fields. It is wonderful to have new cloth for turbans and robes. Praise Allah for his generosity through your father!"

When he opened the second box, he discovered it was full of dried fruits, spices and meats of all kinds. Father had been generous, and made sure that there was enough food to last six people through the winter months. There was goat, lamb, beef and even a small package of dried fish. There were two kinds of dried cheeses, cracked wheat kuskus, dried dates, figs, pears, apricots, and chili peppers, several types of fermented olives, and pine nuts and almonds. A paper wrapped package in the crate held spice packets. There was cinnamon, garlic and cardamom and even a small block of salt. The aromas from the peppers, cheeses and spices filled the air. This bounty would be a fabulous addition to what was fairly routine cooking at the zawiyah.

Sheikh Taqi jumped up and put his hand over his mouth. "Oh thanks be to God! This is a gift fit for a king," he said. He was truly delighted. "We will eat for weeks like the best nobles in the country with all this lovely food! I am speechless with gratitude."

Samir smiled a happy smile. Father would be glad that his gifts were such a big success. He wished that he could stay a few more days and see what the sheikh would cook up with all these new possibilities, but he was anxious to see Mansur.

As the sheikh put the food away in the cooking area, he called over his shoulder, "Samir, I think you will want to ride out tomorrow to see Mansur, yes?"

"Yes, I would, if it is possible," he replied.

"Yes, it is possible. It will be a very nice surprise for him after several difficult weeks. I didn't tell you what he is doing," Sheikh Taqi said. "He has been on a retreat in a small cave I know of quite a distance from here. It is a silent alchemical retreat, where he has had a lot of time to examine his own soul in solitude. He rode his horse. It will take you more than a day to find it on your camel."

"Oh, it's too bad I am coming late. I made a copy of my map for him. I imagine he could have used it on his journey," Samir said.

"There are a few landmarks to go by. He may have struggled a little, but I believe he found the place. Your map will be a perfect gift for him. It will be important for him to have it. Maybe he will update it for the next time he sees you. Do you want to get the map now? I think I can show you how to get there," the sheikh said.

Samir pulled out his treasured map, which was never far away, and unrolled the gazelle skin parchment before the sheikh. For the next hour they studied the map together by candlelight, and Samir made a few light marks on the parchment to indicate a couple of landmarks and the approximate location of the cave. As he traveled, he would be more precise in his calculations, and then add all the information to Mansur's map. Mansur could use maps well, but he wasn't much interested in making them.

Samir was excited about traveling to a new place he had never been. It would help to fill out an empty spot in his map, too. He was glad Amuna would have a full day to rest here first. They would leave the next evening and travel under the cool night sky. Noor had not often been without her mother, so the next few days would be a difficult adjustment for her. He would show Sheikh Taqi how to brush her and give her date treats. That would help her to adjust to the new surroundings.

Sheikh Taqi offered to let Samir sleep in one of the beds in the zawiyah. It was tempting, but he decided he would sleep outside with the camels. It would help Noor to settle down in this new place better, and he was always comfortable sleeping near Amuna. Samir and the sheikh knelt together to chant the night prayers, and then Samir headed outside. He tied a rope across the entrance to the shed to keep the donkey from wandering in while they were sleeping, and within a short time, everyone was fast asleep.

CHAPTER 73

Samir spent the next day inside the zawiyah working on his map and making calculations. He went out to help the sheikh with some farm chores, and made sure Amuna had plenty to drink. They would leave at dark. She could store fat in her hump now and travel greater distances, especially since they wouldn't have Noor with them, and it was always better to have a camel that was well watered.

He left Noor's pack frame in the shed, along with two large water skins. Amuna could carry two skins and Samir comfortably, so he decided to leave the rest. He made sure to bring the skin that had his ten gold dinars in it from Uncle Moosa. He had never taken them out during the past two years. He still had the ten gold dinars father had given him to repay Mansur in his sash, too

Late in the afternoon, he assembled all his items for the journey, and went into the zawiyah. The smells were heavenly! Sheikh Taqi had prepared a delicious sweet and sour stew from goat meat. It had citrus peel, pine nuts, apricots and raisins, along with carrots, garlic and whole grains of wheat. The sheikh made simple kuskus and placed the two pots with a stack of fresh bread on the middle of the eating mat. He also served two fragrant cups of strong mint tea.

Samir could hardly wait to eat. They did the evening prayers quickly, but completely, and came to the food with great anticipation. Samir asked Sheikh Taqi to explain the Surah "Ya Sin" to him. He knew it was the heart surah of the *Qur'an*, and was said to summarize the essence of Islam in the one surah. The sheikh was happy to explain while they ate, and it gave Samir a chance to let his thoughts drift to his journey that night

The cave he sought was in a small sandstone outcropping that was about two days' ride southwest. He would start by heading west just before dawn and then look for a landmark rock around midday where he should turn southwest. He would probably stop there for a few hours to rest Amuna, and then start again in the afternoon

After dinner, he excused himself and went out to load Amuna's pack frame. He had filled the water skins earlier, but went to the well a last time to fill the small water bag he kept on his belt. Sheikh Taqi came out with a small, tightly woven basket with a top tied firmly over it. It was an extra serving of stew and kuskus, with a several bread loaves wrapped separately in waxed cloth

"This is for your dinner tomorrow," the sheikh said. "It should not spoil between now and midday."

"Thank you. This is a wonderful surprise. I will enjoy it again tomorrow very much," Samir said, and he meant it. He found a place where the basket was sure to remain upright, and strapped it and the bread to the frame.

Samir double checked his water supply, his map, his bedroll, his prayer rug, and the burnooses. He had plenty of dried food in his saddlebags. He checked all Amuna's straps. They were ready to go.

He walked over to Noor, who was watching the preparations with interest. She didn't realize she would not be going. She made a coughing sound and a snort as Samir approached. He took her two dates and a fig, and fed them to her one by one, stroking her cheeks and talking in a soft voice.

"This is your new home, little Noor. Mansur will be your guardian now and you will help him. It is hard when the time comes to leave your mother, but you will be safe here. There is plenty of water and food and nice people. You will have a good life. We were very happy to watch your birth, and we are happy to give you a new beginning. I know I will see you again, when you are a grown up camel. Maybe you will even have a baby of your own. I wish you a good and happy life." He patted her neck gently.

He was a little sad. For a long time he had known this moment would come, but suddenly he felt the parting in his heart. Something was changing. Life was moving on. There is excitement and completion in change, but there is sorrow for what is passing, too. He acknowledged his feelings with his hand on his heart.

Samir remembered watching Emir Ibn Yasin turn and walk away as Mansur mounted to ride off to Fez without him. Even though this was just a camel, she was like family to him. He understood how Ibn Yasin had felt now. We cannot stop time from flowing forward, even when we long for it to stand still. He put his arms around Noor's neck one last time, kissed her nose and pulled her ear. Then he turned and walked away, mumbling "Allahu Akbar. Go with God, little Noor."

CHAPTER 74

The sun was almost gone when Samir mounted Amuna and left the zawiyah. He didn't know if he would be coming back here again. The leaving was harder than he had expected.

Noor had bellowed and called a few times after they rode away, and Amuna was restless. Her feet danced a bit, and she turned sideways with anxious distraction. Her instincts made her want to turn back. She had called back to Noor, but she continued in the direction Samir wanted to go. The first few hours that night were uncomfortable for them both.

Samir had plotted his travel line by the stars, and stayed pretty much on a direct path. The land was level and sandy here, and Amuna was moving along at an easy pace in the cool darkness. He wondered if he would overshoot his landmark. After midnight, he decided to stop for an hour to rest. There was no cover on this empty plain.

"Down, 'Muna," he said as they stopped. Amuna knelt down, front legs first, then back, with a noisy squawk. It wasn't as easy fully loaded. "Oh, sorry, girl. I should have jumped off first." He walked around and patted her neck.

He decided to cover her with the brown burnoose for precaution. She could probably be seen for miles in this dark, empty place, if anyone was out here to see.

Samir stretched out on the sand and leaned against Amuna's neck. His attention was starting to shift toward seeing Mansur. He wondered if Mansur had the start of a beard now, or a moustache. He also wondered if he would find the cave. It sounded like a very obscure location. But Shams would be there somewhere, so perhaps that would make it easier. Samir hoped Sheikh Taqi had told him all the right distances and landmarks.

He got to his feet. Unless they were going to camp here, they needed to get moving. The desert chill was uncomfortable without a warm cloak. He decided to walk a while. "Up, 'Muna," he said, and she clambered to her feet, back legs first. He would let her run in the morning. For now they would just walk and generate some body heat.

Toward sunrise the land began to slope upward. It was steeper here. This was the coolest part of the night. Samir decided to ride again, and wrapped himself in the big burnoose. He drank some water from his small skin. He couldn't lean on Amuna's hump for warmth with all the baggage there, but he put a fold of the burnoose over the end of one of the water bags and put his head down there. It was not a bad pillow!

He didn't sleep, because he had to pay attention to their direction while he could see the stars, but he was able to relax and rest. They managed to stay on a straight track through the morning. Before the sun was all the way overhead, Samir spotted the landmark rock in the distance.

There were some small trees smudging the horizon near the rock, so Samir headed that way. He would let Amuna rest a while. When they arrived, he was hungry, and wanted to eat. He started salivating as he unpacked the food Sheikh Taqi had given him, but decided not to go to the trouble to make a fire. The basket had been in the sun all morning, and was warm already. He gobbled it down. It was delicious, even on the second day.

After he ate, Samir unrolled his map and made a few notations. He rolled it again, and slipped it inside his bedroll for protection. From here they would head southwest until they tired. It would be after dark, and he wanted to approach the spot where the cave should be in the daylight. He was afraid he would miss it otherwise, plus it might startle Mansur to have someone unexpected walk up in the middle of the night.

It was a little harder to stay on a southwest path without the stars in this featureless part of the desert. The sand stretched like an ocean in every direction now, and landmarks of any kind were scarce. Finally, he decided to stop. He was starting to feel uncertain about his direction, and didn't want to wander in a circle or get off track.

This was the first time he had ever felt uncertain about his travel direction, and it was a little unnerving. He began to realize how vulnerable he and Amuna were, and how much he depended upon his eyes to keep them on track. His confidence was shaken.

It was very hot. The air shimmered with distortion along the horizon. The afternoon sun is cruel, and there was nothing to break the heat. There was no breeze, and the reflection from the sand made the blinding sunlight even brighter. He walked two paces away and drew a deep line in the sand in the direction he thought they should go. Then he spread out his prayer rug under Amuna to give her a little insulation from the sand. He left the loaded pack on her back because it insulated her from the direct sun.

He took out the big burnoose and tied one corner to the front of the pack frame. He had picked up two long sticks along the way to have as firewood, in case he needed any. He tied another corner of the cloth to one stick and pulled it out straight, then stuck it into the sand. He did the same with the other side. It made a good tent. The cloth was too low for Amuna's head to fit under, but she seemed to appreciate the shade on her body and stayed still. Samir crawled into the shade and decided they would remain there until the worst of the heat broke. He wondered how Mansur had managed this journey without a camel.

The angle of the tent cast a longer and longer shadow as the day wore on. At least now Samir could watch the sun's track to gauge his direction. He checked the line he had drawn in the sand, and discovered his instinct had been right—they had been walking almost straight south, and not southwest.

"Amuna, we were very lucky," he said. "Stopping here saved us at least half a day of tracking back. You are a very wise camel to suggest such a thing." He laughed in a dry voice, and decided he had better drink. His small bag was empty, so he filled it from one of the big bags and splashed a little on his face and arms.

CHAPTER 75

Samir walked beside Amuna for a while, but it was just too hot. He stopped, and got on Amuna's back. As he rested, he noticed that the sand grains around them were bouncing a little.

A hot ground wind had picked up, and there were dust devils swirling out in the distance around them. He enjoyed watching them as they twirled and danced across the sand. Some were thirty or forty feet high. They would come up and move erratically forward for a time, and then suddenly they would drop and disappear with a shoosh. Sometimes two or three of them would combine into a larger one, but then, when the weight of the sand it carried became too heavy, it would collapse.

A hot, steady breeze was coming from behind them now, and a lot of dust hung in the air. Amuna's nostrils were already closed, and Samir pulled the end of his turban around his lower face to make a mask. That helped to keep most of the dust out, but he could feel it between his teeth. His eyelashes were coated with it. It occurred to him that they had never been in a real sandstorm, and he remembered that this area was known for them.

He kept an eye on the surface sand around them, and decided to try and find a place they could stop until the wind died down. Even though the wind was coming from their backs, it was still hard to breathe.

Finally, Samir spotted two small bushes off to the right. He positioned Amuna on the leeward side, and got her to kneel facing in the direction they should go later. This was the best they could do. He decided to make a better windbreak, so he pulled out one of the big burnooses, and wrapped it on the back side of the bushes, tying it at the base of their trunks. He draped it up over the bushes, and the strong wind held the cloth in place.

That helped. The wind was getting even stronger now and the sand stung like needles when it hit bare skin. Samir struggled against the wind to pull out another wrap from his saddlebag, and he draped it over his head and shoulders. Amuna had not been in a sandstorm before, but camels are able to weather storms well, and she seemed relaxed. Her eyes were half closed and her nostrils were closed, so she would be content to sit and wait it out.

Samir didn't know how long the storm would last. He had heard stories of them lasting for days, but usually it was only a few hours. He sheltered between the windbreak and Amuna's back. Now it was just a matter of time. He couldn't sleep. The wind was still intensifying, and it was almost shrieking. Sand was piling up all around them where the wind was blocked. There were already small dunes building behind the bushes and running out on either side of them.

The sun was still out, but the sandstorm was so thick that there was only a dim, uniform golden glow around them—just enough to see that the sand was blowing parallel to the horizon as far as he could see. Occasionally Samir rose up to scoop sand away from Amuna's body, but he had to stay low. They were now in a well of sand. He was afraid the strong wind would blow him away, and he would lose sight of his safe place. Sandstorms were not to be trifled with. Mostly he remained seated and tried not to let the sound of the wind whistling in his ears make him crazy.

It seemed like half a day passed, but the storm subsided after about two hours, almost as fast as it had come up. The air began to clear, and Samir could see that the sun would set soon. He stood to survey their surroundings.

What he saw was shocking. There was a huge dune behind his windbreak now, and it extended about six meters down each side of them. They were in a deep valley surrounded by a giant dune. He was thankful that he had found the bushes in time, but he could see that he would have to leave the burnoose where it was. With the weight of all that sand pressing on it, there was no way to release it.

They needed to get out of the hole they were in and unpack. The load on Amuna's back was almost buried in sand, and she needed a chance to shake off the excess in her fur to lighten her load. Samir's feet had trouble getting traction in the fresh, loose sand, so he told Amuna to stand.

She struggled and clambered to her feet with a mighty effort, and made braying sounds of discontent. The load was quite heavy now. She staggered up and had trouble getting her footing, too, with the awkward slope of the sand

and the much heavier pack on her back. Samir held on to the side of the pack frame and let her walk forward and drag him out of their hole. They walked a short distance to firmer footing, then he unstrapped Amuna's pack and hobbled her. This was not a good place for her to wander away. She shook her whole body, and sand flew everywhere.

The storm had been exhausting. Samir's ears were still ringing, and he wanted to get to Mansur's place as soon as possible now. But first he needed a drink, some food and a chance to stretch out and relax. He could feel the stiffness in his muscles from having been folded and tense through the entire storm. He brushed off his saddlebags, and found some dried figs. He gave two to Amuna and ate two himself. He stroked her cheeks and nose, and brushed sand away from her eyes and ears. Her nostrils were already open again, and she didn't appear to be the worse for wear.

The sun's lower edge was touching the horizon, so the hot winds would not kick up again that night. It already felt cooler than an hour ago. The first stars were blinking into the sky. Samir decided to clear the sand from the baggage, refill his small water bag, and eat a good meal before he prayed, and then he would sleep for a few hours. Yes, a good rest was in order. He remembered that he still had another of Uncle Moosa's burnooses, so he dug it out of the pack and draped it over Amuna's back.

By his calculation, they were getting close to the location of Mansur's cave, but he had lost track of time in the storm. He didn't know exactly how much further they had to go. Around midnight he woke up feeling much better, and loaded up the pack frame. It was much easier to travel at night by the stars in this featureless landscape.

When morning came, Samir looked for a sheltered spot to rest and recalculate their location. They might be able to make it to Mansur before dark, but he wasn't sure. The ground was still sloping up gradually, and had become rocky again. Patches of dusty green shrubs broke the even tan and brown of the sand in places. He spotted a large rock with some vegetation around it, and decided to stop there. A lone scrubby tree offered a little shade, so he took one of the sticks and beat through the bushes to scare off any scorpions or snakes.

It was good that he did. As he moved closer to the rock he spotted a large deathstalker scorpion. It had yellowish legs and a broad, flat back with pale greenish stripes. Its front claws were raised and ready. A sting from the deathstalker would have killed him. He hit it hard with his stick and killed it, then flipped the deadly body far out into the sand away from the rocks. He had heard some scurrying sounds, so there were probably mice or lizards there, too—which meant snakes. Snakes could always be found where there were mice.

"I think we will just rest out here away from the rocks," he decided. "We certainly don't need a snake or scorpion to make our lives miserable, do we girl?." He found a level spot out in the open away from the undergrowth, and unloaded Amuna there, making his usual small tent with the extra burnoose.

Samir didn't sleep, although Amuna seemed to, and he assessed that they would be able to make it to Mansur before dark. Amuna woke when he stood up. She seemed restless and eager to stand. He decided to let her have a short run to loosen up her muscles, since the rocks would remain visible from a short distance. He got on her back, leaving the frame and baggage on the ground.

"Run, 'Muna," he said, and she took off. They headed north a short distance, then doubled back west and then south. They found the rocks again, and he organized his belongings. Samir gave Amuna two dried dates and wiped her face with his hand again. She had a lot of sand in her fur. "You need a bath, lady" he said. "You are as sandy as the desert! Well, that will have to wait until we find an oasis, I guess." He hadn't thought to bring a grooming brush.

Samir loaded Amuna up again, and strapped the baggage down. Then he fished in his saddlebags for some food to munch as they traveled. With luck, they would find Mansur in a few hours. He climbed up on Amuna's back, and as she stood, she screeched in pain. He jumped off and inspected all her straps and harness.

"Ah, sorry, girl," he said, and loosened one of the straps around her middle. He had pulled it too tight and that had pressed the corner of the pack frame into her back as she stood. He pulled a head cloth from one of his saddle bags and put it under the frame edge for padding.

"There, that should make it better," he said. He mounted again and they set off to the southwest. Now he needed to be alert. The last landmark was critical, and he had to be close to it to find the entrance in the formation.

CHAPTER 76

The sun was about half way down in the sky when he spotted another rocky outcropping in the distance. He rode toward it, hoping it was his destination. As they got closer, he saw that the rocks were bigger than they had seemed far away, and higher than others they had passed.

Samir was leery about disturbing any creatures that might be hiding there, so he rode in a wide circle around the vast outcropping to see if it was the right place. There were other rocks in the distance, but this one seemed right. He searched carefully for a hidden defile that opened into the center. Sheikh Taqi said it was on the east face, which was now in deep shadow. He rode back and forth on that side, but could not spot an opening. He went closer, and just where one large rock met another, he finally made out a hint of a trail behind a narrow opening.

Samir dismounted. He led Amuna into the opening. Luckily one of the water bags was half empty, because it was a tight squeeze. After a few meters, the trail doubled back sharply, then opened wider and wound into a large open space. There was a rocky overhang on one side, and beneath the ledge was a pool of water. There was grass near the pool, and Samir could just see a cave opening above the ledge in the failing light. This must be the right place.

Amuna headed straight for the water and started to drink noisily. From behind another rock by the pool, Shams poked out his head. Samir decided all hope of surprise was gone, so he walked over to Shams and petted his long nose to greet him. He hobbled Amuna, even though she was unlikely to go anywhere, and searched for the path up to the cave. As he climbed, his sandals slipped, and little rocks skittered and bounced down the cliff face.

Just as he got near the top of the ledge, Mansur came out of the cave. He was overjoyed to see Samir, and ran over to help him up. "Camel boy! What are you doing here?" His face was one big, toothy grin.

"Mansur! Finally I found you," Samir exclaimed. He grabbed his friend's extended hand and scurried up onto the ledge.

"You climb like an elephant! Any thief within a mile would know exactly where you are," Mansur said. They hugged excitedly. They were overjoyed to see each other.

"Let me see your cave," Samir said. "Sheikh Taqi told me how to find you. How was your retreat? This is a good place. It is really hidden."

"You can see the cave in the morning. It is too dark now. I am tired of being on retreat," Mansur replied. "It's been almost two weeks. The first few days were hard. I had practices to do and thousands of chants to do while sitting still in my cave every day. Sheikh Taqi told me this is the place where he gained his spiritual wisdom. Either I'm not yet ready, or it didn't work for me. I still feel normal." He looked kind of disappointed.

Mansur's hair had grown longer. He had wrapped it on the back of his neck and tied it with a strap. He also had a scruffy beard. It looked thicker than Samir's but it still had empty patches in it. His face was also sharper than Samir remembered. He had lost some of the youthful fat in his cheeks, and his features were more pronounced and more closely resembled his father. He was also very brown.

"You don't look like a rich boy scholar anymore," Samir said. "You look like a farmer with that tanned skin and your rough hands. That's a pretty sorry excuse for a beard though. You look fifteen."

"And you should talk. Look at those few scraggly hairs on your chin. You will be lucky to have a beard by the time you are forty," Mansur retorted. "But you look good." Mansur reached out and gripped Samir's shoulder.

"You have been eating well, I see," he said. "I'm very glad to see you. I didn't know when I would see you again. Where is Amuna?"

"Just below. She was thirsty and headed straight to the pool. We saw Shams there, hiding behind a rock," Samir replied. "How did Sheikh Taqi ever find this place? It is amazing!"

Mansur answered, "A hermit could live out here easily if he had a way to get food. There's nothing much to hunt, though, unless you want to eat mice and snakes," he said. "I was just starting to get low on food, and wondered what would happen next. I didn't know if I was supposed to stay here until someone came to get me or until I had a blinding inspiration."

"I guess I am both," Samir said, holding his hands out wide with a grin. "I am the messenger from Sheikh Taqi that you are to return home, and my presence is blindingly inspiring." They laughed. It felt like no time had passed between them.

"I heard you could have used my map," Samir said. "It's lucky that I made one for you. I have added a lot to mine since I saw you last. I even added the landmarks I passed on the way here, so I will update yours, too. Somehow I doubt you will do it yourself."

"The map will be great to have. You have a gift for map making, my friend. One day you will be famous for it, I think. I will welcome the updates, since for me these landmarks are my neighbors,. And no, I wouldn't do them myself." They laughed again.

CHAPTER 77

Mansur was ready to eat, so they climbed down the narrow path and Mansur greeted Amuna. "And how is the great white racing legend from Fez," he asked as he petted Amuna's neck.

She nuzzled him with affection and snorted, so he fished in his pocket and pulled out a date to feed her. She grumbled happily. Mansur helped Samir to unload Amuna, and set her pack frame off to the side. Deeper in under the ledge, Mansur showed Samir a small fire pit he used for making his food and tea. There was just enough wood around to make a small daily fire, and the flames and smoke didn't show in the distance.

Samir took out some meat and dried carrots and fruits and a few nuts. They boiled them in water from the pool and made a nice stew. Then Samir pulled out the surprise. He had two loaves of flatbread left from last night's meal. Mansur was delighted to have fresh food, and he ate hurriedly. It looked like he wasn't joking that he had just about run out of food.

Once their stomachs were full, it was time to talk about what had happened since they last saw each other. Samir told Mansur about Amuna's twin babies. He was amazed. He had never heard of camel twins, either. He was glad to hear that the little male camel had not been too large for Amuna, and that she had been a good mother.

When Samir told Mansur that he had brought Noor as a gift to Mansur, Mansur was very touched. "My father once told me that I would learn morality from you if I befriended you. There was no obligation on your part to bring a camel to me, as you well know. Yet you did, and it allows you to complete your obligation to my father. It touches me that you would honor his memory in this way. I am grateful for your gift. We will be able to use Noor at the zawiyah."

"That's not all I brought you," Samir said. He stood up and reached into his sash. "Do you remember in Awdaghust when you came down with me to sponsor Amuna for the race? Your father had to guarantee to pay ten gold dinars, which I'm sure he paid at some point. So here are ten gold dinars." He put the money into Mansur's hand. "Without this gold, you and I would never have had our friendship. Maybe you will be able to use the gold for the zawiyah, too," he said.

Mansur looked serious, and said, "Thank you." as he tucked the coins into his sash. "I have used all the gold I had in the past two years. It's nice to have a small sack of my own again. There hasn't been much to buy, but it is still nice to know that I could if I wanted to. I feel less needy for material things now. I guess living with Sheikh Taqi has done that for me. He is a very simple man and doesn't care about things like the quality of a man's clothes or how large a house he has. Somehow he always manages to have just enough for what we need. I haven't reached that point in my training yet, I guess. I still like to have gold."

Samir smiled. "Having gold is much better than not having it." He was feeling good about bringing the gifts to Mansur.

"Sheikh Taqi is a very good cook, too," Samir said. "He fed me a delicious stew when I arrived. Father sent him a box of cloths and a large box with all kinds of spices and dried foods. It was astounding. I didn't even know what was in that box. I think you will eat very well for a while when you get back."

"You have to thank your father for me, then," Mansur said. "Taqi is a good cook and a wonderful teacher, but he tends to cook only a few things over and over again. Maybe your father's gift will get him to broaden his recipes. I guess I really did have a privileged upbringing. I thought everyone ate whatever they wanted. I have learned to appreciate whatever I have now, because I see the effort that goes into growing and preserving food. I can tell you, it is very satisfying to plant a seed in the earth and then watch it grow and produce seeds that will feed many."

Samir nodded in silence. He had never planted seeds himself, but he could imagine the feeling.

"Mansur, do you want to go back right away, or wait here a few more days?" Samir asked.

"Amuna needs a rest, doesn't she?" Mansur asked.

"Yes, it would be good to let her rest for two or three days before starting back," Samir answered. "I don't want to wear her down. It will soon be time to breed her. Father and I will make a trip to Tlemcen soon so she can mate with Qadr again. This time the calf will go to Qadr's owner. I will probably be stuck in Fez for the next two years doing camel business. By the time we get back from Tlemcen, Alama will probably have another calf. Then Amuna will have her calf. Then we have to raise the calf until it is big enough to return to Tlemcen. My navigating skills will shrivel with so little use."

"But you can fill in your map to Tlemcen, at least," Mansur said.

"Yes, that will be interesting. I hear that the desert is less harsh in that direction, and the closer you get toward the sea, the greener the land becomes. It will be nice to explore a new region."

"Let's just sleep down here tonight," Mansur said. "The cave is dark and not as comfortable. I need to feed Shams and get him ready for the night. He will be glad to get out of here and run again. Why don't we do the night prayer before we get settled?" They washed in the pool and knelt under the overhang facing east and quickly recited the prayer.

The darkness was almost complete now, and it was getting chilly. The overhang and rocks kept the wind away, but they would still need something to wrap in for sleep. The small fire was going out, and was not much help for warmth anyway.

"Do you want to explore this place with me in the morning?" Mansur asked. "I need to start gathering my things together for the ride back, and your help would be welcome. Unless you have become old and need a nap after your breakfast." He poked Samir and stood up.

"You are older than me," Samir replied with a grin and scrambled to his feet. It was great to be bantering with his friend again. He would be sorry when they had to part.

Samir and Mansur got their bedrolls and placed them in a sheltered spot, near where Amuna was standing. They took off their sandals and hurriedly pulled up the blankets around their chins. They could see the night sky and the conversation, of course, turned to the stars. Mansur gave Samir new information on his observations, and told him that there would be a comet after the new year if the calculations were correct. Samir told Mansur about the harrowing sandstorm. They were both starting to yawn. Mansur turned over on his side, then turned back toward Samir to say one more thing.

"You know this reminds me of a Mullah Baba story," Mansur said. But it was too late. Samir had already dozed off. The story would have to keep for tomorrow.

CHAPTER 78

The young men spent the next two days in the hidden oasis catching up on all they had seen, heard and done in the past two years. Mansur talked about his daily routine at the zawiyah and the other boys who lived there. No one had come looking for him after his father's death, so he had just adapted to the routine in the zawiyah. He said there were days when he missed his old home in Awdaghust, and the soft beds and the peacocks and riding out with his father and Malik into the desert. But on the whole, he felt nurtured and at home in the zawiyah, and didn't think he would ever go back to Awdaghust.

"I might come to Fez to visit you, though," he said. "I would like to see your father and watch Yasin race. Hey, maybe I will ride him." They both laughed at that idea. "I wonder if he will be able to beat Amuna? If you race them against each other, you have to write to me and tell me who wins."

"I will," Samir said. "It is an interesting idea, but I can't ride both at once, and we don't have another trainer yet. I guess we will have to get someone, since we are getting so many camels now, but I do like being the one who rides in the races."

"Maybe you just like racing Amuna. Maybe it isn't the same if you race other animals," Mansur said. "Besides, you will be too old to be a rider before long. You are bigger than you used to be, and that is a disadvantage."

"That could be," Samir replied. "I guess I will learn that this year. Yasin will be ready to race in a few months."

"What will your father say when he has to give you up?" Mansur said in a moment of insight. "It will be hard for him, I think, when you decide to leave." Mansur's intuition had led him right to a delicate subject.

"Father will be fine with hiring a new jockey to ride. He will want to do what is right for the animals. Amuna is mine, and if she is to breed regularly, I don't see that she will be racing much in the future anyway," Samir replied.

"Well, I didn't mean that. I meant when you leave home and become a navigator. I think that will be very hard for him. He likes your company, and I don't see you becoming a camel breeder."

Samir looked at Mansur with surprise. He should have known his best friend would know the secret worry of his heart, but he had never spoken it.

"You know me too well," Samir said. "I do worry about that time. Father is not old yet, but he is not getting younger. I think in about three years, after we take the new calf to Tlemcen and complete our agreement, I will be ready to begin making journeys on my own. There is a lot to see in the world, and I have an urge to see many new places and add them to my map."

"One thing I have learned from Sheikh Taqi," Mansur replied with a thoughtful expression. "The world is what it is. It is not ideal. It is not going to be ideal tomorrow. If we want to change things we can only change our own lens, our own view of it."

"This is true," Samir replied. "I really hope Allah will present an ideal solution to my father when the time does come for me to go."

The boys sat in silence letting the statements sink in. Then Mansur broke the silence.

"But we must have our own experience to have our own view, yes? Who knows? Maybe I will join you on one of your expeditions," Mansur said. "I think I will be a traveling teacher like Sheikh Taqi one of these days, and my soul may well direct me to go with you to some unknown destination. Maybe we could cross over to Spain and find Ali."

"That would be a great journey," Samir exclaimed.

" Just be ready. You never know when I may show up at your doorstep, a poor, shabby itinerant who needs a meal, a bath, and a trip to a foreign place." They laughed at the idea, but it planted a seed of possibility they would both water.

From Surah 36, *The Holy Qur'an*

Ya-Sin.
By the wise Quran, no doubt you have been sent on a
straight path,
Sent down by the Mighty, the Merciful,
That you may warn a people whose fathers were not
warned, so they are unaware.
Undoubtedly, the word has been proved against most of
them, so they shall not believe.
We have put shackles on their necks raising up their chins,
so they remained with faces aloft,
And We have set a barrier before them and a barrier behind
them, and covered them from above; therefore, they see
nothing, and it is equal for them whether you warn them or
warn them not— they will not believe.
You can warn only him who follows admonition and fears
the Most Merciful without seeing, so give him glad tiding of
forgiveness and noble reward.

Terminology

Adaan – (ah-DAHN) the chant or song that calls Muslims to prayer five times each day.

Alhamdulillah – (all-HAHM-doo-lee-LAH) Praise be to God

Almohad – (all-mo-HAHD) Berber Muslim tribes from northwest Africa and southern Spain. The name means "those who affirm the unity of God". They succeeded the Almoravids.

Almoravid – (all-mo-RAH-vid) an orthodox Muslim confederation of tribes in Morocco whose name means "those who dwell in frontier forts". Strict followers of shari'a law.

Berber - descendants of the pre-Arab inhabitants of North Africa. The Berbers lived in scattered communities across Morocco and northwest Africa.

Caravanserai - a roadside inn where travelers could rest and recover from their journey. They supported the flow of commerce and information across the network of trade routes in North Africa and the Middle East.

Emir – (ay-MEER) an aristocratic or noble title of high office used in a variety of Arab countries and the Muslim world.

Hammam – (ha-MAHM) the Islamic version of the communal Roman bath, steambath, or sauna, distinguished by a focus on water pools, rather than ambient steam.

Ibn – son of

Insh'allah – (een-sha-LAH) if God wills it

Imam – (ee-MAHM) an Islamic leader in a mosque. Commonly used as the title of the worship leader, but may also take on a larger role in providing community support and teaching.

Kairowiyyan – (care-oh-WEE-an) the university, mosque and library complex built about 959 CE in Fez

Madrasa – (meh-DRAH-suh) a type of mosque school or Islamic college, but may apply to any secular or religious educational institution.

Maghrib – (mah-GREEB) the countries of Africa west of Egypt and north and west of the Sahara desert, along the coast.

Mabruk – (mah-BROOK) congratulations

Marhaba – (mar-HA-bah) welcome

Mash'allah – (mosh-all-LAH) God has willed it or by the grace of God

Mawla/Mawlawi – (MAW-la / mah-LAH-wee) a formal title of respect for someone of high, but unknown, station

Mawlid – (maw-LEED) festive observance of the birthday of the Islamic prophet Muhammad.

Muezzin – (moo-eh-ZEEN) person of good character appointed at a mosque to lead and recite the call to prayer for every event of prayer and worship in the mosque.

Salaam – (sah-LAHM) meaning "peace". Used for greetings or goodbye. The formal greeting is As-salaam aleikhum (peace be unto you).

Shari'a – (sha-REE-ah) Islamic canonical law based on the teachings of the *Holy Qur'an* and the traditions (hadith) of the Prophet Mohammed.

Sheikh – (shayk) a patriarch of a family or village, a leader of a Muslim religious organization or group, or a polite title of respect.

Surah – (SOO-rah) a chapter of the *Holy Qur'an*. There are 114 Surahs in the *Qur'an*.

Wadi – (WAH-dee) a small river or creek

Zawiyah – (zah-WEE-ah) a conical shaped hut made of mud bricks or clay, typically found in the desert. Religious teachers or sufis often built a zawiyah and lived there with their students.

About the Author

K. L. Vivian has degrees in Indo-Islamic Art and History, and writing credentials in non-fiction areas of marketing communications and emerging technologies. She has never seen a white camel, but hopes to one day.

Did you enjoy this story?

Additional copies of *The White Camel of Fez* can be ordered as gifts or for classroom use through Amazon.com. Soft cover, Kindle and audio book versions are available.
http://www.amazon.com/books

Please consider writing a review!

Coming soon from K.L. Vivian
the next book in the
Nearly True Books™ series.

The Bronze Mask of Ile-Ife
Publication expected November, 2018

Please join our mailing list to be alerted when new books by this author are published.

http://www.facebook.com/NearlyTrueBooks
(over for more information)

The Bronze Mask of Ile-Ife
by K. L. Vivian

When a beautiful and compelling bronze head of a 13th century Yoruban woman was found among sculptures at an ancient site in Ile-Ife, Nigeria, archaeologists sought clues to her mysterious identity and life. She was the only woman whose likeness was cast in bronze.

The girl was called Netete, Yoruban for "one who is ageless and eternal." Abandoned as an infant, and raised by a priestess in the colorful city of Ile-Ife, Netete was destined to become an oracle, the voice of the gods. After ten years of apprenticeships, she reached the pinnacle of her training –initiation into an oracle's life of service.

"Life moves forward. Leaves wither, die and fall away, and the new growth reaches up into the light. We must be willing to let go of the life we planned to have the life that waits for us." —Ifa wisdom

Netete became revered as a wise judge, seer and religious authority. When an old woman accidentally reveals an unexpected truth, Netete's true destiny emerges. From resourceful child to powerful woman, Netete made a lasting mark on her city, traditions and culture. The mask is all that remains to mark her remarkable life.

Available soon from: http://www.amazon.com/books

Made in the USA
Coppell, TX
27 April 2024